Twist of Fête

SIMON MAIER

This edition first published in paperback by
Michael Terence Publishing in 2022
www.mtp.agency

ISBN 9781800943988

One

As Bardhyl Bardhyly effortlessly climbed the first fourteen floors of the smart apartment building overlooking London's River Thames, he considered again that you could never trust elevators. His view on the topic was that you needed to be in control, not at the mercy of a box that, in his world anyway, often didn't work properly and that invariably stank of piddle, stale sex or old pizzas. An elevator, he reckoned, could be hijacked at any time. As his wingman Colin had said on many occasions, you could easily die in an elevator.

Slight, tough and deadly, Colin was deliberately a floor behind Bardhyl, making sure they weren't being followed. Neither man made any sound – not a cough, not a footstep and not a word. Their breathing was even and silent.

As he took the stairs two at a time, Bardhyl thought once again that things moved fast in his world. He liked that. He was proud of the fact that, two years previously, he'd been put in charge of the Mafia Shqiptare's comfortable, multi-billion pound UK cocaine business. He knew that he had a reputation for getting work done efficiently and, as required, ruthlessly. He also knew that the syndicate bosses were happy in the knowledge that he was adept at keeping the business away from the police.

Thinking about it now as he climbed the stairs, he'd only ever been stopped once by the police – very early on in his career, heading towards London from Leeds on the M1 motorway. It'd been obvious that someone had grassed him up. It happened. He'd always understood perfectly well that you just had to be wide awake, quick on your feet and deadly with your retribution.

He smiled as he remembered seeing and hearing the blues and twos. He'd thrown the car onto the hard shoulder, quickly stuffed a fistful of cash into his passenger's lap and fled. The passenger had been an illegal Somalian with little choice to do anything but take the heat which involved eight kilos of cocaine in the stolen car's boot. Bardhyl laughed silently as he remembered how he'd run off across cabbage fields and, by the time the police helicopter had been airborne, he'd disappeared.

It had been a total surprise when, some months ago, one of the Shqiptare top people had phoned him. He smiled as he remembered the call. A complex deal had been explained the bottom line of which had been the import of a huge quantity of guns and ammunition for a British client, an international dealer in munitions. He chuckled again at how he'd thought at the time that this was going to be a tough mother of a job given that his experience was cocaine not guns. The whole idea of the necessary procurement, theft and transport via half a dozen different countries nowhere near each other had made his stomach churn a little, but not too much.

Smiling, he cast his mind back to the days following the brief when there'd been minute and complicated details from several contacts via coded social media. After that he'd been left to get on with it, the only occasional communication taking place with the client whom he had never met. Until now.

He puffed out his chest a little as he recollected the pride he'd felt at having been chosen to work on this job and was pleased, as were his bosses, that he'd completed it on time, on budget and, he was sure, exactly as the client had wanted.

"If I promise something, then I always deliver," Bardhyl often said to his crews. "It's called besa," he would add for the benefit of any non-Albanians. "Our code for keeping a promise."

But besa, he also pointed out, was always matched with kanun, the ancient Albanian social code of revenge.

"Blood mus' pay wiv blood," once offered a tough, young sidekick who hailed from Basingstoke and had no clue where Albania was.

"You'll go far, Shifty," Bardhyl had said to the beaming teenager who suffered from adenoids and spoke as if he had tight-fitting corks stuffed up his nose.

At the fourteenth floor Colin, ready with a Boker Kalashnikov automatic switchblade, stayed by the stairwell. Simultaneously, Bardhyl unclipped his Ruger SR40c from its holster underneath his lightweight leather jacket. Palming the weapon, he waited for a slow count of twenty before climbing the final flight of stairs to the floor above. He found the door he wanted, waited again for another count of ten as he regulated his breathing and pressed the bellpush of apartment 1543.

The door didn't open immediately. It couldn't, not until five hidden, high-definition video cameras had done their job, recording and facially identifying who was outside. Another set of cameras had picked up Colin waiting by the stairwell on the floor below. Had there been anyone else on other floors or immediately outside the building, then they too would have been duly noted. And managed.

Bardhyl knew better than to ring the doorbell twice. After a few seconds, there was a soft hiss and a double click as the reinforced door swung slowly inwards on hydraulic arms. From hidden speakers, a kindly voice welcomed him, asked him to step forward and put his gun, other weapons and any phone or burner on a glass tray fixed to the wall on Bardhyl's right.

Nobody was in the hallway as the front door closed automatically behind him, but Bardhyl guessed rightly that he was still being watched. He put his phone, gun and the Pro-Tech M2607 switchblade on the tray which withdrew smoothly into the wall. The voice thanked him and insisted that he should stand still and straight. As Bardhyl did as he was told, he heard rather than saw the scanning device. After some brief clanking noises, the sort that an MRI scanner makes, the voice ushered Bardhyl along the corridor to the second door on the left. He was told to open the door and go in. On the floor of the large room was heavy-duty, black, rubber sheeting neatly covering the expensive carpet.

"Decoratin' an' that?" Bardhyl asked politely of the person in shadow sitting at a table in front of a window. Thinking that he'd not been heard, he tried again. "Feller, you gonna do some work on the walls?" There was still no answer and Bardhyl was not invited to sit.

"Tell me what you have."

The client spoke with the voice that Bardhyl recognised, but now there was something, an edge perhaps, which created a frisson of fear in Bardhyl's gut.

Just shy of two million dollars had been deposited in an offshore account nominated by the man in front of him. This sum, accessed solely by Bardhyl, included Bardhyl's partial fee for the job and was totally separate from any of the funds controlled by the client necessary to buy the guns and ammunition, even though many of the consignments had been stolen. The money to which Bardhyl had access was also for paying his team and the greasing of many palms. The man before him had made it clear that he expected Bardhyl to reward his team and contacts well. Good money, the man had said, bred good work. Bardhyl didn't agree with this premise at all, but of course never said as much. He felt that his cut of the upfront money should be sizeable. Unfairly sizeable perhaps but that was the way it was. He felt no guilt whatsoever. In his view guilt was for the weak.

The balance of the money still to come his way was massive and he had been almost salivating on a daily basis at the thought of it. He smiled slightly. The light tap of a fountain pen on the table brought him sharply back into focus.

"Sorry boss. What?"

"I said, tell me what you have."

"The guns?"

"Surprisingly, yes. The guns."

"We have 'em all boss."

The man sighed slightly but the irritation was palpable. "Good," he said, "So… the Magpul FMG-9?"

"Yep."

"Tell me why it's special."

"It folds up into a rectangular block the size of your phone. And… it's mostly made of lightweight polymer, not metal."

The seated man nodded, pleased, although it didn't show. "And?" he asked calmly. "The Armatix iP1?"

"Yeah boss. New. We got one hundred and fifty."

"Tell me why that gun's useful."

"Can't be fired against the guy using it. Never. Not by no one. It's a magazine-fed, semi-automatic pistol what uses smart gun tech."

"And?"

"And… the shooter guy has to wear a special Armatix watch. If the gun and the watch don't connect, the gun don't fire. End of."

The seated man nodded again, but said nothing. Bardhyl's frisson of fear had become fixed now. Edginess wasn't part of his persona but now he felt decidedly uneasy. He thought again about the fee he'd already tucked away plus the sum to come. His nervousness diminished a little. He just wanted to finish the deal, arrange for the weapons and ammunition – all carefully packed in crates with tracking devices supplied by the client – to be forwarded to the end destination. He wanted the cash and to retreat back to the work and world that he knew best.

The client was speaking. "What else?"

"You asked for Chiappa Rhino revolvers. We got 'em."

"And these are good because?"

Bardhyl wasn't stupid and knew why he was being asked these questions – almost like proof of purchase. Having become used to the dim light in the room, he could see that the client was wearing a grey suit and crisp, open-necked white shirt with cufflinks that sparkled, so it was pretty obvious, Bardhyl thought with another small smile, that the guy wasn't doing any decorating.

"I asked you a question!"

"Those guns are good because they recoil straight back into your 'and, not upwards, making 'em more…"

"Accurate?"

"Yeah. That."

"The Remingtons? Bolt-action?"

"No sweat."

"With sniper's rigs, folding stocks, ten round magazines, titan sound suppressors and high-magnification scopes?"

"Yeah."

"Repeat what I just said."

Bardhyl did, word for word.

"You've got one hundred and eighty of those?"

"No boss. You wanted two 'undred and twenty."

"Good," the client said, comforted by the answer. "So, everything's in place? Safe? Ready?"

Bardhyl wasn't sure which question was the important one so he just said, "Yeah."

"And you've kept quiet about this? Just your team? Bardhyl, I shall know if you lie."

Bardhyl knew much better than to lie now. He would always argue that lying had its place, but here wasn't it.

"Sure," he said confidently, "just the guys."

"And everyone got their fair share?"

"Yeah. They did," lied Bardhyl.

"Tell me where the crates are now."

Bardhyl told him. Pleased, the seated man leaned back in his chair, screwed the top back onto his Montblanc fountain pen and smiled; Bardhyl saw the smile, breathed more easily and at last relaxed, the frisson gone.

"Very good," the man said as he shot Bardhyl Bardhyly. Dead.

Two

The front door buzzer snapped Stanley Accrington out of his reverie. He'd been gazing at the choppy, white-flecked North Sea where it met a range of low, pigeon-grey clouds that obliterated the late afternoon sunshine. From the kitchen window, he could see that fat raindrops had started in earnest to buffet the yellow roses in the long garden that stretched down to the sea wall. Shutting the window, he picked up the door phone.

"Mr Accringter!"

"Hello, Mrs Brown," replied Stanley wincing at the voice that sounded like someone finding it hard to swallow several large, spicy Cheetos.

"Mr Accringter, there's a parcel – just bin left outside. Didn't see no one leave it neither."

"Mrs Brown, there aren't any deliveries at this time of day. You know that."

"Well," grated Mrs Brown, "be that as it may, there's a big parcel 'ere. Didn't magic 'isself."

Stanley sighed. "OK, thanks for letting me know Mrs Brown. I'll be right down."

Glancing up at the kitchen clock he realised that he needed to get a move on. He'd promised to see Janine Bishop who thought that a valuable bracelet of hers had been lost and wondered if Stanley could help.

At the entrance to the post office's flat, near neighbour Mrs Aida Brown had already gone. Stanley looked up and down Little Peasen's empty, now damp, high street. He let the rain play over his face for a moment, relishing the fresh and welcome breeze. Stepping back under the porch to the flat's entrance, he picked up the parcel. For no particular reason, he happened to glance towards William Benedict's bookshop opposite. Maybe the parcel was for William, thought Stanley. Nothing unusual in that.

It seemed that there were no lights on in the bookshop, once a Victorian, Methodist chapel. Perhaps someone had tried to deliver the parcel there Stanley wondered but, because there'd been nobody in and, due to the rain, had decided to leave the thing outside the post office. This happened from time to time primarily because the bookshop's opening times were erratic as were its owner's habits. It wasn't unusual for William to be seen popping across the road for a packet of ginger nut biscuits dressed in a Metallica T-shirt, paisley pyjama bottoms and a home-knitted beanie hat that some thought was a tea-cosy. On at least two occasions, people in the shop had found it imperative to point out that the pyjama bottoms were agape to the world.

Stanley looked up and down the road again and back at the bookshop. Something had caught his eye, but what? Had that been a movement through one of the bookshop's large ecclesiastical windows? Nothing definite, but was somebody walking past the window in the dark interior? There it was again. Stanley stared for a moment but there was nothing. Perhaps, he thought, the rain was the cause, creating shapes on the windows.

He looked at the parcel. It was about a metre in length, half that in width and half of that again in depth. The tape on it was neat and the box was sturdy, heavy duty cardboard that looked much like an Amazon package except that there were none of the usual printed labels and no branding, address or addressee. Gently, he shook the package. Nothing rattled. Still puzzled, he brought it into the flat's entrance hallway, shut the front door and put it by the stairs.

Deciding that the morning would be a better time than now to go bothering William, he idly wondered about rain creating shapes on windows or why William might have been moving about with no lights on. Of course, he mused, there was no reason why anyone should or shouldn't move about in the dark in their own home. But the movement had seemed, well, furtive. Could a movement on the other side of a window be furtive? It could, he thought. That darker but indefinable shape seen but not seen, a silhouette that might appear like a possible face in shadow or, more than anything, an indefinable feeling that maybe one was being watched. All of that could be classed as furtive.

As he turned to go back upstairs to the flat, he glanced down again at the parcel and saw in alarm that there was some sort of thick, dark red liquid slowly leaking out all over the hallway's parquet floor. What the hell was that? Oil? Paint? Something edible that had melted? Concerned, Stanley picked up the parcel again and held it at arm's-length, but that didn't help in discovering what the dripping, red goo was, so carefully he put it down.

Hurrying upstairs to fetch a cloth, something suddenly occurred to him. He stopped dead, turning to look down at the parcel and the oozing stuff that in the hallway light looked like blood.

Three men, each dressed in black, stood in front of the village hall near the Little Peasen war memorial. The modest, marble commemoration, displaying forty etched names, was much appreciated by the villagers, many of whom had lost a relative in one or other of the world wars. The memorial was affixed to a concrete base surrounded by a low, metal link fence against which a couple of aged and now faded, remembrance wreaths were leaning.

The grey, rain-filled sky created a surreal light as remnants of late afternoon sunshine tried to break through. The village was drying out from the shower and all was quiet apart from an occasional car or a barking dog.

The three city-dwelling, drug-dealing thugs standing around the war memorial were grim, irritable and didn't like each other much. One of the three men, the leader of the group, began kicking the wreaths.

"We don't wanna be 'ere long," he complained, "This place gives me the fuckin' creeps."

"The guy's late," shouted a fourth man who was sitting in the driver's seat of a dirty white Vauxhall Vivaro, its engine running and radio on. Happily smoking a joint, he was beating the steering wheel with one hand in time with the music.

"Tell me what I don't know," said the group's leader. "An' turn the fuckin' engine off! An' that bleddy row!" He paused, checking his phone again. "Yeah," he said loudly, "the bastard's really late an' I don't like it. Boss or no boss, no bastard's late on my watch! I expec' respec'."

A slim, fit figure, late thirty something and dressed in a lightweight, black suit with open-necked white shirt and black Loake Oxfords, strode up as if out of nowhere. Marching right up to the leader in charge of the small group, he spat his words into the leader's face.

"If you ever say in my hearing – or shout as you just did – that I'm late or if you look more pissed off than you do now, you're a dead man. Call me a bastard – or if I hear from someone else that you've called me a bastard – you're a dead man. Depending on your answer to my next question you might be a dead man walking anyway. Where's the package?"

The gang's leader, showing the bravado that was expected by his small team, didn't flinch.

"Outside the post office mate," he said with a sneer. "We seen one of the truck delivery guys take it there just as we rocked up."

"I'm not your mate, mate and I've just walked past the bookshop and the post office. There's no package. Why didn't you collect it directly from the bookshop? As you were told."

"We didn't get 'ere in time pal," shrugged another member of the gang. "We was late… Traffic an' stuff. Stopped for a brew. And a widdle…"

"Right," said the visitor slowly as he turned back to the gang's leader. "Well now, the future's not looking that rosy for you. Maybe I need to have a chat with your bosses. A serious chat. I think you know how that'll end. I'll get a new crew and you'll be dead. Your bosses are getting a lot of money for this deal. As are you. Think they might be a bit upset if they knew that my job and my cash were in jeopardy. For the second time. Your top guys don't take kindly to deals that go tits up do they? Or clients who don't get what they've paid for. I'm one of those clients. What d'you reckon?"

The gang leader's bravado began to fade and he wasn't sure what jeopardy meant. The client stepped closer, but recoiled and coughed involuntarily at the leader's exhalation of sour breath.

"The parcel," the client managed to say holding his breath and waving the air in front of his face, "has gone. I want it back."

"We'll go an' look, mate."

"I've just told you, it's gone, so why would you go and look, you thicko? It. Is. Gone."

"We'll find it," said the leader whose name was Adidas on account of his preference for certain trainers. "Don't you worry none."

This was a phrase that he'd picked up from some wild west movies for which he had a fondness and almost said it again so much did he like it. The client stepped back a little more and looked hard at the three men in turn. The fourth man in the Vauxhall Vivaro van had turned off the music but not the engine; he edged forward in his seat to see what was going on.

"The package," the client said quietly, "has disappeared and my consignment of guns has gone walkies – and yet here you are standing about smoking dope in the middle of the sodding village!"

"We did what we was told, mate. You don't like it, then tough," retorted Adidas, glancing at his colleagues for approbation.

The client breathed evenly and looked around the empty street for a moment. Turning back, he stepped forwards, grabbed Adidas' ears and pulled the man's head down hard onto a raised left knee. Adidas jerked backwards in shock and pain. As his head came forward again, it was snapped back once more by a fist smashing into his nose.

"Tough you say?" asked the client calmly as if having a conversation with a dear friend over drinks. "Tough?" he repeated. "Really? Don't forget who you're dealing with, sunbeam. Seriously, don't forget. Remember your buddies Bardhyl and Colin? And I already told you once, I am not your mate. Seriously not."

The astonished men either side of Adidas gawked at their leader whose broken nose was bleeding heavily. Their gaze swivelled towards the client who was calmly wiping his hands on a clean, white handkerchief. He stared at each of the three men in turn, something in the look making each man afraid.

"Get the package gentlemen," the client said carefully. "And please believe me when I say I mean it. Plus I want to know that our bookshop friend is done, dusted, wasted… and that we've got my guns back on track to where they're meant to be going. No more cockups. Run and I will find you. Or your bosses will. You'll like it better if your bosses find you first. I hope we understand one another. You do understand, don't you?"

Two of the men said nothing but nodded. Adidas couldn't nod because he knew that to do so would ensure another rush of blood. Checking carefully to see that that his hands were clean, the client looked once more around the empty street.

"The crates," he said fixing his eyes on Adidas, "have in them embedded chips that tell me exactly where they are. You know that. The crates are in the bookshop. You know that too. I want my guns and I want to know that the bookshop guy is out of the picture. And I mean out. There's a fair in this village on Sunday. I want everything sorted out by then. Not really that hard. Even for idiots like you. You know what to do. Be very sure that you do it. No more chances. None."

The client turned to go, but hesitated and handed his handkerchief to Adidas.

"Use this," he said pleasantly. "You're messing up the grass. And your trainers. Mate."

The client walked back the way he'd come towards a new, silver Lexus. The fourth member of the gang in the Vauxhall Vivaro van began to get out.

"Don't even think about it pal," the client murmured after kicking the van's door hard onto the driver's right leg as he passed, "unless, that is, you feel dead lucky."

Three

Janine Bishop thanked Stanley for the prettily wrapped box of homemade jam tarts that Patricia Accrington had insisted her brother take along as a gift. Absent-mindedly, the old lady put the box on a chair. Stanley hoped that she wouldn't equally absent-mindedly sit on the box later and wondered if he should say something, but thought that she might be offended so he didn't.

Janine refused to acknowledge that her lost bracelet could have been misplaced in the house or garden and begged that Stanley should keep his eyes and ears open for information. She emphasised the fact that the bracelet was silver with small porcelain flowers evenly spaced and that at the centre of each flower was a tiny diamond.

"Edelweiss," she smiled in a girlish sort of way. "Nothing to do with the *Sound of Music* of course, but everything to do with…" She halted for a moment and Stanley was wise enough not to fill the gap. "My initials are on the inside and so are those of Tobias. Entwined you see."

Janine explained with great care that sometimes she took the bracelet off when she wrote something and that may have been what had happened at the post office. Mr Accrington would have a good look once again wouldn't he, just in case? Stanley promised that he would. They finished the conversation by speaking of Tobias' funeral a few weeks before, after which Stanley said that he needed to be on his way. Again, he reassured Janine that he would do his best to find the bracelet.

"I know you will," said the old lady gratefully as she saw Stanley to the front door. "Tobias gave it to me for our silver wedding anniversary and," slipping into a language that she rarely used, said, "Es bedeutet mir aus vielen Gründen sehr viel. You speak a little German I think Mr Accrington?" She smiled slightly and then, thought Stanley, for her own sake as much as for his, said, "It means a lot to me for many reasons."

"You gave her the tarts?" asked Patricia later of her brother over dinner.

"I did."

"And how is she… in the circumstances?"

"OK, I think. Coping. Wants me to help find a precious bracelet, but I'm not sure where to start. Tobias gave it to her as an anniversary present. Valuable in many ways. She thinks she may have lost it in the post office but we'd have found anything like that so…"

"Tobias was such a lovely man. Did the police discover any more about his fall?"

"Not as far as I'm aware. I was told in no uncertain terms that the case was closed. But… he was only on a two-step ladder fixing some low wisteria. He wasn't ill by all accounts and the fall wasn't what killed him. Bee stings did that." Stanley pushed his fair hair back and sighed. "The police and medics thought it was anaphylaxis… although Janine says that the poor chap had no record of being susceptible."

"And you think what?"

"Last week when I went over to see her with that box of fruit and vegetables, I asked if I could have a look at the back of the cottage. There are no beehives there or close by. I don't know anyone who has bees in the village and, anyway, bees don't really attack unless they're disturbed. Someone brought the bees to the garden. Not sure how or, more particularly, why, let alone who. But that's what happened I'm certain. Everyone liked Tobias. It just seems odd that…"

His sister interrupted. "Let this one go Stan."

"The police think it was just unlucky, but…"

"You know," interrupted Patricia to change the subject, "Janine's going to have a special silver cup made in Tobias' memory? For the winner of one of the main sugar beet wheelbarrow races. It'll replace the rather knackered wooden plate that he made and donated eons ago."

"She didn't mention that," said Stanley reflecting on the fact that the old lady was both lonely and alone, something shared by many villagers.

"Flan?" asked Patricia.

"Please… I've not really thought much about the fête," he said guiltily.

"Well," commented his sister as she put a large slice of homemade fruit flan in front of her brother, "you need to get your skates on if you're going to be a decent MC again. Talk to Graham Lambert asap I would. Have some crème fraiche."

Stanley agreed to the addition to his dessert and was enjoying a forkful when the kitchen door was pushed open. A barefoot blonde playing air guitar and singing snatches of a song appeared in the doorway.

The girl stopped playing the biggest rock gig ever, put her air guitar away, glanced at what her uncle was eating and smiled.

"Any flan left?"

"Loads," said her aunt. "Help yourself."

"This fête you're talking about. When is it?"

"Sunday."

"You guys need any help?"

"Seriously?" asked a surprised Patricia.

As Bethan cut herself a huge piece of flan, she asked. "It's not like dancing round a wicker man thing, is it?"

"It's just a village fête," Patricia said, smiling. "A fair. We do it every year. Started when villages round here celebrated sugar beet crops."

The girl grinned, licking an errant bit of plum off a finger. "Still sounds like a wicker man thing."

"It isn't. It's good fun."

"OK. What's fun about it then?"

Patricia was, she knew, sailing into dangerous waters. "There's sugar beet bowling, beet throwing, races with wheelbarrows full of sugar beets, a beet shy instead of a coconut shy… and everything else you'd find at a village fair… rides, a roundabout, two swing boats – remember those? Loads of music – no really, some great music! Games, face-painting, huge bouncy castle, donkey rides… masses of all sorts to eat and drink. Oh yes and this year there'll be a new kite flying display, subject to wind, courtesy of the WI and Mr Berkley. The kites not the wind, although…" She grinned. "It's just an old-fashioned, family day. You must've seen the posters; there's one in the window downstairs."

Patricia waited for an acerbic response as did her brother. A piece of flan topped with crème fraiche plopped in sympathy from Stanley's fork onto his shirt.

"Cool," Bethan said, "Count me in. Course I'll help," she said.

Patricia checked to see if there had been any hint of sarcasm. Feeling that there hadn't, she said with care, "I always do the fifty-fifty thing. You could help with that."

"Fifty-fifty thing?"

"Yes. People buy a ticket for a pound and the cash goes into a bucket… I suppose next year we'll just have to walk around with a credit card machine. Anyway, when the cash gets totted up at the end of the day, half goes to the winning ticket and the other half goes towards stuff for the older folks in the village. That and the profits from the fair usually make up a tidy sum."

Bethan looked less enthusiastic. "I wouldn't have to do that all day though, right?"

Her aunt laughed. "No. An hour or so would be great. Really appreciated."

"OK. I'm in."

Patricia wondered if her niece was oblivious to the fact that she was the dream of many an adolescent in the village and quite probably some folk not so adolescent. Would, Patricia wondered, the fact that her current short shorts and skimpy top didn't meet in the middle be an advantage or disadvantage to fifty-fifty sales? It depended, she decided, on which way you looked at it. Or them.

Once Bethan had made herself a cup of herbal tea to go with the flan, she plonked a kiss on her aunt's head, sat next to her uncle and grinned at him.

"So, Mr Berkley and kites?" asked Bethan.

"It's a new thing he's set up in conjunction with the local WI. Some of the ladies are making kites at Darkwater Hall and the money from the sales is going towards helping local, disadvantaged kids."

"He's a creep," offered Bethan.

"So," asked Stanley changing the topic, "is climbing Kilimanjaro still on once you get your results?"

"Nah," Bethan said smiling and then with a straight face added, "I'm thinking of training as a commercial pilot."

Stanley laughed. "Go for it, but don't you need decent maths to fly commercial jets? And even a smattering of geography?"

Bethan shrugged, grinning back. She paused and studied her uncle for a moment. He would have made, she reflected, a great leading man in a Netflix thriller. He didn't look, she thought, his thirty five years.

"Actually," she said, "I'm seriously considering drama school."

Stanley, pausing to finish his flan and tidy up his crème fraiche stained shirt, turned to look at his niece. "Really?"

"Yeah. I've been told I'm not bad. It was always my favourite subject. And you said I was pretty decent too when you saw me in

As You Like It last year."

"Not just decent. You were a really good Rosalind… You've been good in a few things we've seen you in… Talked to mum and dad about it then?"

"Pa yes. Ma not yet. Dad thinks it's a good idea. What do you think?"

Stanley avoided looking at his sister.

"Beth," he said, "I think that whatever you decide to do, you'll do it brilliantly well. That's not just uncle rubbish either. I mean it. If you want to make acting your life, then go for it."

Bethan wolfed down her flan and finished her tea. She sprang up.

"Out tonight?" asked Patricia.

"Nah. Reading… Oh yeah… I found a book of yours Uncle Stanley – *An Actor Prepares.* Constantin Stanislavski. You don't mind do you? I saw your name written on the flyleaf. From someone whose signature I can't read. It says RADA, London but I can't make out the rest. And there's a message I can't work out either. What was that for then?"

Stanley's surprise was covered by a sudden veil that fell across his face. His niece didn't notice but his sister did.

"Beth, help yourself anytime. Let me know though what you think when you've read the Stanislavski."

"Cool."

Bethan gave her uncle a kiss on his head and left the room exchanging her air guitar for dance movements and singing the song she'd been singing on her arrival into the kitchen. Patricia looked at her brother for a moment, thought about saying something but changed her mind and said something else.

"I hope Martha and Pete are OK with Bethan staying here so long."

Martha, older sister to Patricia and Stanley, had suddenly

upped sticks from London and had left her job as an engineer and her husband, Pete, six months ago. Pete had coped badly. Martha was somewhere in Italy now with her wine importer lover. Patricia had stepped in quickly and offered to be in loco parentis for a while, an offer that Pete had accepted gratefully so that he could focus on the divorce and building up his design agency. The 'for a while', initially assumed to be a few months, had no agreed end date but neither Stanley nor Patricia minded and, truth be told, Bethan had happily fitted in to their and Little Peasen's lives.

Stanley looked at his sister, smiled reassuringly and said, "She'll be OK. And I reckon her results'll be good too. Martha…"

Any further discussion on the subject of their niece was interrupted by the front door buzzer. Stanley let in a police officer. A cup of coffee was accepted, a fruit muffin was refused and the mysterious package, now double wrapped in clear polythene, was examined on the dining room table which for protection was covered in layers of more plastic sheeting.

"You didn't try and open it?" asked the police officer.

Detective Sergeant Evie Harris had known the Accrington siblings for a while and liked them both, but had a strong preference for Stanley whom she regarded as sexy, although she had never overtly shown or shared her feelings.

"No."

"I'm pretty sure that the red stuff is packing grease," commented DS Harris as she looked down at the now dark brown substance on the package. "It's likely to be something called Cosmoline, a corrosion inhibitor."

"Used for what?" Stanley asked, already guessing the answer.

"If it's what I think it is, this kind of grease is used to keep weapons clean and untarnished. I'll take the package away. Can't open it yet of course and, even if I could, I couldn't open it here. Obviously I'll give you a receipt and then we need to see if it can be traced at all." She finished her coffee. "By the way Mr Accrington, any more views on Mr Bishop's demise? DCI Poole mentioned that you thought something wasn't quite right…"

"Isn't the case closed?" asked Stanley.

"Well, if you know of anything further…"

Stanley was about to say something but didn't and shook his head.

"Mr Accrington?"

"No, nothing."

"Sure, sir?"

"Dead sure."

Four

"It's government-funded you know," commented Mrs Margaret McFlintock in the village shop and post office, tapping a nearby tin of baked beans to get customers' attention.

"What I hear," she declaimed, "is that Mr Berkley's business is producing kites. For what purpose nobody yet knows. But that's what I hear."

Her audience paid close attention as they always did to Mrs Margaret McFlintock's prophesies, despite the fact that few came to pass. Nobody moved. Shopping stopped as she gave one of her regular verdicts. At this point she would frequently shut her eyes as if in fervent and determined prayer.

"Whatever it is," she went on once her eyes had opened again, "might be let loose at any moment. Germ warfare is what I'm thinking. Plague!"

At this information, as if expecting a marauding horde of germs to descend upon the village, many people in the post office and shop clutched handbags or played anxiously with house keys.

Mrs Margaret McFlintock, once a Girl Guide leader, now administrator of the local Mothers' Union chapter and maker of the most bitter of marmalades, had been long convinced that it would be only a matter of time for a plague once more to envelop the whole of East Anglia. She was a firm believer that SARS, bird-flu, coronavirus or indeed any viral, air-born or germ-driven strain of anything, was the will of God bearing down upon the wicked. She casually dismissed the argument often put to her that such diseases tended to catch the good as well as the bad without discrimination.

Long ago, she had seen a film called *The Ten Commandments* starring Charlton Heston as Moses and Yul Brynner as Rameses II. Particularly taken with Mr Heston, she thought that he would have made a very good husband, although she readily accepted that such a view was based on slim information. Her own husband, now long since departed for foreign climes – some said with an uplifted heart – had in her view been a very poor partner. Certainly, he had left her reasonably well-provided, but she felt that he was no great loss. He simply hadn't had what she called the gumption that undeniably she knew Mr Heston possessed. After all, as she often thought while making marmalade or gazing out of the kitchen window at her fish pond, who wouldn't want to be married to Moses? In fact, on some occasions she almost expected the pond water to divide allowing a troop of beetles, a battalion of ants or even a large family of hedgehogs to pass safely across. On the basis of the one film and the allure of Mr Heston, she read avidly about the ten plagues and thought that each was a just punishment following the wickedness of Yul Brynner. Dreadful man, she thought.

"The Lord," she would often declare, "promised plagues and what the Lord promises he will deliver. So, plagues there will be. Of that have no doubt, no doubt at all."

Invariably, when addressing a group of people, she would invite her listeners to mark her words.

"Mark my words," she commented now to the post office congregation tapping the can of beans again to ensure undivided attention.

Anyone who was fidgeting or making a move to leave the premises stopped.

"If the Lord promises something," Mrs Margaret McFlintock said, pointing to the ceiling, "then there will be no escape from the poison that will one day punish the wicked amongst us."

She shut her mouth at this point with an almost audible snap as if to avoid the avowed poison and only opened it again to point out an ominous conclusion.

"And," she said emphatically to her audience members many with mouths agape, "that will be that."

If she remembered, she would regale her audience with her thankfully succinct treatise on the ten plagues with which God is alleged to have struck the Egyptians for not letting the Israelites go free. She was always at great pains to repeatedly tell Richard Threadgill, Little Peasen's long-suffering vicar, that her favourite plague was that of boils.

"You can't beat boils," she would say, a little fearfully as if half expecting even herself to be struck down with the affliction.

"You can't?" asked the vicar.

"You see," she would explain, assuming her man of God to have only limited knowledge of the book of Exodus, "an affliction of boils is evidence that the afflicted have been wicked. However," she would aver, eyelids fluttering with excitement and well before the vicar could protest, "as you know, I'm also rather interested in the plagues of darkness, locusts and pestilence; they too have much going for them."

Reverend Richard Threadgill, extraordinarily patient as he was, had once pointed out to Mrs Margaret McFlintock that all-encompassing darkness, locusts, pestilence or indeed boils were unlikely in Little Peasen. He had also been keen, on at least three occasions, to tell his excitable parishioner that what had been written about the plagues may contain some small element of truth, but was likely to be based at best on a mix of mostly apocryphal stories. Smiling weakly, he had said that in those days the nights might have been rather long.

Mrs Margaret McFlintock would have none of it and was privately irritated that the vicar, whom she equally privately adored, could not follow what she felt was simple logic. Some aspects of the relevant biblical texts troubled her though and she regularly asked the same questions. Did the vicar, for example, know precisely what pestilence actually was and, further, how might one recognise it when it arrived?

The vicar, often praying for his religious sanity, had sometimes wondered whether to refer Mrs Margaret McFlintock to ancient rabbinical commentaries on the subject of plagues. However, he had quickly dismissed this train of thought believing that such a referral wouldn't be a solution or provide any closure.

What usually diffused the topic, if they were meeting at the vicarage, was the offer of a second, large slice of caraway seed cake and a third cup of tea, an offer that had never been refused.

Stanley Accrington liked Mrs Margaret McFlintock despite her zany mania. She was, he thought, one of those women who was simply tough and determined. Her capacity for helping people was well-known. She was also a stalwart of the village, not least in currently preparing for the forthcoming fête. Stanley liked her for her strength, fortitude and friendship. A plus in her favour was her distaste of Ray Berkley, something that many shared, Stanley included.

Stanley felt that any unjustified open ridicule was wrong in his book and it was a fact that Ray Berkley regularly and openly derided Mrs Margaret McFlintock's good works, her support for the Mothers' Union, her marmalade, her fluttering eyelids, her love of Little Peasen, but mostly her innocent, religious fervour.

At a dinner that Ray had held at a redecorated Darkwater Hall some months ago when his wife Stephanie had been in situ for all of three weeks – the sum total of her residence – he'd looked carefully at the twelve guests as wine glasses were being replenished by a butler hired for the occasion. Not for the first time, he'd patted a hired waitress' bottom as she'd passed.

"Oh for God's sake," Stephanie had muttered not so quietly into her sixth large glass of Savennières which had been preceded by four equally large pink gins. Gazing blearily round the table, she'd smiled to herself thinking, probably out loud, that the evening was a bit like *The Last Supper* painting by that bloke what wrote *The Da Vinci Code*. It wasn't until days later that she realised with a jolt, that in many ways, the dinner party had been her own last supper.

The dinner hadn't been a success on many counts.

"Ray," had piped up a keen-to-impress accountancy firm junior partner carefully putting down his knife and fork. "Is it true," he'd asked brightly and in the hope of currying favour, "that you're developing devices for the armed forces?"

Noise around the dinner table had ceased almost on cue as people had begun fiddling with their linen napkins. Some had glanced surreptitiously at Ray for a reaction. Their host's face had darkened, his eyes flashing with anger. The accountant, realising that he may have lost a hoped-for client and possibly his job, had blushed deeply to the colour of his half-eaten langoustines. His putty-faced wife, dour as a rule anyway and with a mouth like the puckered end of a German sausage, had resolved there and then to deprive her husband of conjugal expectations for a very long time, if not forever.

"You may regret that question Cyril," Ray had spat, sharing the contents of his mouth with those sitting nearest. "I've not invested in expensive facilities and some of the best engineers just to make kites!"

Refilling his mouth, grease dribbling down his chin, he'd wiped his oily lips with his neighbour's napkin and waited until he had the room's attention although he knew that he'd lost Stephanie's.

"Suffice it to say," he'd said pointing a greasy finger at the red-faced accountancy junior partner from Clerkenwell, "what we're doing at Berkley Technologies will change the way some things are done. And, to answer your moronic question Cyril… well, let's just say… what we do could affect all aspects of life. And death. Maybe even yours Cyril."

At that moment, every single person in the room, including the hired butler and waiting staff, would have cheerfully liked to have seen Ray Berkley drop down dead.

"Lend me a few quid then."

Dr Malcolm Carmichael, one of Berkley Technologies' top engineers, rolled over in the bed, found his wallet and removed a twenty pound note. Inadvertently three came out at once, each of which were snatched from his hand. He said nothing.

Amber Cooper's mouth smiled but not her eyes. Malcolm knew that he was this beautiful woman's private bank. He knew he was being a fool. She liked his money, his car and more of his money. He supposed that she might like his intelligence too, although he doubted it because when he tried to explain something, she was always thinking about or doing something else. Neither did she much care and often said so.

He knew that he'd found himself a gorgeous girlfriend. He didn't mind treating her to dinners, jewellery and clothes. It made him feel good, momentarily anyway. It annoyed him that she kept nagging that she wanted to be invited to his house something that wasn't ever going to happen and he had no intention of explaining why. But the upside for her it seemed was being treated to overnight visits twice a week or so to one of the many coastal hotels.

Malcolm watched Amber dress and wondered what on earth he was doing with this twenty eight year old woman who was anything but kind. Was it, he wondered yet again, his own fault? He arrived at no conclusion other than it was.

On his drive to work, he thought about Amber and why she was attracted to him. He knew of course that he was no great looker and had the general demeanour of a world-weary man. Tall and appearing much older than his thirty four years, he knew that he tended to walk with a stoop, invariably facing the ground as if in perpetual, deep thought. From childhood onwards he'd been very clever, but always unnoticeable and ordinary. Here in Little Peasen though he'd been astonished to find that he was noticed and, at least in the eyes of some single and a few married women, found to be extraordinary. He felt used but, on the basis that this was the first time that he'd had regular sex, he wasn't keen to change the scenario, although he knew that the status quo would lead only to more emptiness for him.

At the front gates of Berkley Technologies, he didn't even bother to nod at one of the unsmiling security guards who always seemed to be halfway through a thick, jam sandwich. Malcolm was a aware of her first name not least because it was on her name badge, but never felt brave enough to use it and no friendship had ever been offered or encouraged.

He stared at the tall, triple Gallagher M10000i electric fence in front of his car. Tapping his steering wheel impatiently as he waited, he knew that this morning had brought with it another large helping of self-pity. As the gates slowly opened and the duty guard impatiently waved him in so that she could go back to discussing… well, Malcolm wondered, what would the guards be discussing? Sandwich fillings maybe? Football? The prime minister? Sex? Some social media scandal? Dr Carmichael's receding hairline?

At the second set of security gates, he sat impatiently while the video sensors and millimetre wave scanners went to work. For reassurance, he felt underneath his seat and touched the small, osmium-lined box designed to look like the first aid kit it replaced. That he knew would not show up on the scanners. He noticed that, on the passenger seat, at some point Amber must have left a flyer boldly advertising The Annual Little Peasen Fête. Malcolm stared at it before folding it neatly and putting into his jacket pocket.

As he waited, he smiled much as a small child might at the sheer cleverness of the technology at work in front of him. Another train of thought struck him as it did nearly every day and any vestiges of any smile on his face fled. Ray Berkley had known Malcolm's father from days when they'd both worked in the same firm. They had never much liked each other and their paths diverged when Ray went off to pursue his entrepreneurial career and Malcolm's father left the world of commerce to become a housemaster at a well-known London public boarding school. One day, out of the blue, Malcolm's father found himself falsely accused of sexual abuse against two pupils. The case had seemed water tight at the time and he'd lost his job in ignominy. Months later he had committed suicide.

A few years after that, Ray had been in touch with a job offer.

Malcolm's prowess and burgeoning engineering brilliance was of interest. Malcolm had refused. The very next day, Malcolm's mother, unwell with a serious illness, had received a phone call from Ray.

Ray had explained to Malcolm's ill mother that it had been he who had fed the stories about Malcolm's father to the school with cleverly fabricated but damning photographs. He'd made it clear that one of his business colleagues had wanted a serious accusation against his son dropped. The son had badly beaten a much younger child at the school. It hadn't been simply a beating, but the younger child had been left with horrific injuries. The case was extreme and, if not dropped, could have resulted in a prison sentence for the perpetrator. Certainly it would have put the kibosh on the young man's planned legal career. The business colleague needed Malcolm's housemaster father to stand up for the business colleague's son and ensure that all records showed that he had always been a star pupil which had most definitely not been the case. Malcolm's father had refused point blank.

Ray once again tried to lure Malcolm to join his firm. The offer had been excellent with good money, a top of the range car and great perks. Again, Malcolm had refused. Within a week, a pack of photographs had arrived at the house that Malcolm shared with his mother. They were of Malcolm in compromising positions with various men and women. They were all bogus, but Malcolm knew that they looked very real and would appear so to anyone else. Ray rang Malcolm threatening to show these photos to Malcolm's sick mother and to his current employer unless he joined Berkley Technologies.

Malcolm was jolted into the here and now by a multiple-jointed automatic bomb detection system which had begun moving along the underside of the car. Other mechanical arms scanned the vehicle's contents as well as everything inside that was human. The noises of the equipment suddenly stopped and there was a pause. Malcolm held his breath. One by one, the six warning lights blinked red, hesitated at amber and finally displayed green as the huge metal anchors were lifted from the tungsten gates. He drove through and breathed.

As he parked and set up a charge for his Tesla, he thought of his burning hatred of Ray Berkley. He thought about his mother. He knew in his heart of hearts that she'd seen the photographs, but had said nothing. Within a month of the photographs being sent, she'd been admitted to hospital and one morning not long after that, there'd been a telephone call to say that she was dead.

Five

Specialising in a few antiquarian texts, but mostly tomes on local history and books bought at house clearance auctions, William Benedict had been on a mission to replenish his bookshop stock. The popular New and Second Hand International Book Fair of Stockholm, not to be confused of course with the Svenska Antikvariatföreningen, was an occasion that he'd always much enjoyed, even though he could only afford to attend once every couple of years.

Although he felt under the weather due to his hangover, William was excited at the prospect of receiving his new purchases. He had ordered, or rather thought he'd ordered, a quantity of titles by a Swedish author called Edmond Sergusson, written in English and mostly about early settlements in East Anglia. This was because William had felt that he should branch out and cater for a wider variety of public tastes although, on his own admission, understanding his buying public was more miss than hit. Instead of the Edmond Sergusson titles on early East Anglia however, what he had actually purchased, although he didn't know it yet, was a large number of Swedish cookery books written in Swedish and English by a woman called Engegärd Sergusson. In addition, he had also bought twelve large crates of new paperback novels written, he had thought, in English by Swedish novelists. However, what the crates actually contained was an eclectic mix of science fiction written in a variety of European languages, the majority thankfully in English.

William, an easy victim to flattery, had been persuaded to buy a quantity of beautifully illustrated hard copies of the *Pippi Longstocking* stories in English which he had been told were destined to be remaindered. He was a great fan of the eponymous series of children's books by Swedish author Astrid Lindgren. His nieces had long ago delighted in giggles when he'd read them the tales – and he well remembered their three and five year old faces glowing with excitement at the protagonist's escapades.

Remaindering such beautiful and possibly collectible books would have been a terrible waste he'd thought, although he hadn't been at all sure if the threat had been true. However, there was an issue with the books which the dealer had openly explained. In every copy, pages thirty three and therefore thirty four were missing. William hoped that customers might not notice this until it was too late and then, if challenged, he imagined that he would express horror at the error, but shrug his shoulders. He'd already planned his approach and had practised this under his breath on the plane home from Stockholm much to the voluble consternation of the woman sitting next to him.

"Sorry," he planned to say to any complaining *Pippi Longstocking* customer. "I really can't reimburse you the money. The books are extremely rare and, like other collectibles, well… any missing element will only enhance future values. Of course, these were sold to you at a very reasonable price and, well, caveat emptor you know, caveat emptor. Mind you," he avowed to add quickly to any customer threatening violence, "you must agree that the illustrations on their own are worth having."

William had assumed that what he'd ordered were three hundred copies of the book, but he was to discover that the number was actually one thousand three hundred. His last purchase had been thirteen cases of mixed hardback novels written in English. Many were dubious in that they were soft porn under the guise of historical fiction. Well, he thought, they'd been cheap, were brand new and local care homes along with a few private buyers always liked to buy risqué books. He'd ensured that all of his purchases were wooden-crated since, in his experience, despite the extra cost, this meant less likely transport damage. All in all, he'd flown home reasonably satisfied with his trip, despite the aquavit hangover and an overdraft.

The Albanian driver of the P220 Scania HGV collecting William's crates of books was happy. The discharging of the crates at Immingham Docks had been straightforward and the sun was shining. While waiting for the truck to be loaded, the driver had on rare impulse arranged to take a small but unofficial detour. This deviation was for the purpose of meeting a good Albanian friend at the Banham service station on the A47. The driver was looking forward to having a catch-up in the café there about whatever was going on back home. However, immediately after agreeing to the meeting, the Albanian friend had been arrested for an altercation with a traffic warden and he'd been temporarily relieved of his belongings including of course his phone.

At exactly the same time, a Mercedes-Benz Actros articulated lorry loaded with a huge cache of arms and ammunition was making its way along the same A47 road, London bound. The Boeing CH-47 Chinook helicopter had landed at Brancaster Bay on time in the very early hours and the transfer had been perfect. The driver reflected that his now demised pal Bardhyl Bardhyly would have been pleased with the speed of the transfer. His good humour fled. Despite the sunshine and low traffic volume, the driver frowned at the thought that he had to break his journey.

He and his co-driver had been instructed to meet a Mafia Shqiptare gang contact at the Banham services on the A47. There the contact was to tell the driver the precise destination for the delivery of arms and ammunition in London. This was a security precaution and quite the norm amongst the Shqiptare's operatives. The arms' delivery driver, annoyed at having to stop – always a risk he thought – had been ordered to go to cubicle number two in the men's lavatories at precisely three-thirty in the afternoon. He was to knock and say nothing to whoever was waiting for him in the cubicle except, "Shqiponja ka zbritur." He thought it odd to say that the eagle has landed, but he knew that doing what one was told meant that one stayed alive. He also knew that, following the utterance of the eagle nonsense, he would receive by way of instant reply the precise delivery address in London for the arms' delivery.

It turned out that the gang member who should have been waiting in cubicle number two with the precise London address was, at three-thirty, in bed with a lady who hailed from Grimsby. Anyway, as it happened, and as is sometimes the case in the world of happenstance, at exactly three–thirty in cubicle number two of the Banham services' men's lavatories, the book delivery driver was literally minding his own business and making himself comfortable. Without warning, someone barged in, breaking the cubicle's lock in the process. Surprised and not a little annoyed, the book delivery driver shouted something in Albanian to the effect of, "Now, you've made me wet my trousers!"

The man who had barged in, an Albanian supermarket delivery driver on his way to his depot, was genuinely embarrassed at having disturbed a fellow citizen while at his lavatorial endeavours. In an effort at reconciliation, the supermarket delivery driver handed the book delivery driver a twenty pound note towards the repair of the damaged trousers. Reluctantly he also handed over a colourful London club flyer the presentation of which would entitle the user to a decent discount, some private dancing and two free drinks.

The book delivery driver, still upset, accepted the money and the flyer. In his distraction, he assumed wrongly from the gabbling supermarket delivery driver that there had been a change of plan and that the club in London's Soho was now where his truck of books had to go. Honour of sorts reinstated, the two men bade each other farewell with customary hugs.

The book delivery driver stayed behind to focus on cleaning his trousers – much to the consternation of others using the sinks – and emptied his trouser pockets to better enable the process. Unnoticed, he accidentally dropped the piece of paper on which was written the original book delivery instructions and address in Little Peasen. Feeling able to face the world once more and, following attempted phone calls, he disappointedly assumed that his Albanian friend had either given up or had something better to do. He shrugged and went off to find his co–driver to tell him of the new direction for the journey which was now London and not Little Peasen. His co-driver, who was chatting up an American student at a coffee outlet, stared at the book delivery driver's trousers, wet in all the wrong places. The American student, also seeing the state of the trousers, made her alarmed excuses and fled, much to the annoyance of the book delivery co-driver.

Meanwhile, five minutes after the book delivery driver had left the service station washroom, the arms' delivery driver arrived at cubicle two anxious and out of breath. That the traffic had become worse as the journey had continued irritated him to the point of headache. Sweating profusely, he swore out loud when he discovered that nobody was in the cubicle. With absolutely no clue as to where he was to deliver the valuable cargo of arms and ammunition, panic had begun to overtake his headache along with the thought of what would shortly become of him. Glancing down he noticed a piece of paper on which he could see were some details comprising of an address and something else written in Albanian. Picking the note up and reading it carefully twice, he raised his eyes and arms heavenwards, noticing the filth on the washroom ceiling. He thanked all the world's deities, a relieved grin spreading across his face.

An Albanian professor of history, visiting the UK for the first time and now washing his hands in the same washroom, heard the arms' delivery driver repeatedly say, "Brilliant!" in Albanian. The professor turned, greeted the driver and, enjoying the ensuing conversation, offered coffee as a gesture of Albanian goodwill. Delighted, the arms' delivery driver nodded and sidled up to the professor while whispering the words, "Shqiponja ka zbritur." The professor, surprised, wasn't at all sure how to answer the question as to whether any eagle had landed somewhere.

"A ka vërtet? Sa interesante!" was what he said. For the benefit of practising his English and partly to show off a little, he provided a translation, "Has it really? How interesting!"

This was more than good enough for the arms' delivery driver, who was just enormously relieved to have found, he thought, someone senior in the Mafia Shqiptare's hierachy. For his part, the history professor, who had never been in a gang of any sort, apart from once at school aged six, was simply pleased to meet a fellow countryman interested in ornithology, something he himself knew little about.

The arms' delivery driver was privately beside himself with joy at avoiding death now that he had a target address, although unknown to him it was of course the wrong one. He thought it very clever that the man before him had deliberately put the piece of paper on the floor so that it could be easily seen.

On the way from the washroom to the cafeteria, it transpired that both the arms' delivery driver and the history professor knew the city of Tirana. The professor proudly declared that he worked at the university there teaching history. The arms' delivery driver smiled knowingly at the professor and considered that this was a great cover story. He accepted of course that cover stories had to be kept, even with colleagues in the same gang. The professor, generous with his time, was pleased to meet the arms' delivery driver's co-driver and immediately offered and bought Danish pastries and coffee for them all.

Both the arms' delivery driver and his co-driver were keen on football and, once the professor had returned with a full tray, they tried to engage him in talk about the game. After ten minutes, the professor had heard enough about the pros and cons of the Vllaznia football team, famous in Shkodër, but possibly not elsewhere. The arms' delivery co-driver sensed that the man in front of him, clearly a clever gun-running maestro masquerading as a professor, was becoming impatient. Fearing the possible consequences of that, the co-driver, an avid reader, thought it best to change the subject and, in some desperation, wondered out loud where he might find some Albanian books to read in this part of the world, not really expecting a helpful answer. However, anxious now to wrap up the conversation and be on his way, the professor was delighted to be able to help.

"As it happens," said the professor standing up ready to bid the two men farewell, "there is a bookshop in a village called Little Peasen not far from here that might be able to help. Actually," he enthused as he fished about in a jacket pocket, "I have a card with the address. Here, take it. You could go there quite easily. I drove through there not so long ago in my blue hire car you know. The bookshop is reasonable and the owner helpful. A pleasant man. He will offer you some coffee or lemon tea and maybe a ginger biscuit. He certainly has a few books in Albanian. I myself bought an interesting book there on Iceni tradecraft, although that was in English of course."

The arms' delivery driver thought for a moment and carefully pulled out the piece of paper that he'd picked up in the washroom. He glanced at it below table height and then at the card that the professor had just handed him. Yes, he thought, Little Peasen! And the address was a bookshop! Exactly the same address! That's what the professor had just said and that's what was written here! The arms' delivery driver knew beyond any doubt whatsoever now that before him was a brilliant mastermind. He grinned at the professor, but toned it down a bit when he thought that perhaps grinning was the wrong thing to do.

A hiss of air brakes announced the arrival of a large truck outside the bookshop. William's delivery was later than advised, but he didn't mind. He imagined that getting through ports these days, what with various issues including terrorist threats and the increase in people-smuggling, was a drawn-out process and delays would be normal. Excitedly, he opened his door with a welcoming beam. The driver stared at William but said nothing and neither did the co-driver. Standing at the front door, they both looked rather serious and William was taken aback to notice that one of the men possibly had a gun stuffed under his T-shirt.

The co-driver suddenly smiled and insisted on going into the actual bookshop, chattering now in Albanian to which William could only listen but not interpret. He guessed that the language was Albanian because the co-driver's T-shirt bore the word Shqipëri which William knew was Albanian for Albania.

He felt his stomach churn a little in trepidation as he and the delivery driver just stood looking at each other in the hallway while the co-driver perused books. Within minutes though the co-driver handed over five pounds, the correct money, for two out-of-print hardback books in Albanian. One was about manufacturing in Liverpool and the other seemed to be an out-of-date treatise on the conquering of Everest, but with some decent colour photographs.

William started in alarm when the two men seemed to expect him to unload the truck himself, something nobody could do on their own. He panicked and began speaking loudly and slowly in the hope that he would be better understood. The men stared at him. Trying poor sign language, reinforcing the fact that William knew how awful he was at charades, he half invited and half led the men into the kitchen where he bade them sit. Hastily giving each man a cold can of Coca Cola and glasses filled with ice, he decided to put two more cans on the table and added a plate piled high with ginger nut biscuits.

Using Google Translate, William looked up what he needed on his phone. Once the driver and co-driver saw what the message read, they nodded. Chattering to each other for a bit they came to a conclusion. The co-driver made the international sign for money by rubbing a thumb against a forefinger. William understood, but had no clue what he should offer. He was also annoyed because he had been promised by the Swedish transport company that the crates would be unloaded free of charge. Swallowing any disappointment, he got up to grab his wallet and sat down again in front of the men who had by now eaten all the biscuits. Extracting two fifty pound notes he looked up expectantly. The men stared back. Gulping, he took out two more with the same result. He only had three twenty pound notes left in his wallet and began to panic again. The co-driver looked pointedly at the wallet. William withdraw the last three notes. All the notes were plucked neatly from his right hand and, grinning, both men gave him a thumbs up sign as they trooped off to unload the truck.

Whistling and joking amongst themselves, the driver and co-driver took the wooden crates down to what had once been the chapel's crypt. The job took well over three hours and, once complete, the men left with a case of Evian, another of Malbec, five large unopened boxes of shortbread left over from Christmas, two bumper bags of twenty four variety flavoured packets of crisps, a huge carrier bag of Braeburn apples from the bookshop's garden and a return of the money that had been paid for the hardback books on Liverpool and Everest. He was relieved to see the two men go on several counts, the main one being that he'd spotted the gun sticking out of the driver's belt, exposed by the exertions of the unloading.

Closing the door in some relief, there had been a screech of brakes and William's stomach had somersaulted when the co-driver, looking apologetic, had returned to hand over a large parcel, perfectly packaged, neatly taped and unlabelled. William didn't know what to do, but the co-driver smiled, offering up the package and indicated that William should take it. Pretty sure that the parcel couldn't be for him, William shook his head vehemently and pointed across the road to the post office. Anxious to be on his way, the co-driver took the parcel across the road and placed it carefully outside the post office door under cover just as it began to rain.

Relieved at the men's final departure, the disappearing roar of the huge diesel engine and the diminishing underlying fear, William's current issue was whether or not he should try the vegan sausages that Sheila Prewer, his military hobbyist neighbour and vegan par excellence, had bought for him.

"Try 'em, Willy," she'd said on many an occasion. "They're dead good."

Six

Mr Grise, a divorce lawyer of some experience, was obliged to listen yet again to his client explaining that it was her looks that had first hooked Ray Berkley just over six years ago.

"I was takin' someone's coat at the club, Mr G. London's best y'know… Bin clubbin' much 'ave you? No? Well, no worries. One day… Any'ow, Ray rocks up wiv 'is then girlfriend. She didn't even give me the time of day. Silly cow. Let me tell you Mr G, by the end of the evenin' the snotty woman 'ad been put in a taxi alone and I'd been asked out for dinner for the following evenin'! Le Gavroche it were!"

Initially this story had been told by Stephanie Berkley to the lawyer as one of pride but, as their meetings had gone on, Mr Grise felt that the pride had become replaced with anger, frustration and misery at what once had been.

Mr Grise of Grise, Doughty and Pantile explained the detail of the latest offer put forward by Ray Berkley's legal team. Stephanie tried to listen but listening wasn't her strong suit. As she attempted and failed to gather what her lawyer was trying to explain, she thought back to when she'd first met her husband.

"I'm twenty-three," she remembered telling her then best friend Susie after her first date with Ray, "and I've been on the lookout for a man like Ray since God was a girl."

Stephanie hadn't been daft and knew that Susie had been bored rigid and had spitefully blown across the top of her cappuccino hoping that the chocolate detritus might make its way onto her friend's white, Natori blouse.

"The bloke's not 'andsome in the normal sense," had extolled Stephanie, ignoring Susie's efforts at blowing chocolate shavings at her, "but 'e's got summat… and Suse… Suse babes," Stephanie had squeaked, "I reckon 'e's seriously loaded!"

Stephanie had always known that she was bone idle. She'd

also always known that with patience she could, as she'd always put it, grab some rich pillock by the goolies and marry him. It hadn't been a description that she'd shared with Ray of course, but when he'd asked her to marry him, no thinking time had been necessary. The icing on the cake in addition to the dinners, clothes, cars, jewellery, fabulous trips abroad and the apartment in Devonshire Street, had been the cup of Earl Grey tea and small cucumber sandwiches with the crusts cut off at the prime minister's home in Downing Street.

At the time, Ray had been happy to have been hooked.

"I'm not stupid. I know what's going on," Ray had said with his mouth full of sauté potato to the managing director of a supplier company over dinner at Boodle's.

Without appearing to be rude and because he'd wanted a new, substantial contract to be signed, the managing director had spent time surreptitiously avoiding spat particles of potato flying at speed in his direction. He'd put Ray's behaviour down to alcohol, overfed ego and lack of manners with manners perhaps taking the lead.

"I grew up with not a lot of cash in a big city like Steph did," Ray had said speaking as if wanting to share his views with the whole room, "and I'm no better. I understand her and I admire her spunk… Oh, sorry. Too loud? Determination's a better word, is it? Alright, determination then. She's just an attractive woman who's got enough… determination to sort out her life using whatever attributes she's got."

The managing director of the supplier company hadn't been asked his opinion and would have offered none had he been invited to have a view. But he'd met Stephanie and had thought privately that Ray had been and was making a big mistake. But, he'd considered, it wasn't his mistake and therefore he couldn't have cared less – as long as his contract got signed before the evening was out. He'd also realised that within a day or two he would have to apologise to the club secretary in person and then in writing for his ill-mannered dinner guest.

"Anyway," Ray had gone on, thumping the table for emphasis and causing all the cutlery to jump, "she looks good even after some rough an' tumble." He'd sniggered. "Know what I mean? Course you do! And she understands more or less which knife and fork to use. And how to eat an artichoke."

With that pronouncement Ray had shoved the last of his Kobe steak into his mouth and had washed it down with a half glass of Domaine Etienne Guigal, all seemingly in one movement. He'd continued to further embarrass his dinner companion and had also irritated a visiting African bishop who'd been having a hoped-for quiet meal with senior members of the British clergy.

"Sure she wants to spend my money," Ray had concluded before turning the conversation to business, "but that's OK for the time being. Once we're married she'll toe the line. You not going to eat that beef?"

Once married, everything had gone as Ray and Stephanie had both planned.

"It's great babes," Stephanie had said on the phone to her latest best friend Lottie, a Premier League footballer's wife. "I can allus butter up Ray's business people. Yeah, it's a bit of a felafel really, but dead easy. Wiggle me bum and they'll do anything. Whassat? Love? Nah, course not, but the money's great, the sex is OK and, to be fair babes, we both understand each other."

Later in the marriage the rows had become a fixture. Daisy, her then best friend, a TV weather presenter's partner, had been obliged to listen.

"Daze, Ray wants kids! I told 'im to eff off Daze. I don't want no kids, Daze," she'd whined. "I seen what 'avin' a kid does to a gels' figure. Yeah, I know you got kids Daze."

Daisy had listened but knew better than to respond very much and so had just picked over the expensive lunch of lettuce leaves, half a ripe avocado, a teaspoon of Brie de Meaux, two firm cherry tomatoes, a carrot cut into the shape of a flower and three slivers of thin wholemeal French toast.

"And, Daze," Stephanie had complained to her friend who'd been much more interested in an Italian waiter, "it bloody 'urts! And them nappies! Don't mean to be a damp squid an' that but, if I gotta look after someone, then that someone's me – end of."

Following the receipt of divorce papers and various legal meetings, a fog of financial gloom had fallen over Stephanie. Mr Grise had explained in words of one syllable that she was due to receive a modest, but by most people's standards very decent, one-off lump sum in settlement and a two-bedroomed flat in East London that Ray had kept as a rental for years.

In front of Mr Grise, she had argued and wept explaining that she knew that there were more properties off grid. Her lawyer had folded his hands and explained that all other properties would have been leased or sub-leased with eventual ownership disappearing into Switzerland, Belize or the Bahamas. Hard and very expensive, if not impossible, to trace. As for Ray's financial status, while Stephanie was sure that her husband had bank accounts where she or indeed the inland revenue would never find them, Mr Grise again pointed out that any search would be costly. Whatever the scenario, he indicated as delicately as he could, she had little muscle with which to fight. He had also been obliged to explain that, after the divorce, she would have four weeks to vacate the smart, four-bedroomed, Devonshire Street apartment in which she had spent the last six years and had regarded as home.

Mr Grise coughed loudly which forced Stephanie to tune back into the present. Her stomach turned to ice as she heard her solicitor repeat the next steps in the divorce proceedings. She realised that she had little time left to do anything to scupper her husband. When Mr Grise finished, she once again made it clear what she thought about her position.

"Mr G, when Ray bought Darkwater 'all, 'e said that the plan would be to move to Norfik permanent like, keepin' the London place as a cafetière."

Mr Grise wondered. "Do you mean pied-à-terre?"

"S'what I said."

Mr Grise was desperate to get away from the partly exposed breasts and ruination of grammar in front of him and go for a walk in Hyde Park after which he might enjoy a sandwich and a flat white in a café where he could be alone with his own company. Perhaps, he mused, a hearty plate of spaghetti bolognaise, a decent side salad and a half bottle of Chianti might be better.

"Please go on," he said.

"That place!" Stephanie exclaimed. Mr Grise knew very well what that place meant. He hoped that his client hadn't seen that he'd involuntarily rolled his eyes at the thought of the ensuing ennui of the next half hour or so.

"Why the bleedin' 'ell Ray bought that place I still dunno. Nobody in their right skull would wanna buy a manky Tudor 'ouse wiv fields and whatnot. And 'e spent a fortune doing up that 'ouse and then forked out even more dosh buildin' that factory thingy! All from money that I want!"

Stephanie had tapped a manicured nail on her front teeth, a habit that Mr Grise still found irritating. He reflected that he had aged since taking on this new client and now felt considerably older than his fifty three years.

"Mr G," his client grumbled, "I stayed in that 'ouse for free 'ole weeks and I can tell you it was more than enough for a gel to know that I bloody 'ate the place, the stupid gardens, the one shop village, fick people wiv turrets what never wash and the brown, bloody sea." She shuddered.

Mr Grise couldn't help himself asking the question.

"Turrets?"

"Yeah you know when them people what shout an' swear an' they can't 'elp it."

"Possibly you might mean Tourette's syndrome. That's an illness Mrs Berkley."

"S'what I mean. Them lot. And Ray actually reckoned I'd wear green wellies and make jam! Me! Make jam!"

Mr Grise wanted to say that he'd heard the majority of this before, but he didn't. Instead he closed his eyes briefly and fervently wished that one of the other partners of Grise, Doughty and Pantile had taken this case.

"I jus' want some fun," Stephanie whined, "not oiled rain jackets and a dirty little pub what stinks of stale beer, old people, diesel, sweat an' chips."

The lawyer gently pushed a box of tissues towards his client as he asked her again if there was anything at all that Stephanie could think of that might help her case. She shook her head, but suddenly brightened.

"Mr G, maybe there is summink! My 'usband wants to be chair of the Little Peeing Paris Council. And I know for a fact that the pillock 'as allus wanted a gong."

Mr Grise boggled. "You mean perhaps the parish council… and… er… possibly an honour of some sort?"

"S'what I jus' said."

"Mrs Berkley, it'd be best advised to call the village in which Mr Berkley resides Little Peasen I think."

"Yeah, yeah. Whatever. Listen… I reckon I could cause 'im some damage. Get some of what you calls leverage."

What, enquired her tired lawyer did Mrs Berkley have in mind?

What she had in mind, his client said, delighted with the development of a plan, was a visit to some cruddy fair.

"A fair?" Mr Grise asked, bemused by whether a fair might be what his client called cruddy, a word that wasn't in his vernacular.

"Yeah, the Liddle Piddle Sugar Beet Fête."

"I'm sorry?"

"There's a village fair. Big one an' all. I'm gonna go."

"Go?" asked Mr Grise hopefully.

"Yeah. On Sunday. Mess up me weekend but never mind. Wurf it. Mr G, I do fink we might be able to do summat."

She stood up, straightening her short skirt, pleased with her burgeoning plan.

"Won't your husband be there?"

"That's the bleedin' idea mate," she called from the room's door as she twiddled a few fingers at her legal advisor. "I want 'im to be there. Cos after that 'e's gonna be a dead duck!"

Seven

In the Cromer beach hut to which he and his gang of three had no entitlement, Adidas, still nursing his broken nose, had just been reading a small poster pinned up on the inside of the hut. It was advertising what it described as 'a fun occasion for all the family' and was due to take place the next day in the village of Little Peasen. This, he thought dismally, was the deadline that had been set for him and his small team to retrieve the guns and ammunition and get them to where there were supposed to have gone in the first place. On pain of death. His nose hurt in sympathy with his bowels which fluttered in fear.

Never one much able to make decisions if matters could be put off, Adidas blew out his cheeks, took a deep breath and stared out at the blue and grey North Sea, the wind causing white flurries on the gentle swell. Sitting on the horizon's ledge, there were two container ships, one red and the other yellow, that had seemingly not moved at all, although, when Adidas glanced back at them, of course they had. He looked up at the sky wondering at a cloud that looked a bit like his grandmother, although he reflected that it wasn't a particularly complimentary thought. Somewhere someone's radio was playing a Keith Jarrett number, pleasant on the warm sea breeze.

"We're now in the harms business," Adidas said, more bravely than he felt as he regarded a squadron of brightly coloured kites moving this way and that over the beach.

"Once this deal is done," he reflected, "well, then I reckon we should do some more harms business. Bigger an' better deals." Proudly he added, "That's what it would say on me business cart if I 'ad business carts: 'Bigger an' better deals'. Waddya think?"

"Yeah, whatever, boss," muttered Wilf irritably, not really interested in the process of arms dealing or, for that matter, business cards. "Why don't we go an' wipe out the bookshop guy now? Like the man said. Could've done it already instead of sodding about at the sodding seaside!"

"Yeah," agreed one of the others whose name was Kreshnik and who, despite his poor English, was very quick to verbal anger and eventual violence. Right now, he was keen to finish the job, get back to London and rejoin the drugs' trade.

Adidas sighed. "We," he said patiently as if giving a tutorial in leadership, "are jus' waitin' till I sort stuff out. Can't afford to make any mistakes. Remember Bardhyl and Colin? Yeah? Do ya? Wanna end up like them? No you don't! Besides, if we lamp this book guy, the gun crates need to be ready to rock an' roll and so far we got no wheels."

Before Terence, the fourth member of the team, could join in the discussion and ask whose effing fault that was, a small child walked past the beach hut licking a huge ice-cream cone with a chocolate flake inserted between the soft, vanilla ice-cream and partly up the child's nose. The boy stopped and stared at the men.

"Terence, tell that thing to fuck off," commanded Adidas.

"Jus' take no notice of 'im boss," said Terence who had small nephews. "He'll go in a minute."

Adidas looked away from the boy and at the two container ships still making their slow way across the edge of the world. He whispered hotly and loudly to Terence without looking at him, a confusing gesture at the best of times, but one that Adidas thought presented firm leadership and one that Terence thought presented idiocy.

"You checkin' my instructions, man? My instructions? You sayin' I'm not the boss?"

Terence wondered again why Adidas was in fact the boss. "No boss."

"Then tell the child to disappear."

"Hey, kid," called out Terence waving at the boy. "Go 'way."

The big-eyed child with soft vanilla ice cream running down his chin mixing with the green coming out of his nose, just stood and stared at the men.

"Oi, Fidel," came a woman's voice further along the promenade. "Come over 'ere right nah!"

The child turned to look but shook his head. Adidas took a gun out of his jeans' waistband and waved it at the boy who promptly squeaked, dropped the ice cream and ran away.

"Boss, showin' your piece ain't cool!" said Wilf, who, being the biggest and strongest of the four, felt that he could speak more openly than the others.

"Shut it. I do what I want. You do what I say."

Nobody had anything to add as Adidas replaced the gun in his jeans' belt. He felt more in charge now that he'd dealt with the ice cream child and general leadership matters. He pointed at the poster on the beach hut wall.

"Wilf, you nick a car and go to that village Little Pee whatever. You wait overnight and then go to the bookshop in the mornin'. You talk to the Willy Benedict guy and you explain the mistake which I reckon by now 'e knows. You offer Willy three grand cash just so that we can take the crates away without any fuss. No trouble. He shuts up and we get out."

"But boss," said Wilf shaking his head, "first, we got no wheels and second, the man said we got to toast the bookshop guy. Third why wait till tomorrow? What's wrong with now?"

"Well," replied Adidas looking theatrically round the hut, "I don't see nobody else in charge. The man ain't 'ere. I am. 'sides," he said holding the bridge of his sore nose, "we may need the bookshop guy as a 'ostage and we can scare 'im big time so 'e won't talk. Wilf, if I says you go now, you go now. You don't wanna rile me! Go buy some sandwiches or summat, nick a car in Cromer – any ol' banger'll do – an' you get some kip an' wait. Tomorrer, there'll be noise around so it'll be better."

Wilf couldn't untangle all that he'd been told. But he tried. "Why don't we all go tomorrow then?"

There was a pause. "Because I want to sort out wheels and

because… I fuckin' said so!"

Wilf wanted to hit his boss. "What if the Willy guy does blab though? Don't we need to nip this one in the butt?"

Adidas stared for a moment at Wilf. Collecting himself, he barked angrily, "If 'e blabs, 'e blabs. We'll be gone. Maybe we thump him a bit. Tie 'im up. We'll tell 'im we know where 'e lives an' such. Maybe we'll take 'im with us."

Wilf said nothing but just stared at his boss, seriously concerned now about Adidas' sanity, his leadership qualities and the wisdom of his instructions. He missed Bardhyl Bardhyly.

"What if he tries to be difficult?" he asked.

"For fuck's sake Wilf! Then you do 'im. But quiet like. No red. Get me? Clean. First, just chat. If there's a fuss, make the scratch four thou. Anything else, do 'im."

Again Wilf stared at his boss wondering if they were on the same planet never mind the same page.

"You want me to go on me own?"

"Yeah. You frit?"

"I ain't frit."

"Yeah, you frit."

"I ain't frit. I'm never frit, you know that."

"I don't know bollocks. It's a doggy dog world Wilf."

Wilf gaped again at his boss for a moment. "So, you lot staying 'ere?"

"Sure, why not? We'll wait for you to call and tell us all's clear. I'll talk to the client and tell 'im to organise a truck for tomorrow night. Tell 'im I couldn't sort nothin' else. No trucks aroun' an' such. Spin a line. Easy. There's that village thing goin' on tomorrow, so nobody'll be any trouble. We load the truck, wait till late and go. Easy. Wilf, you don't talk to nobody unless it's the bookshop guy. Gimme your phones."

The others handed over their mobiles as Adidas took four fresh burner phones with new SIM cards out of his holdall. He made sure that the only numbers they had were each other's and then he added an app on one of the phones. He took out the SIM cards from the old phones and scrunched them with his gun, then hit each old phone very hard twice, neatly putting the debris into a plastic bag which went into the holdall.

Resentfully, Wilf trudged off pocketing his new phone while the other three, with no embarrassment at all, changed into recently purchased fluorescent swimming shorts. They stuffed their weapons and phones into blue, green or red plastic bags to identify which belonged to who and stashed those into the holdall. Quickly covering that with towels, one of them grabbed a pink and yellow beachball, another locked the beach hut with their own Abus Granit Plus padlock and all three ran to the sand.

William Benedict sat on a wooden crate in his crypt, looking aghast at the sea of crates around him. He now knew with sickening clarity that something had gone very badly wrong and, as a result, he felt ill, compounded by the remains of his hangover. He had always thought that acquiring fresh stock was much like deciding where and how to hang new pictures. It was a wonderful period of well-spent time, time that he had always relished both in the anticipation and the doing. The shock of seeing rows of weapons, covered in red grease and some sort of oiled paper, was immense. The shock had turned to icy fear as he thought about the fact that someone somewhere was missing a great number of armaments and would definitely want them back.

William wondered if he should ring the Swedish transport company or maybe someone at the port. But, while he'd be able to find numbers, he had no real clue as to whom he should be speaking. In his experience it would probably be like calling a utility company or a large store with a complaint. Lots of time listening to *Greensleeves,* large chunks of Vivaldi or even Boy George for hours on end. He had no appetite for any of that.

He stood up, wiped his damp hands on his T-shirt and stared at the contents of the two crates that he'd just prised open. Sitting down on a third, he quickly stood up again wondering if pressure on a crate might make something explode. The opening of another crate just exposed boxes of ammunition. In a vague but unjustified hope, but mostly in panic, he opened another two crates knowing well before he'd opened the second that he was in dead trouble.

Eight

The evening before the fair had witnessed the traditional barbecue on the Little Peasen village green – always an idyllic scene with coloured lights making the striped marquees, the bunting and the event's staging all look professional and a touch magical. Music had been on offer by an excellent, local cover band much to the delight of villagers and visitors alike, particularly a Norfolk chapter of Hells Angels.

During the earlier part of the evening, children and, actually, a fair few adults had been treated to Marvo the Magician who wore a yellow mask and a purple cloak. To everyone's delight, Marvo had produced long strings of coloured handkerchiefs out of various ears and, to his audience's further delectation, had made a variety of personal belongings disappear and appear again some distance away. Taking watches and wallets from people without them knowing caused dismay and subsequent relief. To many oohs and aahs he'd also cut up someone's twenty pound note and made it whole again by blowing on the pieces. He'd made red balls become green and green ones become white, all with the wave a magic wand. And then he'd made the wand disappear and reappear in someone's jacket pocket. At the end of the magical display, the fair's committee had ill-advisedly handed out small bags of sweets resulting in the children and one Hells Angel running riot amongst the haybales that outlined the sugar beet race course.

The music had gone on until late and revellers took their time to repair to beds, either their own or not as the case may have been. By three in the morning the village green had been empty, only a modicum of food debris littering various parts of structures and grass.

The morning of the fair found several villagers at prayer. Mrs Margaret McFlintock was making her heavenly petitions as she did every morning, although today she additionally spent some time over a cup of tea thinking about what to write in the next issue of the North Norfolk Mothers' Union newsletter. She favoured a change from the theme of maternity in biblical times and thought perhaps that the topic might well have run its current course. Neither could she see how plagues could become part of a relevant treatise, particularly since the firstborn featured, but not necessarily in a good way. Perhaps, she enthused to herself, it might pay dividend to examine an idea that had originated from one of the vicar's recent sermons. The homily had mentioned the story of Samson and Delilah and, fortuitously, Mrs Margaret McFlintock had recently watched a Cecil B. DeMille film called *Samson and Delilah* on TV. While Victor Mature was possibly not in the same league as Charlton Heston, she admired Mr Mature's demeanour if not his gumption. She trembled slightly with anger as she recalled that the Saran of Gaza, played by George Sanders, had a great deal of guile and, she had to admit, some gumption, but he had been particularly unpleasant to Mr Mature. Of course, she considered, there was that nagging concern she had about Samson's obsession with the jawbones of asses. She wondered if the vicar would be able to explain.

If the Reverend Richard Threadgill had known of the possibility of having to explain Danite Hebraic detail to his enthusiastic parishioner, he would have quaked in his flip-flops. At the moment he was saying his own prayers in the church; his were of a very different sort to Mrs Margaret McFlintock's and considerably longer. This was a favourite time of day for him and in summer months he always found the cool of the church reassuring. His wife Jessica was still in bed, but not asleep.

The dawn of the fair found Captain Horsham tired since he'd slept badly as was often the case these days. For the first time in a very long time he was saying prayers or, rather, trying to. The requests to the almighty were many and, as a result and in his keenness to get them in the right order, he'd had to restart his attempts at least three times.

He wanted the recipient of his prayers to know that every morning he was obliged to look out of his bedroom window at what had been the home of the Horsham family since 1564. All that remained of the estate under his ownership were about two acres and the small lodge and this was another issue on which he wanted some ethereal guidance. Every day brought with it a poisonous mixture of dismay, bitterness and hate against Darkwater Hall's new owner and that too was of course not good for his general well-being or relationship with any higher order. If Ray Berkley had presented himself by the big bushes of delicate, pink dog roses at that very moment, then Captain Horsham would cheerfully have fetched his rifle and shot the man. However, he assumed that this thinking wasn't particularly beneficial to the selling of any petition to a divine being.

He opened his eyes in readiness to begin his prayers again. Not a particularly religious man and generally of mild hue when it came to categorising his beliefs, he regarded the riot of purple and lilac azaleas. He recalled his grandmother having planted those. As he looked through the window at what was still his, now fenced off from the main estate, he noticed Sydney Baxter who lived with his wife Rosie in a little grace and favour cottage within the curtilage of the land that he still owned.

Sydney was sitting on a bench next to an aged bothy which had been unused for years. Unusually, noticed Captain Horsham, the bothy's door was ajar and he idly wondered why. Normally nobody ever used it, not since his wife Dorothy had passed away. He recalled with a rare smile that she'd kept tulip bulbs and shallots there during winter months and had been at pains to tell him on many occasions never to confuse the two boxes.

He glanced again at Sydney and felt deeply sorry for the man. Losing contact with someone, in this case a son, must be, he imagined, excruciating. Not knowing was terrible enough and the captain was aware that there'd been no contact with or from Paul Baxter for nearly six months. The captain sighed and decided to add Paul Baxter and one other item to his long list of supplications.

Sydney Baxter had decided to sit up very late the previous night and, after a few glasses of pale ale and a large helping of Rosie's homemade shepherd's pie, he'd stretched out on the bench on which he now sat and had smoked the remains of a small cigar while considering the stars. He liked looking at the heavens in the summer months and delighted in seeing something occasionally shoot across the clear, darkening skies. Rosie knew that her husband found sleep difficult. She didn't care for the idea of him spending the night outside, but it wasn't a new occurrence and so she'd put out a couple of rugs and had made him a small pack of sandwiches as well as a flask of vegetable soup in case he needed warming up.

It had been a fine night with a wonderful Sturgeon Moon and Sydney had delighted in the vastness of the canopy that we all call sky. He'd wondered again where on earth his only son could possibly be and whether Paul too might be looking at the world's umbrella at the same time as his father. The music in the distance had soothed him with its regular beat and he'd quickly drifted off to sleep. When he awoke, one of the rugs, the pack of sandwiches and the flask of soup had gone. He assumed that Rosie must have taken them inside. He sat on the bench in view of Captain Horsham's lodge and sighed. When the captain saw him next through his kitchen window, Sydney was holding his head in his hands refusing to believe that his son, Paul, might be dead.

For many of Little Peasen's villagers, the day of the fête began early, not long after dawn's cloudless sky. Freshly made bacon sandwiches, vegan buns, mugs of tea, cups of passably decent coffee and a warm breeze put almost everyone in a good mood.

The red and white striped marquee that was to be the fair's tea tent became a hive of activity. What had once been the pub's stables were emptied of the fête's paraphernalia. The wooden wheelbarrows used for the races had their wheels oiled and any rough wood was smoothed out. The sugar beets to be used for the various competitions and races were inspected, counted out, weighed and numbered. Signs, chairs, tables and all sorts of utensils were cleaned. The scattered detritus from the evening before was collected and the hay bales marking the wheelbarrow race were tidied and straightened. Lost items were found while others were lost again. Someone opened a newly purchased box of bunting only to discover that the contents were hundreds of metres of 'Happy Birthday Gran' rather than the requested triangles of red, white and blue.

The St John's Ambulance people were briefed for the third time. Jeff Cattermole was reminded to be ready by the village hall with his spotless, red 1936 Riley Lynx. He was charged with his one task – that of motoring slowly on cue along the village green carrying the fête's prince and princess, Travis, aged seven and Travis' sister Sharon, aged four along with their mother, grandmothers and a random, smiling visitor from New Zealand whom none of them knew.

Food outlets were in plentiful supply including, for the first time, a stall selling Sheila Prewer's much favoured, vegan sausages. Two ice-cream tricycles, one in sky blue and the other vivid green, had been set up, each with opposing colour parasols and battery-operated freezers attached. A popcorn stall had been erected as had an outlet selling toffee apples, although Mrs Margaret McFlintock had wanted to know whether the fête's insurance would pay out on any claim for broken teeth.

More than forty kites in various sizes and designs flew over the village green, some with animal faces, others with words, stripes, dots or a mix of all the rainbow colours. Mrs Barbara Monteith JP, in charge of the tea tent and also head of kite production at Crazy Kites, murmured a brief prayer for sunshine and breeze. Running the Crazy Kites charity, the production of kites and today's tea tent were all heavy responsibilities each of which she took very seriously.

Games and activities of all sorts in vivid, primary colours were up and running. A small merry-go-round was being tested and its twirling disco balls caught the morning sunshine. Three sad-looking donkeys were being readied for rides and already a child had fallen into a donkey deposit much to the amusement of everyone except child, parent and donkey. Splat the Rat was being trialled, although not successfully given that the woollen rat had been grabbed by a small French bulldog. Punch and Judy were being put through their paces with the operator, a retired librarian, already finding his hip flask empty and speech difficult. Various dance troupes and musicians set up or argued over set lists. A large brass band arrived by coach from Cardiff for a reason that nobody could explain and a number of its tired membership looked queasy and hot in their maroon, serge outfits.

Two fire engines were parked to allow children the eventual delight of wearing helmets and pressing buttons. The paramedics had to keep shooing people away from their ambulance where three villagers with hangovers were trying to lie down on the two beds. Norfolk Coast Radio was taking up position at a stand surrounded by large pull-up posters extolling the virtues of early morning listening.

By ten o'clock it was blazing hot and Stanley, readying himself for his MC role, signalled that the Household Cavalry CD that had been playing loudly should stop, which it did rather brutally.

"As far as I'm aware, nobody's Trooping the Colour today," Stanley heard Captain Horsham's brittle mutter as he walked past.

"Captain Horsham! That, I'll have you know," admonished Juliet Corbell, the fair's secretary, "was my choice. One never knows who's in attendance!"

Juliet Corbell, responsible for the beefy pamphlet outlining the complex sugar beet race rules, meant well, reflected Stanley, but invariably made more foes than friends on account of her lemony comments. Shrugging, Stanley began the first of his announcements concerning parking, lost and found, first aid and lavatorial arrangements, as well as the broad order of the day. That done, he heralded the arrival of the town crier.

Kevin Stringer walked towards the stage, trying hard not to stumble in the pointed, red shoes provided by the amdram society's secretary who thought the shoes best emulated town crier footwear. Thin as a rake and over six feet tall, Kevin bore no relation to the traditional town criers favoured by film-makers. Wearing a white collarless shirt and green waistcoat along with white leggings plus the red shoes, Kevin seemed to be more suited to the role of a reticent Pied Piper. Behind Kevin came Jeff Cattermole's gleaming, red Riley that at walking pace carried the fête's young prince and princess accompanied by their various relatives and the antipodean whom nobody knew.

Following the car were a dozen or so children trudging along as if to some sort of doom and wearing a variety of fancy dress costumes. In the line were a few adults also decked out in fancy dress, each hoping that they or their children would win the tasting menu dinner for two offered by the Michelin-starred King's Head. A tiny Batman was holding hands with a tall Snow White and a large fairy kept trying to trip up a small Robin Hood who was happily waving a bent, cardboard sword. Goldilocks, having already fallen over twice, was crying for her mother who was dressed as Nell Gwynne and had no time for sobbing infants. In any case, she was struggling to keep a shallow basket full of large oranges from tipping one way or another.

Striding along, looking straight ahead and concentrating hard, Kevin rang a school bell with one hand as if insisting that people should bring out their dead. Occasionally the ring would result in a dull thud as the clapper hit his thumb. In the other hand he held a large roll of pale green anaglypta wallpaper that was meant to be a scroll and had written on it his short speech in black felt-tip pen.

The wide stage to which the entourage had arrived was covered in red and white gingham cotton which the soft breeze tried to lift up like a saucy Wild West skirt. Stanley introduced Kevin enthusiastically and, after light applause but mostly whistles, the fête's town crier climbed up to the stage as if he was about to be guillotined. Handing the bell to Stanley for safekeeping, he unrolled the pale green anaglypta wallpaper leaving the assembly to focus on the orange underpants under his tights. He read in a nervous monotone and someone mistakenly started the applause before it was properly due. Eventually, Kevin bowed deeply, stepping backwards as if, exhausted, he'd just delivered the final solo number in a West End musical. Grabbing one of the man's arms, Stanley stopped him from toppling off the rear edge of the stage.

Ushering the now happy Kevin offstage, Stanley quickly introduced the guest of honour. To desultory applause, renowned theatre director and local celebrity Sir Jon Appleyard took the stage and, with the microphone slipping down its stand and him moving his head down with it, began his speech.

For whatever reason, Sir Jon had often claimed that occasions like this were not dissimilar to life in the theatre. It had been his opening gambit for most of his public speaking engagements, infrequent as they were these days. Such a notion rested, he thought, on the principle of art reflecting life. This tenet absorbed this particular audience not at all following which, in a hope that he might engage his public better, Sir Jon talked about his work directing Shakespeare. He quoted what he felt were amusing lines from a number of plays none of which resonated with the few listeners. Suddenly, or perhaps eventually, realising that his was a vertical, uphill struggle, he decided mid-sentence to declare the event to be open.

People did clap now, mostly in relief, as Sir Jon stared at the red, nylon tape held up by two posts either side of the gingham-covered stage and struggled with blunt scissors. The frustration of the moment was best made manifest by Sir Jon, who shouted a rich profanity and rasped the tape violently in half with his house keys.

Stanley quickly beckoned up to the stage the fair's young prince and princess in order to receive memento certificates from Sir Jon. Having undertaken this task and with recipients departed, Stanley put his hand over the microphone and, after an urgent whisper, the now peevish theatre director looked down at the unsmiling children and adults below the stage each of whom was wearing fancy dress of sorts. In a sudden wish to be somewhere else, Sir Jon pointed at the small child dressed as Robin Hood holding the bent, cardboard sword. Tersely declaring this child the winner, the famous theatre director tossed his hair and flounced from the stage. It was left to Stanley to present the winner and happy parent with the envelope containing the dinner voucher along with an enormous bar of pink nougat, already bending in the heat so that it matched the curvature of the child's sword. The woman dressed as Nell Gwynne threw down her basket of oranges and stomped off in search of alcohol.

Stanley cleared the stage and thanked everyone concerned. Announcing the first sugar beet wheelbarrow race between The Basin of Porridge pub and The King's Head restaurant, the fair's activities got underway with bonhomie and gusto.

Around the periphery of the village green, neatly set out stalls offered, amongst other things, pottery, paintings, etchings, knitted clothing, joinery items of dubious use, arrays of house plants, bric-a-brac, vinyl records, hemp products and second-hand books. Film makeup designer Daphne Pennyweather, a Little Peasen second home owner, but very much part of village life, eyed with some trepidation the lengthening queue of excited children and yawning or arguing parents as she began a day's work of face-painting. Crockery could be heard being destroyed at the smashing crockery stall and someone had already threatened violence over a suspicion that the sugar beet shy was a fix.

"Hot don't you think?" observed an elderly gentleman to his carer who wasn't really listening but was, instead, making eyes at a young woman who had her guitar slung over her back.

"Oh yeah," murmured the carer, hoping upon hope that the target of her flirtation would smile back at her, "dead hot."

Nine

Shop now closed, Patricia Accrington's duty as a roving seller of fifty-fifty tickets was going well although her niece had yet to show up to offer promised help. Patricia managed to stop for breath, some water and a brief chat with her brother who turned his microphone off and stepped down from the stage.

"Good turnout," she said in Stanley's left ear as she put down her heavy bucket already full of cash. "Might be a record. D'you want me to get you a… bloody hell," she grunted, as a hefty shove had her staggering.

Stanley stopped her from falling, but Patricia was bent over in pain and clutched an elbow. Her brother turned to seek out her attacker and saw a teenager with blue hair, jeans, leather jacket and Converse trainers running away with another teenager similarly dressed and carrying the bucket of money. Patricia, grimacing and rubbing her bruised elbow, looked around for the perpetrator.

"You OK?" Stanley asked putting a protective arm around his sister's shoulders.

"Yeah. Bloody hurt though. Little buggers."

"That was Anthony Helliwell. Been in all sorts of trouble. You've seen him before. D'you remember when Dad barred the lad's parents from the post office? The father's doing time in Wandsworth now and the mum scooted off to Manchester with some bloke. Tony lives with his grandmother these days. She's alright. Tony's sidekick, that's Stevie Devonport. He's another little terror, but less of a little terror than Tony's a little terror. And, by the way, they've taken your bucket of money."

Patricia whirled round to see that the bucket had gone.

"Bastards!" yelled Patricia. "Bastards," was all she could repeat in frustration and rage. People turned round to look, keen to see any drama. Patricia stared them down. She turned to her brother. "I… Why are you smiling?"

"Because in a moment I'll announce that the administration has been handed a set of motorbike keys, a wallet, a small packet of dope, roll-up papers, some tobacco, a lighter and a new iPhone. I shall also thank the two boys by name for helping to collect money for the fifty-fifty competition. I'll ask them to come up regularly during the day and tell the good people here roughly how much has been collected so far. I shan't mention the dope, but will allude to the fact that I could at any time and that the police would be interested if I did."

"How did you get those things?"

Stanley smiled. "You forget that my prowess in magic and sleight of hand is well known to… ooh all of say four people. Christmas revelries, kids' parties, office socials, weddings… they all cry out for… I thank you… Marvo the Magician! Who, they ask in amazement, is that masked man in the purple cape?"

"Idiot," said Patricia grinning with relief. "I know you're good at magic tricks and you did a great job last night getting hankies out of people's noses, but how did…?"

"Onstage, it's easy to see what's going on around the green. You see the slapped child, the one who's lost, the couple in love or lust, a dropped ice cream, the rows, an indiscrete star of stage and screen… I guessed that those two'd be trying their luck. The bucket of dosh was too good to miss. And with these crowds they knew that an easy getaway was guaranteed."

Stanley climbed back up to the stage to make the promised announcement. Sure enough, three minutes later two sullen youths stood staring up at him. One held the bucket of cash.

"Simple choice guys," said Stanley switching the microphone off and stepping down to face the boys. "The police… there're two over there… I can call them over now or you do some work for me… your choice. And of course you will apologise to my sister."

"What d'you mean, work for you?" asked Anthony, looking as

tough as he could.

“I’ll keep your indiscretions quiet including this one. But in return, from time-to-time, I’ll call on you to help keep Little Peasen safe and sound. A civil service if you like. Deal?”

“What’s that mean then, safe ‘n’ sound?”

“And what’s civil fuckin’ service?”

Stanley explained what he meant. “Any more attitude by the way and the offer’s off the table and you’re nicked. OK?”

There was no reaction from the boys.

“Fair enough. I can get Alfie Scott over here in a jiffy and I reckon he’d take you both away in cuffs. Want people to see that?” He paused. “Folk in the village lose things,” he went on more kindly, “stuff goes missing and people do things they shouldn’t. You know the form. And people, decent people, people you know, become upset. I help the police sometimes. You help me. Simple.”

“We can’t grass up our mates.”

“Agreed, but I’d expect you to let me know what’s happening if I ask you and if something really bad was going down.”

“We’d get paid?”

“Possibly. We’ll see. Depends on you. But mess me about, lie, cheat or steal – just once – and you’re history as far as I’m concerned. No three strikes. Not even two. Out first time. So. Deal?”

The two boys looked at each other for a moment and both nodded. They turned as one to Patricia and mumbled low apologies. Anthony handed the bucket to her and Stanley gave back his belongings, but not the dope.

“Hey…” began Anthony.

“You don’t need that right now.”

Stanley held a hand out and the boys looked at him for a

moment and then the hand.

"You're meant to shake it," said Patricia. "It signifies a deal."

As the two left, Anthony said to Stevie, "He's OK the post office bloke. He stood up for my dad in court."

"So?"

"I wouldn't have stood up for my dad in court. Dead straight I wouldn't."

Having ensured that her fiefdom, otherwise known as the tea tent, was still working efficiently, Barbara Monteith JP, Little Peasen's WI capo di capo and boss of the Crazy Kites initiative, approached the stage. The heels of her white shoes, bought for the occasion, collected small divots of grass. And she was uncomfortable. The shoes pinched as did several undergarments. Her emerald green dress made of thick material, a bit like the anaglypta wallpaper that town crier Kevin Stringer had used as a scroll, was far too hot.

She looked up and smiled openly but nervously at Stanley who beamed reassuringly back at her. He invited her onstage, immediately making an announcement that joining him was Barbara Monteith JP and chair of the district chapter of the local branch of the Women's Institute. Barbara blushed underneath her face powder and cleared her throat nervously.

"Er… ladies and gentlemen," she began hesitantly. For some reason the PA system blasted out a loud burst of *Stayin' Alive* from *Saturday Night Fever*. Everyone jumped but not in a good way and looked at the stage in wild surmise. Stanley, making urgent hand signals to the sleepy or inebriated technician, introduced Barbara Monteith all over again.

"Hello, everyone," she started once more, pausing briefly just in case. "Thank you so much for coming to our annual Little Peasen Sugar Beet Fête. It really is appreciated. As you know, the WI is an organisation that sits at the very heart of the village and my colleagues and I are delighted that once again we can lay claim to supporting this lovely occasion in but a modest way. I'd also like to say that it would be a delight for me and for my WI friends, if you bought one of our very reasonably priced Crazy Kites."

She pointed to the assortment fortunately still flying high and people dutifully looked up at the remarkable display.

"Money we earn from these kites is in aid of local children with learning difficulties, a worthy cause I hope you'll agree... But, ladies and gentlemen, I digress... There are two people to whom we are all indebted for truly supporting the fête from its inception. One, alas, was sadly taken from us very recently, but the other... I'm delighted to say is here now. Please welcome Mrs Janine Bishop."

So saying, Barbara did a sort of pirouette off the stage carrying the microphone and its stand with her. Stanley, retrieving the stand and microphone, helped Janine up the stage steps.

"Good afternoon," the old woman said clearly. "Mrs Monteith is very kind. I promise to be brief. And I shall certainly buy a kite in support of such an important cause." Lightly, she cleared her throat. "Many years ago my late husband donated a wooden shield for the sugar beet race between the village pub and The King's Head restaurant. It wasn't actually that well-made and he was no carpenter, but he made it with love. As I am often reminded however, the shield has seen far better days. All I wanted to say was that it was my husband's ambition to replace the shield with a silver cup. I would like to see his wish come to fruition." She paused for a moment. "My plan is to provide a new cup, suitably engraved, with the committee's approval of course, in time for next year's fête."

There was genuine applause and Stanley was impressed that people had listened to Janine's clear voice of dignity.

"I have," the old lady went on, "many good friends here in Little Peasen and I value them all." She paused and smiled. "They mean a great deal to me and have been so kind. My husband loved this village… as do I… very much. Tobias was a great supporter of the fête and he admired anyone who could control a wheelbarrow up and down the green here without losing a single beet." She smiled again as did many in the audience. "He…"

"Was a bastard!" came an angry, deep-throated yell from somewhere towards the back of the crowd. "Bloody good job 'e's dead an' all. You'll be next. Go back to Germany, you dried up ol' Nazi bitch! We don't want none of your shitty silver. Give it to your friend, 'itler!"

Janine froze and Stanley could see the utter confusion on her face. He looked out over the myriad of stunned people, but could see no culprit. Quickly, he strode across to the old lady, took one of her arms and, at her own pace, walked her offstage and down the steps. Patricia took over and led Janine away as another even louder shout from the same source could be heard.

"That's it, run away, you bleddy coward! Bugger off an' die you stinkin', ol' maggot. Nobody wants you 'ere. Sieg 'eil!"

Constable Scott and another officer could be seen making their way through the crowd, but the culprit seemed to have vanished. Stanley quickly introduced the next race, one for the mums and dads and, as is often the case after a shocking moment which has been and gone, the mood relaxed in relief and voluble opinions.

More races followed, as did varieties of music and the full menu of entertainments. Anything cold on the drinks' front was already in low supply and most of the WI baked goods had gone, much to the delight of Barbara Monteith who now wished fervently that she'd worn a better girdle, less makeup, a summer dress and flat shoes.

"People often say stupid and nasty things when they've been drinking," Patricia was saying helplessly to Janine Bishop as they walked towards the old lady's cottage, the noise of the fair diminishing behind them. "Please don't think that we're all like that. We just aren't."

"Oh, I know that… but it's hard to… and in front of all those people… and so soon after Tobias… and…" Before she could add any more, Janine was interrupted by a breathless Mrs Margaret McFlintock.

"Mrs Bishop, you're to come home with me this instant," Mrs Margaret McFlintock commanded, "and I shall give you tea and crumpets or buttered toast with my homemade plum conserve. It's an acquired taste but nourishing none the less. You're to put your feet up or we can sit in the garden. The choice is yours. But this is what you are going to do!"

Mrs Margaret McFlintock's eyes were wet with tears, her voice choked and on the edge of total distress.

"Such a terrible thing," she said, her voice shaking, rising in anger, "and I'm so ashamed that it was said today. Or at all. And here in the village. And so soon after your husband…" She checked herself. "But, the perpetrator will be punished. Possibly," she said in all seriousness, "by a plague. Now… Patricia will need to go back and help her brother and you dear Janine will come with me. Barbara Monteith might join us. She's had enough of the tea tent anyway and, you know, I suspect that the tea tent might have had quite enough of her!"

Janine could do nothing but smile, not at the rather daunting prospect of trying Mrs Margaret McFlintock's comestibles or at having to talk to both her and Barbara Monteith for hours on end, but because of the sheer kindness which is what she needed at that moment. And Patricia thought that, yes, kindness – that commodity which costs so little, the welcome balm, the blanket of care that everyone craves one way or another – was exactly what was required.

Patricia looked at the old lady. "What do you think, Janine?"

"Oh, a cup of tea," said Janine quietly, smiling slightly but absolutely meaning what she said, "with Margaret and Barbara along with a crumpet or two would be lovely." She paused. "With or without plum conserve."

Spectators were still watching the races and it was as one of these was ending that Stanley noticed three men dressed in black. He kept an eye on them as they weaved in and out of the crowds one behind the other at a slow pace, as if waiting for something to happen or as if going somewhere to make something happen. If you were making a TV series, Stanley thought, and wanted thugs from central casting, then each of these three would be a dead cert.

Ten

Wilf thought that Adidas was a total dipstick. He wondered if there was a way that he could let the Mafia Shqiptare know that this enterprise was at risk and that the client was going to be even more mightily pissed off at the gang's failure to deliver than he was already. He knew of course that he couldn't tell anyone anything. He wasn't in the inner sanctum. He wasn't Albanian and wasn't even close to anyone who was either Albanian or in the inner sanctum. He knew he'd somehow just have to try and ride this one out. He missed Bardhyl Bardhyly.

He was fed up because he'd spent the night in a beaten up, dusty, old Ford Focus and in the knowledge that his so-called buddies had probably filled their faces with seaside fish and chips the evening before. Even with the sandwiches he'd bought in Cromer along with the fruit, boiled sweets, five bars of chocolate and bottles of water, he wasn't in the best of moods. Bardhyl, he reminisced, had always made sure that his crews had decent, regular meals when they were on a job. He'd been a good planner had Bardhyl, Wilf thought, not an attribute to which his current boss could lay any claim whatsoever. However, he noted with a sigh, Bardhyl wasn't around to glory in any attributes of any sort.

As instructed, Wilf had waited until after nine o'clock before seeking out the green and gold sign next to the Little Peasen Bookshop's front door. There was no answer when he yanked the old-fashioned bell-pull although he could hear the bell's tinkle from inside the building. Nobody appeared. Irritated, he went to the side of the property where there was space for three or four cars and access to a large, walled garden. He couldn't fail to notice the shape of a large truck under a tarpaulin parked at the rear of the neighbouring house. He knocked on the bookshop's back door and this time William Benedict answered almost immediately.

"Hello. Yes?" William asked, perturbed by the tall, broad-shouldered and threatening figure in front of him. Wilf too was slightly taken aback. Before him was a man wearing a faded green T-shirt and a pair of well-worn striped pyjama bottoms.

"You William Benedict?"

"Yes, I am he."

"Your thing's hanging out, man."

"What? What thing?"

"That thing. Your willy."

"I am yes."

"Your thing!"

"What? Oh, I see. Oh dear. Well, there we are. All fixed. Now, what can I do for you?"

The unwashed menace terrified William and he thought for a moment about trying to shut the door.

"You've got something that doesn't belong to you," declared Wilf as he stepped forward making William's fleeting notion of door closing an inapplicable idea.

"What… do you mean?"

"Crates."

"Crates?"

"Yeah, crates."

"Crates?"

"If you make me say it again, pin'ead, I'm gonna break your fuckin' arms," growled Wilf.

"I see. Well…"

Wilf pushed William aside, walked in and planted himself by the kitchen table.

"So, where are they?"

The insides of William's already nervous stomach turned to

mush.

"Where are they?" repeated Wilf intimidatingly as he put a Taurus Model 85 Ultra-Lite on the table. William knew something about weapons, his education on that subject having been gleaned from neighbour and military expert, Sheila Prewer. The Taurus, he knew, could do a great deal of damage. Wilf saw William looking at the gun and grinned wolfishly.

"Would you…?" began William, playing for time, although to what end he didn't know. "Would you like a cup of tea? A biscuit perhaps?"

The grin disappeared. "What I want are the crates. You're in deep shit, pal."

"Oh yes and why is that do you think…?"

William didn't finish the question because the man stepped forward and slapped the bookshop owner very hard across the face.

"The crates," snarled Wilf, readying his hand for another strike.

"OK, OK… alright. No need for that. That bloody hurt that did," wailed the anguished bookseller. He'd actually seen stars. "They're downstairs in the crypt."

"What? What's a crip?"

"The cellar. Follow me."

Picking up his gun, Wilf gave William a push. "Show me this crip."

"What?" asked William.

"The crip!"

"What do you mean?"

"You said the crates are in the crip! Let's go. Small warning though pal," said Wilf pointing his gun at a shaking William, "I don't need much of an excuse to kill you. Trust me, I don't."

As they walked down the stone stairs to the crypt's entrance, William thought hard about what he should do. Not much came to mind. Nobody was expected and, because of the fair, the shop had been shut all day.

The door to the crypt was made of thick, solid oak reinforced with huge iron hinges. The well-oiled double lock was massive as was the key.

"Open it," instructed Wilf.

As the door swung open, William leaned forward to switch on the light. Wilf gazed at the myriad of crates stacked neatly in rows and, relieved, pushed past William. At a speed that resulted in his pyjama bottoms falling to his knees, William swung the heavy door shut and locked it. Immediately there was muffled yelling followed by two shots as the man reacted in a way that William hadn't really thought through.

"Now I'm in dead trouble," William said to himself as he pulled up his pyjama bottoms.

Reluctantly managing the raffle stall for a while, a bored and testy Amber Cooper was on her fourth large vodka and not much tonic when she saw Dr Malcolm Carmichael wandering past. Abandoning the stall, she strode over towards the engineer as he headed in her direction. Once he saw who was coming towards him, he smiled in greeting. He waved with both hands, one low and the other high. Fleetingly, Amber thought that odd. But she had other fish to fry.

"You bastard!" she shouted, her face red with anger and alcohol.

Malcolm stopped walking and looked behind him, uncertain as to whether the shout had been at him or someone else.

"Yeah, I'm talkin' to you, dick'ead. What you playin' at? I ain't good enough for you? That it? Look at me when I'm talking to you, you fat arse!"

"I'd like to think Amber," said a firm voice from a gap between two stalls, "that my backside isn't fat even though in this underwear it does perhaps appear a tad large."

"Not you, Mrs Monteith. That bastard."

Malcolm had turned away and walked off still waving at somebody. Amber tried to see who it was but couldn't and so began to trudge back to the raffle ticket stall. Mrs Monteith stopped her.

"A word if you please. Over here's quieter… Everything alright is it with Dr Carmichael?"

"Not as it goes, no," an agitated Amber shot back. "I just wanted to 'ave a word or two with 'im, not that it's any business of yours!"

"You're quite right, it isn't, but I'd like to think that one of my possible Crazy Kite recruits was behaving herself and not shooting off her big mouth too much. Rumour has it that you're becoming what you people might call gobby."

"Bit too much to drink probably."

"Maybe stop drinking for a while."

"And maybe you should mind your own fuckin' business?"

"Well," said Barbara Monteith quietly, "I can do that of course or I can call one of the two police officers to come over and have a word if you prefer. Or maybe you could have a chat with someone else. What do you think?"

Amber shrugged vaguely, walked away and almost bumped into Dr Carmichael who was now holding a bottle of sparkling mineral water in one hand. The other seemed to be employed waving at waist height as if he was encouraging someone to follow him or overtake. She stood firmly in front of him.

"You tosser!" she yelled. "You reckon you can two-time me? Me? You 'avin' a laugh? You don't know when you're well off, mate. What they say's true ain't it? You really are a jumped up fuckwit."

Interested observers formed a circle around the two, keen to discover what the disturbance might be about. Malcolm was taken aback, irritated generally and annoyed specifically that he'd been stopped. Amber stepped forward and shoved him hard so that he nearly lost his mineral water.

"You're a loser," Amber yelled into his face. "You think I don't know you've been shaggin' my mate Julie? But I do, right? You do 'er again and you're a dead man. Got that? Dead!"

The threat hung heavily in the air and it was one that many heard.

Suddenly Malcolm stepped backwards forcing Amber to stumble forward awkwardly. He turned away and, waving a hand, accidentally clipped her nose with a fingernail. Amber, taken aback at the sudden move, yelped in shock and pain.

"Leave us alone," Malcolm shouted with a venom that surprised his adversary as well as the small group of onlookers. "You know nothing," he called as he walked off. "Nothing! You're a moron. Always were. Always will be. Thick as mince. Just leave us alone!"

"What didjya say?" asked Amber surprised, slightly bloodied and humiliated. "Fick as mince? Me? You're dead mate…" She stumbled, about to fall.

A strong arm stopped her tumbling over and gently led her away from prying eyes between the two stalls where Mrs Monteith had been.

"Y'know Amber, I'd be careful about threatening people like that," said a quiet voice.

Amber couldn't see to whom the voice belonged because the whole figure was hidden in the shade and the sun was behind the man.

"I hope you understand," the voice said still in a sympathetic way, "that when you speak out of turn, as you've been doing recently, well – it puts things and people at risk. That upsets me."

Amber, hot, bothered and confused, tried to make out who the man was but he stayed in shadow. Something frightened her and she stepped backwards. The man grabbed a wrist.

"We've been watching you and we don't much care for what we see. Or hear. Time for you to behave," the man said all benevolence gone.

"Ow! That 'urts."

The man squeezed the wrist harder and could see pain in Amber's eyes. The wrist was released and the girl rubbed the red weal. The man turned sideways as if to walk away but stopped and backhanded Amber twice very hard across the face and neck. That done, casually he walked off into the crowds.

From his vantage point onstage, Stanley noticed the famous theatre director holding court with admirers. Way beyond Sir Jon Appleyard, his lady wife and acolytes, Stanley also observed one of the tough-looking men dressed in black, standing next to the large oak by the village green shed talking to a person who was partially hidden by the tree. They were discussing something in an animated way it seemed and, just as Stanley was about to look elsewhere, the man in black was handed something. People walked in front of the pair blocking Stanley's view. Focussing back on the famous theatre director, he watched as Sir Jon was given a pot plant by someone. From where Stanley stood, the plant looked very much like deadly nightshade. Surely not he thought with a smile. He recalled a dramaturgy tutor explaining how the real eleventh century Macbeth had probably used belladonna to poison Duncan's troops.

"Dead in minutes," the tutor had said.

Eleven

The loudspeakers suddenly squawked after which Stanley could be heard announcing that the awards' ceremony would begin soon, followed by the fifty-fifty and raffle draws. As Jessica Threadgill walked over to the stage area to watch her husband preside over the fifty-fifty, she thought that Stanley had exactly the right manner to be an MC. Nice voice too. An actor's voice. She glanced at her watch. And dead on time.

She felt her head swim. It was so hot. She wanted to go home, have a cooling bath, a decent cup of tea, a home-made scone and a light snooze whilst watching some reassuring rubbish on TV. Or, if not TV, then a listen perhaps to something like Smetana's *Má vlast*, one of her favourite pieces. But of course, she couldn't do that. It would be letting the side down… letting Richard down and his parishioners. Even now, another worried soul was walking past. It was someone she knew well by sight and she smiled at him. He was holding his right hand which had a handkerchief over it and the handkerchief was covered in something red. Something that looked like blood. The man, her near neighbour, that quiet Dr Carmichael, looked very calm she thought. Dead calm.

Hurrying to attend Captain Horsham's awards' briefing, Richard Threadgill had just managed to disentangle himself from the clutches of two parishioners when, once again, he found himself being hailed by another. He was hot, a little weary and just wanted to enjoy himself even for a short time. But, as he had often said to himself, and indeed as his bishop had frequently remarked, the life of a country vicar running several churches at once, was not one's own.

"Ah, vicar… Richard," Ray puffed as he grabbed one of the vicar's arms none too gently. "There you are."

Richard Threadgill disliked both the familiarity and having his arm firmly held to the point of pain.

"Mr Berkley, good afternoon to you," he said stiffly. "I'm going," he said, anxious to make his escape, "to be briefed on the awards' process."

"Yes, I know all about that. Doing what I should have been doing in actual fact!" Ray toned down his approach. "Vicar… Richard… look, this isn't your pulpit of course. It's much more mine. I was just wondering if you'd allow me to give out the fifty-fifty prize… I will of course make sure that the church funds benefit. So, a deal?"

Richard Threadgill breathed out slowly and drew himself to his full height. "No deal, Mr Berkley," he said slowly. "I'm looking forward to giving out the fifty-fifty award and I shall do just that. Now, if you…"

"Listen… Richard… The photographers and media people will focus on the fifty-fifty and the cash handover. I'm keen as you know to… to reinforce my position in the community and hopefully beyond. Soon I'd like to offer my modest services to chair the parish council and… What can I do to persuade you?"

In the administration marquee, there was a corner barricaded by tables and boxes of merchandise where Juliet Corbell was counting up some of the day's takings, alternately tutting, mouthing numbers and crashing a nicotine-stained finger on a large, aged calculator. Captain Horsham checked his watch again. Damn it to hell and back he thought and possibly even said it out loud. Where the bloody hell was the bloody vicar? He knew that Accrington always ensured that the last of the races started on the dot of four. Which meant the awards ceremony would begin promptly at four forty-five.

Sydney Baxter, who shouldn't have been in the administration marquee but was, edged closer to the long table full of neatly set out awards. He stopped in front of a worn, almost shabby, wooden shield for the race between the pub and the Michelin-starred King's Head. He peered more closely. At the bottom of the shield there was the inscription, 'Made and donated by Tobias Bishop,' followed by a date. Sydney stiffened and glanced carefully about him. Satisfied that nobody was looking in his direction, he took out his sharp Burgon and Ball gardening knife.

Bethan was eating a delicious vanilla ice cream as she gazed admiringly at a child's face being made up to look like a frog. She'd surprised herself and was really enjoying the day with its colour, sounds and vibrancy. As she looked around, she happened to notice a man dressed in black standing by the big, old oak tree next to the shed at the top of the village green. For some reason she thought the man looked out of place. He was smoking and watching the current sugar beet race with no great enthusiasm. Her gaze roamed round the fair's activities again but landed back at the man dressed in black. She froze. His eyes had locked on hers.

Sir Jon Appleyard was also gazing at Daphne Pennyweather's make-up creation. The theatre director was in the process of asking Daphne and the child's parents if he could take a photograph or two. That style of frog, thought Sir Jon, was exactly the kind of make-up he wanted for his open air London production of *A Midsummer Night's Dream.* This, he knew unequivocally, is what would bring in coachloads of middle England. This was where the money was and he badly needed money. Yes, he drooled mentally, it would have the same pull as *War Horse.* But that thought bubble was pricked by a small devil on his shoulder pointing out that he still couldn't find a producer to fund the project. Excuses had been wide and varied, although only one possible theatrical angel had been honest - or cruel - enough to tell him to his face that his reputation had become tired, dull and not particularly bankable.

Sir Jon sighed. He'd asked relations, friends and Ray Berkley but they'd all refused point blank and, as a very last port of call, he'd almost begged Tobias Bishop who had turned him down as well. Idiotic little man, Sir Jon thought and reflected how pleased he was that the idiot was dead. He knew of course that all these people had no idea what a talent his was. He was, after all, Sir Jon Appleyard.

Fair enough, his last production, which he had part-financed himself, had failed and had all but broken him financially. And, yes, his two investors had been less than pleased and had only last week threatened legal action for the return of their original outlay as per contract. Debtors had begun to knock and writs were starting to mount up. He sighed again. It was true that the production had been derided by some critics while others had given it and him a little credit although, he'd been mortified to read, the comments had been meagre and unenthusiastic. His wife was putting pressure on him too and he knew that he could no longer re-mortgage their converted barn.

Doubts settled once more like a fine dust as he wondered if he could actually raise the money for *A Midsummer Night's Dream.* Even if he could, he knew that he needed the production to be not only financially extraordinary, but also to be the definitive version of the play, the one that people would talk about in perpetuity. Forget Michael Boyd, Peter Brook, Trevor Nunn, John Barton et al, he thought. His, Sir Jon Appleyard's, had to be the only one that people remembered.

Bethan, knowing nothing of this, was absorbed again in what the face-painter was doing. She didn't notice Sir Jon sidling up to her. He'd already double–checked to see that his wife was somewhere else on the other side of the village green.

As he got closer, Bethan became aware of his presence and moved back slightly.

Sir Jon moved to close the gap again. He pointed at the child being face-painted. "Clever, isn't it?"

Bethan shot him a startled look, taken aback by the fact that, surprisingly, the famous theatre director's teeth were like an assortment of carelessly scattered Polo mints.

"Very clever," she said.

"Jon Appleyard," he introduced himself as charmingly as possible.

"Yes, I know. I recognised you. Bethan Gill. Hi. You're the theatre director."

Sir Jon preened slightly and shrugged as if being Sir Jon Appleyard was nothing much.

"Well, you'll certainly do," he said openly looking Bethan up and down, something that made her step back again, her skin beginning to crawl.

"Have you seen the band playing over there? They're very good. I'll go with you if you'd like to have a listen."

Sir John, as he waited for a reply, moved even closer. Bethan smiled and stepped away again but as she did so, caught a fingernail on a loose thread from one of Sir Jon's denim shirtsleeves.

"I'm happy just where I am thanks…" she said trying to extricate her finger. Playing for time, so she could remove her digit with dignity, she tried to make conversation.

"I saw the Almeida Theatre interview you did a few years ago. My school took a group of us… fabulous!"

The occasion, she recalled, hadn't been remotely fabulous. Everyone in the school drama group including her teacher had thought the interview drab and uninformative. However, the famous theatre director glowed.

"Y'know I'm always on the lookout for the next Brie Larson," he said silkily. "I'm casting soon for my new production. It's *A Midsummer Night's Dream*, you know. Let's go over there behind the tea tent where it's quiet and we can chat."

Bethan had no intention of going anywhere with the man who was again quite openly eyeing her up and down.

"It's really good isn't it?" Bethan said, pointing with her free hand at a little girl who now had her face made up to look like a fish.

"Very," said Sir Jon without looking at the child. "I'm thinking of using that kind of style in my production of *A Midsu…*" Sir Jon stopped speaking abruptly as if he'd been struck in the back with an arrow. Behind Bethan, Jon Appleyard's wife, Lady Appleyard or actress Talulah Bancroft as was, stood with two cups of coffee in her hand.

Bethan, guessing precisely who was behind her, thought quickly. "Sure," she said in a loud voice. "As you say, behind the tea tent would be great for a chat. Let's go over and get to know each other better."

"Well, perhaps…" mumbled Sir Jon, his shine now markedly dulling.

"I'd really love to hear more about your work," Bethan gushed. "Casting for *A Midsummer Night's Dream* must have started I suppose? How exciting! Have you found your Helena yet?"

The famous theatre director seemed unable to speak and only had eyes for the person behind Bethan's left shoulder.

Bethan ploughed on. "So, Mr Appleyard, what part d'you think I might play?"

"It's sir, not mister," cut in a brittle, ice-cold voice that froze the hot air. "Also, my husband doesn't offer parts to snots like you. If he does, it'll be the last thing he does this side of a divorce court."

Bethan turned round and, as she did, the caught nail tore making her gasp in pain. The woman in front of her was dressed in a cream blouse, black jeans and a pair of Christian Louboutin low-top trainers. Apart from the red hair with sunglasses perched on top, the only other things that Bethan noticed was an angry slit of a mouth and glaring, even angrier eyes. The woman thrust a cup of coffee at the hapless director.

Bethan planted on her face a sunny smile while thinking that

Lady Appleyard moved her mouth much as a camel would. "Hi," she said. "Do have your very creepy husband back."

Walking away, she poked around in her bag, eventually feeling the point of her nail scissors. "These'll do," she said grimly to herself. "Dead sharp."

Sydney Baxter shuffled out of the administration marquee, holding his gardening knife the long blade of which was open and glistening with something red. Captain Horsham glanced impatiently at his watch, tapped a foot and loudly cleared his throat. He was still short of the vicar! He heard Stanley declare that one of the races had been a draw and therefore the prize would have to be shared. The captain grimaced. For the first time ever, he thought dejectedly, a dead bloody heat.

William Benedict sat at his large, stripped pine table in the middle of his kitchen wondering what he should do. Exhausted, he pressed his knuckles to his head and tried to focus. Still dressed in old T-shirt and pyjama bottoms with errant fly, he was nursing, but mostly spilling, a mug of strong, sweet tea.

His heart was racing. He'd thought about getting as far away as possible, but where? William's partner, Vedansh, was an artist of some renown who lived separately in a converted coastguard cottage overlooking the sea near Cromer. It was an arrangement that suited them both. Vedansh was widely known in Norfolk for his successful business selling Indian objets d'art. Much of his own work, local seascape paintings mostly, were also in demand. Both William and Vedansh had decided that marriage was outmoded or unnecessary, one of the two certainly. They felt blessed with their families and were regularly visited by relatives from both the British and American varieties of Norfolk as well as New York and Mumbai. William wished that Vedansh was with him right now but immediately abandoned that thought, given the serious nature of his current position.

He considered contacting Sheila Prewer next door but, despite her toughness, she was in her eighties and it would have been wrong to put her in danger too. He thought about the police, but how could he possibly explain the cargo of weaponry in the crypt? The thought of the crypt and the man in it caused William to wince followed by a whimper, even though there'd been no sound from below for a while. He came to a decision, spilled more of his tea and stood up at exactly the same time as he heard a hammering on the front door.

The presentation of the rosettes, cups, shields and plates had gone more or less smoothly. Some awards had been given only for the purposes of photographs, but winners were mostly content in the knowledge that their names would be etched, albeit in a very small font, on the silver plate. There was however an unusual glitch in the awards' process. When it had come for the old, hand-made wooden shield – carved and donated by Tobias Bishop many years ago – to be given out to an excited villager, even if only for photographic purposes, it seemed to have gone missing. Captain Horsham had been livid, such an occurrence having never happened before. The disgruntled winner had been obliged to make do with apologies, a red rosette and a decent bottle of wine. The offer of a large bar of nougat was refused accompanied by an expletive.

The large crowd, including the local media, had moved closer to the stage. Everyone was hot and bothered, but all were now anxious to know who'd won the fifty-fifty and after that the raffle prizes. Stanley had already told the audience that there was a grand sum of one thousand eight hundred and twenty four pounds in the pot, the highest amount ever collected and half that amount, he'd declared, was for some lucky winner.

On his arrival in the administration marquee, Richard Threadgill had admired a cake and wondered if he might have a piece given that he'd not had much to eat all day. Someone had immediately cut him a generous slice, wrapped it carefully in a paper serviette and thrust it into the vicar's hand. Richard managed to wolf the cake down in three big bites before he thanked his benefactor, wiped his mouth with the serviette, grinned at Stanley and took the stage.

Richard Threadgill was enormously proud to be facing this sizeable audience many of whom he knew were part of his flock. This though he felt was very different from his work in the church. Today was just a way of celebrating… celebrating what exactly, he wondered? Kinship perhaps, togetherness and… well, maybe avarice and possibly greed? Perhaps greed and avarice were not to be celebrated, but that thought didn't dent his feeling of being amongst people whom he liked and, he hoped, who liked him.

He too had been absolutely horrified at the terrible accusations shouted at Janine Bishop and he'd wondered then as he did now what had caused an individual to do such a thing. The poor woman had only just buried her husband too. While officiating at the funeral had been a duty, he had been genuinely saddened to see a decent man like Tobias go. He promised himself that he would visit Janine immediately the fête had finished.

Applause had welcomed him onstage and it was a genuine welcome. To people who knew him he was seen as a man for all religious seasons – not only in Little Peasen, but for other churches in the parish. His was a role, people felt, of quiet care and virtue.

Stanley was there to assist with spinning the yellow drum which he did after Richard had built up some tension with harmless banter to an over-excited audience. As the drum came to a clattering stop, Richard, as eager as his audience, beamed again at the throng which held its collective, bated breath. The vicar's left hand opened the slot and his right dipped through into the drum. Enjoying some faux drama, he fiddled about trying to find a ticket which he did and tantalisingly drew it out. There was not a sound anywhere. Music, games, rides and chatter had all ceased. Richard glanced at the number and, standing close again to the microphone, grinned.

"Are you ready?" he shouted.

A collective, loud affirmation came back at him.

"I said, are you ready?"

And of course the crowd was.

"Ladies and gentlemen, boys and girls… for the sum of nine hundred and twelve pounds, the winning number is… two… one… eight! Two one eight!"

Richard, relieved that he'd done his job well, helped himself to a small bottle of water from the dozen or so on a small table behind him, opened it and took a long draught. There was no sound from anyone in the audience. Nothing happened. Perplexed, Richard looked questioningly at Stanley. A sudden whoop could be heard from the back of the crowd and a bald-headed man wearing a string vest and long, bright blue shorts, pushed his way through. The man, sunburnt through the holes in his vest and with arms aloft as if he'd just completed a marathon in record time, rushed to the stage. Bounding up the steps, displaying a quantity of underarm hair, he turned to the crowd for approbation. To his surprise, there was none and neither was Richard Threadgill there to greet him with an expected handshake and the envelope of cash. Richard Threadgill was in fact lying on his back, staring sightlessly at the sky as the crowd remained dead quiet.

Twelve

Some people gathered and others went on their way as if nothing had happened. The St John's paramedics had established beyond doubt that the vicar was dead and one of them had called the local GP. They had driven the ambulance over to the stage and stretchered the now covered body away from prying eyes. As the ambulance retreated to a quieter, shaded area, Stanley made some announcements which he hoped would reassure people that the matter was being managed without actually saying what the matter was, although quite a few people knew or had guessed. He explained that the raffle would have to wait momentarily, although until when or how he had no real clue. Incongruous, loud music began again and, while there were no more races, most of the stalls and activities remained open.

Patricia had an arm around Jessica's shoulders as she was led away following the ambulance. Doctor Ellis Bindman was talking to Stanley, bag in hand.

"Any idea what happened?"

"Not sure. I'm no expert, Ellis."

"Unwell? Alcohol?"

"No to the first and I doubt it to the second."

Stanley remained outside the ambulance with Patricia and Jessica while the doctor made his examination.

"Jess?" Stanley whispered as he took one of her hands in his. It felt ice-cold.

"He's definitely dead, isn't he?"

Stanley struggled. "Yes, he is. I'm so very sorry."

Patricia had a protective arm around Jessica's shoulders although, Stanley thought, those who comfort others often seek comfort themselves and receive it by being comforting.

"Jess," Stanley said softly, "the doctor will be out in a moment and then of course you must go in."

He thought back. There had been an expression of sudden pain on Richard's face, but also surprise as if an unwelcome Grim Reaper had turned up unannounced at the vicar's doorstep while he was in the middle of Sunday lunch.

Captain Horsham strode up. "I'm so deeply sorry for your loss Mrs Threadgill," he said. "Terrible thing."

"Excuse me," said Stanley as he turned away, "but I need to ring the police. Nobody can seem to find the two constables on duty here."

"The police?" asked the captain with some anxiety in his voice.

"Of course… an unexplained death…"

"Unexplained? I thought…" But it wasn't clear what he thought. The captain had nothing further to add and stepped away. As he moved back, he trod on something shiny and hard. Looking down, Stanley saw that it was a thin, metal knife, the type a surgeon might use or maybe a model maker of some sort. The captain bent to pick it up, but Stanley grabbed his shoulder and pulled him away.

"David, stop. Don't touch that!"

Captain Horsham looked up at Stanley, puzzled.

"It could be important," muttered Stanley as he used his handkerchief to pick up the blade.

"Bit melodramatic Accrington, don't you think?"

Stanley said nothing. Walking away, he wrapped the knife in his handkerchief and put the result in a small Jiffy bag he found in the administration marquee. As he waited for someone to answer his call to the police, he looked over towards the stage. In his mind's eye he could see Richard fall. He could still hear that dreadful, animal-like noise. There was something else, but he couldn't think what it was. At the very moment Richard had begun reading the winning number, something had happened. Stanley tried to think what the something had been but couldn't. Then his phone call to the police was answered.

Ellis Bindman was in his thirties, of medium height with a perpetual suntan and a ready smile that always showed a warmth. As he came out of the ambulance, carefully closing the door and loosening his tie, he gestured for Jessica to come forward to spend a few minutes inside with her dead husband.

Captain Horsham stepped forward to address the doctor. "What's your view Bindman?"

The doctor looked at the retired soldier. "Captain Horsham," he said sharply, "I have no intention whatsoever of discussing any medical matters or, indeed, anything else with you."

The captain started slightly, stared at the doctor for a moment, coughed behind a fist and walked away.

Ellis beckoned to Stanley. "Stanley, you organised the stage area to be taped off?"

"Yes," Stanley said, surprised by – and curious at – the doctor's abruptness with the captain. "Tony Helliwell and Stevie Devonport saw to the taping up of the area… and Graham there… you know Graham Lambert? Runs the whole shebang. He's standing guard, shooing away anyone who comes too close."

"I'm impressed that you've got those two lads to help," murmured the doctor. "Normally they'd do anything but."

"Let's call it a debt being paid."

"Police on their way?"

"Yes."

"Bit of a tough one this," said the doctor.

"It is Ellis. He was a good man."

The doctor nodded and looked towards the stage area. Stanley followed the doctor's gaze. Once again he knew with a start that there was something that he'd seen just before or around the time when Richard had read out the winning number. But, what the hell was it? He shut his eyes and tried to visualise the vicar chatting to the audience, the drum spinning, more chat, the opening of the drum's slot, the pulling out of the winning ticket, the announcement of the number – twice – the draught of water from the water bottle, the sudden startled look, the clutch at the throat, the collapse. And that terrible sound. But what was it that he'd missed?

The doctor interrupted his thoughts. "Stanley?"

"Sorry Ellis," muttered Stanley, shaking his head as if to clear it. Remembering the knife found by Captain Horsham, with great care he handed the Jiffy bag to the doctor.

"A Swann-Morton by the looks of it," commented the doctor. "One that only a surgeon would use. I'd say this is brand new. Costly. On the ground you say? Odd. Not the sort of thing that anyone would normally drop even if the person was a medic of some kind. Who the hell carries scalpels around at a village fair?"

Carefully the doctor wrapped up the knife again and handed it back. The two duty constables arrived on the scene, spoke to Graham Lambert and took over the management of the area. One, having had a quick word with the doctor, instructed that the St John's ambulance should stay put for the moment. The other helped Graham with keeping people at a distance. Much to the relief of both officers, a second ambulance arrived along with a police car containing much needed support.

A little less than ten minutes later, Detective Chief Inspector Julian Poole and Detective Sergeant Evie Harris arrived. It was just after six o'clock now, but the early evening was still airless and sweltering. An officer was striding purposefully towards DCI Poole.

"Scotty, good to see you," said the detective chief inspector and meant it. "What's the score?"

"Sir, unexplained death. The deceased was a Reverend Richard Threadgill. The local vicar. Lived with his wife Jessica in the vicarage. No children. Vicar to a parish of five churches, the one here being the main one. Just collapsed and died apparently – on the stage over there. Doctor's here. The body's in the St John's ambulance there sir. I…"

DCI Poole raised a hand slightly. By his side, DS Harris smiled encouragingly at the young constable and waited for her superior to snap orders. However, Julian just looked over the scene through three hundred and sixty degrees. Many people were staring openly at the good-looking young man in a lightweight black suit and open-necked white shirt who was accompanied by an attractive woman wearing black jeans, a white top and faded pink ankle boots. Gossip prevailed over most conversations as onlookers wondered who they were and what, if anything, might happen next.

Constable Alfie Scott, freckle-faced, tousle-haired and known for his ready grin, waited but without the grin. Evie stirred restlessly at her boss' side, sensing a mere routine investigation stretching ahead of them. It was Sunday and her shift finished in two hours' time. She was anxious to get home, shower, change into something loose, put her feet up, have a couple of cold ciders, pick at a dish of salted cashews or pimento olives and have a natter with friends on the phone for an hour or two before watching Ryan Reynolds on Netflix.

"Hot in the tea tent, is it Scotty?" Julian asked quietly.

"Yes, sir. Boiling."

"The vicar – an oldish man was he?"

"Fifty five sir."

"How many people here at the fair would you say?"

"About three thousand for most of the day I reckon sir."

"And you've called us in… why?"

"I didn't make the call sir… The vicar was reading out the fifty-fifty winning number sir. The fifty-fifty is where…"

"I know what it is."

"Well sir, just after he'd read out the winning number and the bloke who'd won had made his way to get the cash, the vicar sir, well apparently he just keeled over. On the stage there."

Julian Poole nodded. "And who moved the body?"

"The paramedics who were on duty here sir. Before me and Gus Chambers had a chance to intervene."

"And the paramedics are still onsite?"

"In their ambulance's cab."

"And…?"

"The guy who runs the post office reckoned that this might not be a natural death… sir." Constable Scott lowered his voice. "Him and the local GP were unhappy with what had happened."

"The GP? Ellis Bindman?"

"Yes, sir. That's the one."

"And Stan Accrington?"

"Yes sir, Mr Accrington. They're both over there, sir."

Julian nodded. If a doctor had raised a question about a death, it had to be investigated. If Stan Accrington thought something wasn't right, then Julian knew that something wasn't right.

"And where were you and Chambers when this bit of drama was going on?"

"Sir, we was trying to sort out some parking stuff."

"Were."

"Were what sir?"

"Never mind. Go on."

"Some bloke… sorry sir… a member of the public had parked his vehicle where he shouldn't and there was a bit of an altercation with the person whose drive he'd blocked."

"Right," Julian said, not interested in local parking issues, "let's see what we've got. Lead on."

The relieved constable began to make his way towards the St John's ambulance.

"Scotty."

"Sir?"

"I want the officers by the stage to stay by the stage and I want more tape around the area. At the moment it looks like a playground, not a possible crime scene. The others plus you and DS Harris, get so-called witnesses together in that red and white striped marquee over there. By the signage I'm guessing that's the tea tent. Leave one officer by the village green gate. Bit late I guess, but nobody gets in as of now. We clear?"

"Sir."

"Then, once in the tea tent, after half an hour, less probably, they'll all want to leave. It'll be hell in a handbag. But they can't. Got it?"

Alfie Scott and Evie Harris both nodded.

"Evie, chase up SOCO please. And forensic. Possible homicide."

Julian Poole turned away and looked around again at the remnants of the fête. As some jolly music started up, he noticed that one of the donkeys was staring at him. He stared back and smiled.

"No offence old son," he said to the donkey, "but I just hope we're not flogging a dead horse."

The doctor led Julian and Evie towards the St John's ambulance where one of the paramedics was standing guard. Julian indicated with a flick of his head that Stanley should join them. At the ambulance Dr Bindman invited them all to put on surgical face masks and gloves just as he'd asked Jessica to do.

Over Richard Threadgill's body, the doctor said, "Look at his mouth and nostrils."

Julian leaned forward. "Those tiny black specks you mean?"

"What are they Ellis?" asked Stanley, looking away. He felt that there was something wrong for his dead friend to have people peer down at him.

"I don't know, but whatever they are they're recent."

Julian peered down again. "And you think that these black specks, whatever they are, might have caused his death?"

"No idea," replied the doctor. "Your people can work out what's what though. But I've never seen anything like this before."

Julian turned to Stanley. "Did you notice Richard Threadgill blowing his nose or sneezing just before he collapsed?"

"No. But he did take a long pull from one of the bottles of water that were onstage."

"The bottle was already open?"

"No. He opened it and…"

"What?" asked Julian.

"He had three large bites of cake just before he came on stage."

"And?"

"And it might have been caraway seed cake. He's… he was very fond of that. Those specks could be seeds."

Dr Bindman looked at Stanley. Julian looked at nobody but, as the three left the ambulance, he took out his phone, pressed some buttons and made a call.

"Well, interrupt his bloody game then and tell him it's urgent. And I want more uniforms over here toot sweet. Don't know, but could be a murder."

Julian finished the call and rang his DS. "Evie, there'll be more boots here shortly. I want the area properly cordoned off. I want a full search of the village green and everything on it. I want to get statements to hurry up, particularly of people I choose, starting with Captain Horsham. You have? Good. Draw up the list. All statements accompanied by fingerprints, photos with permission and check any previous."

Three police vehicles pulled up by the green. Behind the police vehicles, an old 911 Porsche noisily scrunched to a halt on roadside gravel. Out climbed a man dressed for golf. He put on a white, protective boiler suit plus slipover boots and stuck a Hazchem helmet under one arm which made him look, thought Stanley, as if he was carrying a spare head.

"Doctor, my team's here," said Julian. "Thanks for your help. Appreciated."

"Not a problem," Ellis Bindman said. Raising a hand as he turned to go, he called out, "TV tennis and a cold beer beckon. I'll have a quick word with your chaps and then I'll be away."

"Stan," Julian said, "over here a moment." There were only very few people who got away with calling Stanley Stan and Julian was one. The DCI knew that witnesses, like all people, each had different mindsets that unintentionally or intentionally added bias to viewpoints. What he needed was someone who told it how it was and nothing more.

"OK, I need to brief my guys but, before I do, give me the gist of anything you know of the vicar's demise." He switched his phone to record. For five minutes or so Stanley gave Julian his overall view of the vicar's death.

"Indulge me Stan. How do you think he died?"

"No indulgence necessary. I have no idea."

"Apart from the seed cake and water, did he eat or drink anything else?"

"I've just told you that."

"Tell me again."

"Apart from the seed cake and the bottled water, that's all I saw. There are always things in the admin marquee for people to eat. It's traditionally one of the perks – WI sandwiches, cakes, jugs of juice – that kind of thing. The captain insists on it. He won't have a clue what was there but Juliet Corbell might. She counts up the fair's takings. Bit of a grump but she's good on detail. She'd have been in the marquee at the time."

"The water the vicar drank on stage. From one bottle or more?"

"One. As I said, now wrapped in a piece of red and white gingham. Tucked underneath the stage."

"The surgical knife. Let's have it."

Julian took the offered Jiffy bag.

"And the captain trod on it?"

"Yes. On the ground over there. Ellis Bindman identified it as new, top of the range."

"Any thoughts as to why this was there?" he asked, carefully studying the vicious-looking metal.

"No."

Julian noticed the hesitation, wrapped up the knife, took out a tamper-proof evidence bag from his pocket and dropped the knife into the bag.

"Reverend Threadgill was last to arrive at the admin marquee. Why do you remember that?"

"He was hot and bothered. He'd just had a run-in with the guy I told you about who badly wanted to give out the fifty-fifty prize. I saw that from where I was onstage and heard the conversation. Prior to that, Richard kept being waylaid by several villagers. Par for the course – and he'd always stop for his parishioners."

"Anything odd about his behaviour during the day?"

"Not as far as I could tell, no."

"The Cooper girl who was pushing for a scrap with the Carmichael guy, you know her well?"

"A bit."

"You said that the vicar didn't seem frightened, worried or distracted when he put his hand into the drum. Nothing?"

"Nothing. Correct."

Julian noticed the sadness in his friend's eyes. Loss is hard at any point in life Julian thought and it can't be easily managed, no matter when it happens or to whom. He'd seen his share of horrors in his time and in all cases there was of course a deep sadness left behind somewhere.

"Was the vicar a religious man?" asked Julian.

"I'd say so. A sensible, dutiful, faithful, religious man. An honest man."

"Any enemies?"

"Apart from the few to whom he couldn't guarantee a seat in heaven, no. Some people may have found him annoying, but that goes with any man or woman of any cloth."

Julian nodded. "You said that officers Scott and Chambers weren't around?"

"I told you. Wasn't their fault. They were run a bit ragged with an idiot motorist parking in the wrong place. And they may have been following up on Mrs Bishop being accused of being a Nazi."

"The guy's voice?"

"Loud, clear, confident, angry and meant every word."

"This Mrs Bishop…"

"Her husband, Tobias, died some weeks ago. You'll recall the case. Stung by bees. So everyone said."

"You think someone's got some sort of vendetta against the Bishops?"

"Can't imagine why they would."

Julian switched off the recorder on his phone, tapped out a number and spoke quickly. Within two minutes, Evie Harris returned with a uniformed sergeant and Constable Scott. Evie smiled at Stanley.

"Sir?" asked the uniformed sergeant.

"I need to talk to the teams," said Julian. "Get them gathered please. Over there will do. Someone chase the incident unit. Get all the stallholders to pack up right now and leave unless they're witnesses to anything. Some are just messing about hoping to see something to talk about over their cereal tomorrow. I want them out. They've got twenty minutes max. Understood?"

"Sir," said the sergeant.

"Hold on. I want all the folks in the tea tent who haven't yet been interviewed to be interviewed pronto. Speed it up."

"Sir, if they've given statements, can they go?" asked the uniformed sergeant as he turned to leave.

"Yes, but they can't leave the village."

As the sergeant and officer Scott left, Julian looked at Stanley.

"OK Stan, what?"

"Over here."

Julian and Evie followed Stanley to the stage area. The wrapped water bottle was handed over to the SOCO team with strict instructions from Evie.

"Look at the aperture. The lip," Stanley said standing on the stage as close to the yellow fifty-fifty drum as the crime officers' presence would allow.

Evie asked one of the team for face masks and gloves.

Julian turned to Stanley who was snapping on his gloves. "What am I looking at?"

"You have to move a bit closer," Stanley said. "I only saw it myself after Richard died."

Julian stared at the drum's opening, but could see nothing out of the ordinary. Then he did and stiffened.

"Evie, get one of the forensic guys over here," he said quietly. A short, stocky man in blue overalls, mask, boots and matching hair hat came over.

"Steve."

"Sir?"

"Bag up all the stuff in the admin marquee – bottles, comestibles, the lot – and I mean absolutely everything, including the money. Tell your guys to be toxic careful. We don't know yet what's involved."

Steve Benson turned, snapped some orders and began to leave.

"No, hang on a minute. Look at this."

Julian stood a little to one side to allow the forensics' officer to stand beside him. He pointed a rubber gloved finger at the drum's aperture.

"Steve, see the slot? Look around the immediate edge. Tiny, black dots? Those there. Like a sprinkle of pepper."

The man peered down, eyes squinting a little. "No, I can't… OK, yeah. Got you."

Julian was in a hurry. "I want to know what those are."

Steve Benson glanced sideways at Stanley.

"It's fine," said Julian testily. "This gentleman's here at my invitation."

Steve Benson grunted, scowled, tutted and looked again at the drum's aperture. He said nothing but reached into one of his overall's pockets and brought out a loupe and, using it, looked again. He let out a long, low breath.

"Not sure without closer examination," he said at last.

"OK, but likely to be what?'

"Unsure, sir."

"Seeds maybe?"

"Maybe."

"Hazard a guess."

"I don't hazard. Sir."

"Have you seen anything like this before?"

"Not as such no."

"Not as such?"

"Then, no."

"Odd you think?"

"Yes sir, odd."

"In what way?"

"In the way of not knowing what it is."

"And you're sure that you can't hazard a guess?"

"Yes sir. Dead sure."

Thirteen

William Benedict was sitting naked, tied to a kitchen chair. His bottom was sore and one of his legs had gone to sleep. A rag which stank of something unpleasant had been taped over his mouth.

Wilf, angry and hungry, had wanted to damage William very badly for locking him in the crypt.

"No, we wait and then we snuff the guy when we're ready," snapped Adidas. "That's what's called an order. Get me? Anyway, you could've got out of the cellar. You 'ad a fuckin' gun. You 'ad boxes of fuckin' guns!"

"Yeah, right boss," replied a more than peevish Wilf. "I could've, should've, would've. I 'ad no bleedin' silencer did I? And it's a good job I didn't fire me gun off more'n I did. In the middle of a village? Then we'd've all bin screwed! And the client wouldn't have bin very much chuffed if I'd used one of the new pieces!"

Fuming, ready to break protocol and thump his boss, Wilf shut up, eyeing both William and Adidas with equal malice. William in turn was pretty sure that he understood what the word 'snuff' meant in this context. The situation, along with the acid in his stomach, were running riot making him groan in discomfort and despair.

An agitated Terence, keen both to get on with the task in hand and collect the rest of his share of the money, changed the subject. "Boss," he urged, "we need to get the crates into a lorry and scoot."

"Like, you think I don't know that, Terence?"

Terence persisted. "The client won't take kindly to another screw up. And he could rock up any time."

Adidas' mood was more than sour and whatever small, remaining patience he had now disappeared.

"Shut it Terence! I know!"

Adidas' foul breath caused Terence to recoil violently so that he almost sat on William's lap and any further debate on the subject of screw ups ceased.

Adidas sighed inside. The massive problem was verging on a massive headache. He knew very well that thinking about getting the crates of guns and ammunition away wasn't the same as making it happen. He also knew that he should have already made the call some time ago to get transport sorted. And the third thing he knew was that their client, the arms dealer, would now offer no help, if he'd ever been interested in offering any at all in the first place which Adidas doubted. What the arms dealer was paying the gang to do, mused Adidas, the gang wasn't doing. Absent-mindedly, he massaged his still sore nose which was now supported by a large plaster decorated with butterflies helpfully supplied by William. That had been the only type of plaster that William kept in his bathroom cabinet amongst the plethora of medication for indigestion, a condition to which the bookshop proprietor had long been prone.

Adidas swore and smacked his own leg and then William's in frustration. His tension increased as he considered that further mistakes would mean much more than a broken nose. He was in a hole and he knew that the hole could soon be a literal one. Why, he admonished himself while cracking his finger joints, hadn't he arranged the transport when he could have arranged it? His London contact could have laid on a truck within hours. Ten trucks if necessary! It had only needed a phone call and cash. But he'd delayed too long and the commodity of time was running out fast. He realised yet again, this time with a hot flush, that he'd screwed up big time and that his weak leadership would mean strong punishment. He licked his lips and thought some more which resulted in him taking out his disposable phone and dialling a number.

"Kresh, you OK?" he demanded of the fourth member of the group who was happily smoking dope in the village green shed.

"All good, man. I got us a 'ostage," said Kreshnik merrily.

"What! Why? Who?"

Kreshnik currently found it hard to answer one question at a time so three definitely made his head spin.

"Just in case," he said slowly. "You never knows."

"How?"

That was easier to answer. "This babe saw me smoke coming out the window. Keepin' me company now."

Adidas ground his teeth. "You fuckin' crazy? You wanna get caught? You got the controller thing? Kreshnik, tell me you still have the controller thing!"

"You wan' me to press the button now?"

"No! No, no." Adidas ground his teeth so hard he felt one give a little. "Just wanted to check you still safe, man."

Adidas hated Kreshinik at this moment and would cheerfully have shot him between the eyes.

"Kreshnik, listen mate," Adidas wheedled, but the wheedling quickly turned to frustration. "Don't press the button until I sez! And stop chasin' the weed now bruv. Serious. No smokin' anythin'! Otherwise you're out? I mean it. Straighten up or else! Dead man walkin' feller. Get me? Focus Kresh. Kresh? You still there? Tell me you understand."

"No probs. Chill."

Adidas breathed heavily, sweating. "Who's the hostage?'

"Dunno. A gel. Nosy. Nice. Neat. S'cool."

"OK." Adidas breathed out and softened. The damage was done. "Kresh, listen mate… you need to keep 'er there now. You can't let the 'ostage go until I give the word. OK? Get me?"

"You want me to…?"

"No!" interrupted Adidas knowing where the conversation

was leading. "You do nothing without my say-so. But keep 'er there."

"She ain't going nowhere boss."

"Good." Adidas cut the call and breathed in deeply almost forgetting to breathe out.

"Kreshnik's the weak link boss," advised Terence who'd heard both parts of the conversation.

Adidas was about to admonish Terence once more for his insolence and was also going to warn him that turning on a colleague could result in a poor outcome. However, in this instance he agreed with Terence and was about to say so when his thoughts were interrupted by a series of loud knocks on the front door. Everyone froze.

"Who might that be?" asked Adidas of William in a loud whisper.

"He can't speak boss," said Wilf not unreasonably.

"Untie 'is gob," Adidas instructed as he screwed a silencer onto his gun.

Cheerfully, Terence ripped the rag and tape from William's mouth causing the bookshop owner to yelp in pain for which he received a sharp slap.

"Shut it if you wanna live," Adidas whispered malodourously into William's face.

"Wills, 'ello dear. You there? I know you're in there," called an old woman's voice from outside.

"Answer normal and see what she wants," breathed Adidas warmly into one of William's ears. "Do it, now!"

"Hello, Sheila love," called out William in a tremulous voice. "I'm a bit tied up at the moment," a comment for which he received a kick from Wilf. William nearly cried out in pain, but turned the anguish into a cough when Adidas' gun prodded his naked stomach.

"Sheila," William called out, "I'll pop over for a chat soon. Bit busy at the moment."

"I saw someone come in to see you," shouted back Sheila. "Ages ago. A big man dressed in black. He 'asn't come out. Wills, you OK?"

"I… I'm fine Sheila. He's a…"

"Frien'," muttered Adidas. "Say frien'."

William pulled his head away from Adidas' breath. "He's… a distant friend from er…"

"Say from Albania. Durrës."

"Um… he's from Albania. Durex."

Adidas poked the barrel of his gun harder into William's stomach and hissed, "Door. Us!"

"From Doris," said William a little more confidently.

Kreshnik pressed the gun harder still. "Doorus, you fuckin' idiot! Doorus!"

"From Doorus, Sheil!" William squeaked. "In Albania."

"Say some more," urged Kreshnik. "Visitin' and such."

"Sheil, he's over here… over here on holiday. He's just… looking at some family photographs."

"In the kitchen?"

"Yes. On the table…"

"You don't have no Albanian relatives, Wills."

"That's… true, Sheila, I don't. But… but friends of the family from… way back. Pre-war."

"What war?"

William realised that mentioning anything military to Sheila Prewer had been a big mistake.

"Wassisname, your friend?" prompted Sheila.

"Er… it's… he…"

"Say Erag," whispered Adidas.

"A rag?" William whispered back, desperate to get his nose away from his tormentor's breath.

"Yeah!" hissed Adidas irritated at the way events were going. He kicked William's nearest leg. "Say it fool."

"Arag, Sheil. His name is Arag."

"Not a rag! Erag!"

"His name is Erag. You can talk to him later, if you like. Nice chap. He'd like you Sheil."

Adidas nodded, pleased at this additional piece of play.

Sheila was not to be assuaged. "A rag? You're 'avin' a laugh Willy. That ain't a name. That's a dish cloth." There was a pause. "Ask him to shout 'ello."

"Look, Sheil," said William wearily, at the end of his amdram capabilities now, "it's difficult at the moment." Adidas gave him a thumbs up. "Sheila, I'll give you a ring in a bit and you can come round for some tea and a piece of Dundee cake. You can meet my friend… Erag. We can look at some gun mags if you like. He likes guns too."

"Let me in so I can meet him. This a rag person."

Adidas pressed his gun into William's temple now. "Tell 'er to piss off!"

"Sheila, later," William stuttered. "Please," he begged.

"Wills, you sound weird. Shall I fetch one of the police? There's loads of 'em on the green. The vicar's dead y'know."

Stunned, for a moment William couldn't speak. "The vicar? Dead?" he asked eventually.

"Yeah. Jus' collapsed."

Adidas had had enough. "Tell 'er to bog off. Now!"

"Sheila… really… let's… meet up a bit later…"

"OK, Wills. Say 'ello to your friend for me. Lookin' forward to meeting him. Erag you say."

They all heard Sheila go.

The gun was removed from William's head.

"What… are you going to do to me?"

"Who was that?"

"My neighbour. Sheila Prewer. She's an old lady… What are you going to do to me?"

"Maybe we'll shoot you. Maybe take you with us. Maybe someone else'll finish you." Adidas shrugged. He had other things to worry about.

"But I haven't done anything…" William paused. "Did you… kill the vicar?"

"No! Why would we kill a man o' the church?"

"Boss," said an agitated Terence. "This don't sound good with all the fuzz around. Maybe you need the client to sort out the transport now? Speedy like. You say sorry and tell 'im we don't want no more cash…"

"Can't do that. Too late. We'd be in big trubs if I ask him now. Remember Bardhyl? And Colin? Remember my nose?"

Wilf stood, teeth and fists clenched. "What about the Shoreditch guys? They got vans and trucks. Loads."

Adidas grimaced. "It'd cost a heap… and they don't like me much."

Wilf and Terence currently shared the Shoreditch guys' view of Adidas. There was a slight lull in chatter while each person thought. Eventually, Wilf pointed at his boss.

"This is down to you Ad! We're gonna be in dead trouble and dead if we don't get goin' soon. And all the fuzz round 'ere ain't good."

Adidas thought about squaring up to Wilf but decided against it. He considered shooting him too but that thought didn't really fly either.

"I've done nothing wrong," wailed William.

Adidas was pleased at the change in conversation. "You swiped our guns man," said Adidas with menace. "That ain't nothin'. Shut it before I smack your 'ead with something solid."

"But... please..."

"Shut your cake 'ole!" said Wilf. Irritably, he turned back to Adidas, "So, boss, what's the plan? Where you gonna get transport now?"

Everyone, even William, noticed the 'we' had become 'you' and that wasn't helped by the testy addition from Terence of, "Yeah. Where?"

Adidas looked at his crew and then their captive. He poked William's thigh with the end of the silencer. There was a pause.

"Willy boy, you got a car or a van?"

"I do have a small van," said William vaguely thinking that being as helpful as possible might be a way out of this mess. "It's in the garage behind..."

"OK," said Terence with some hope in his voice, "Ad you got your van and Willy boy 'ere 'as wheels. That's a start. Mebbe you could do this thing in shifts? Or you could nick some more wheels?"

Adidas growled. "What's wiv this you stuff?" Glancing quickly around at all the crates. "And Terence, use your 'ead man. I mean," he added less vehemently, not wishing to lose his gang or any remaining, thin thread of control, "we need a big truck. Do the thing in one go."

"That lady," said William, "the one who came to the door, she's got a big truck. I could ask if you could borrow it. It's an old army vehicle. Surplus. Painted RAF blue. Her nephews got it for her. They're in the forces you know. Pilots. She uses it for war games and…"

"Shut your mouth," said Adidas. He paused, "The truck, it works?"

William, petrified, just stared at Adidas not sure whether to be quiet or answer the question. Adidas slapped William's face hard. Blood oozed from William's mouth. There was a whimper and a silence.

"The truck. Where is it?"

"At the back, next door," William said quietly with a quivering voice. "Under tarpaulin. It's in very good condi… Please don't…"

"Wilf, Terence – get out there and take a look. But quiet, real quiet, okay?"

"You want us to open it up? Make sure it works?"

"No, not yet. Just see if it looks decent, but be quiet. And don't be seen."

"Right," said Terence. "Oi, Willy boy, back door key?"

"Hanging up there. I'm getting cold, so can I…?"

"No you can't," snapped Adidas.

Kreshnik, sprawling on an old, dusty settee in the village green shed, stubbed the reefer with his fingers and put the remains into a pocket.

He yawned. "So you an' me need to wait."

"What for?"

"You'll see."

"Can I have my bag back?"

"No."

Bethan had one hand in her suede jacket pocket. At the same time as checking that her nail scissors were there, she switched her phone to silent. She offered a comprehensive, silent prayer of thanks to any listening deity that she'd kept her scissors in her jacket pocket after cutting her torn nail.

She looked at her captor. "What is it you want?"

"Me?"

"There's nobody else here, idiot. What do you want?"

A red spark lit in Kreshnik's eyes. "Nothin' much," he said. "Yet. You're good callatel."

"Good what?"

"You takin' the piss?"

"No. I didn't understand. What's callatel?"

"Co…lat…al…el. Same in Albanian."

"Oh, collateral. For what? I mean why do you want me as collateral?"

"None of your business… You're pretty ain't you? Boyfrien'?"

"No. You?"

The red spark lit brighter in Kreshnik's eyes. He popped some M&Ms into his mouth, flicking any green ones away. Glancing at Bethan from time to time, he relaxed, deciding that the day had improved. Spending time with this girl with not much to do except hold a remote control with only four buttons in one hand and alternately his gun or M&Ms in the other was, he thought, dead easy.

Fourteen

Sir Jon and Lady Appleyard were standing amongst the people still hanging around behind the police line hoping for some more drama to unfold. Sir Jon had just given a radio interview, although he was peeved that it had only lasted for two minutes and he knew that this would be cut down to a maximum of fifteen seconds on local news if it was used at all. Lady Appleyard was irritated at not having been asked to give her opinion about art following life or, of course, death on which she had important views.

Sir Jon reflected. He felt that the moment when the Bishop woman had been humiliated onstage had been one of glorious retribution. It meant that perhaps there was indeed a reckoning for people who crossed him. However, his smile fell and his ire rose when he considered that he still had no funding for what was going to be the ultimate production of *A Midsummer Night's Dream*. His anxiety and resultant digestive disorder caused excess wind so he was pleased to be outside at the moment as he thought dismally of the rising pile of debts, settlement demands and threats of legal action.

Stanley saw the couple and thought that it would be a friendly gesture to thank Sir Jon again for giving up his time. As he walked towards them he could see the pair staring at him. Lady Appleyard's clear, cold and loud voice begged to be heard.

"Seriously Jon? He's the village postman, for God's sake. Why on earth would we ever want to speak to him? Village trash."

Stanley stopped, looked at the couple, turned without saying a word and walked away.

Unafraid, but still understandably upset, Janine Bishop had decided that a short walk would do her good. She knew that Tobias would have been horrified at today's occurrence. He had always been her rock, strong and unflappable. His death had been a terrible blow and she still couldn't understand why or how he had been stung by so many bees. It had happened, she remembered, the day after that famous theatre director had visited. The two men had been talking quietly in the garden about a new Shakespeare production and she'd brought them coffee and generous slices of homemade apple cake topped with whipped cream and a sprinkling of cinnamon. After a short while, she'd left the two men to talk. To begin with, according to Tobias when he'd later related what had happened, the famous theatre director had been full of charm, but had left rather abruptly and rudely. When Tobias had told her why, her opinion of the famous theatre director had fallen to rock bottom. Had he, she wondered now, been the person who had shouted those horrible things?

Her reverie was interrupted by sudden, distant cheers from the direction of the fête. She sighed. The ever attentive Mrs Margaret McFlintock had walked her home and had left her with a jar of bitter marmalade and an insistence that she was but a shortish stroll away should Janine need assistance or a good cry in company.

Janine hadn't wanted to cry. That she knew would lead to no useful outcome. Home at the moment held too many strong memories so, despite the fact that Mrs Monteith had advised caution, she decided that another stroll might be beneficial. As she walked, her thoughts turned to poor Richard Threadgill – and it was now that she did weep unashamedly for someone who had always been an invaluable companion to her when she and indeed Tobias had ever needed solace.

Arriving at the top of the village green near the old oak and shed, she decided that it was time to go home, have two poached eggs on wholemeal toast accompanied by some camomile tea followed later perhaps by a small glass of brandy and definitely an early night. As she began to walk away, she heard a cough from inside the old shed. She also noticed a strange smell. Walking quietly to the shed's only window, standing on tiptoe and peering in, Janine pulled back quickly in surprise because looking at her from the other side of the pane of glass was a face. The next moment, the shed door had opened and a man dressed in black had grabbed the old lady and bundled her into the hut.

"Ouch," was the first thing Janine said and the second was, "What on earth is going on?" Indignantly, she shook off the man's hand as he held her shoulder. "Bethan, what is this?"

"Sit!" said the man in black.

"Why? What do you want?" asked Janine shakily. Was this, she wondered, the man who had shouted at her?

"Janine, humour him," said Bethan, shocked and immediately concerned to see Janine. "Apparently I'm a hostage for some reason and I suspect that now you are too."

Kreshnik nodded. "Hostage, yes."

Bethan smiled encouragingly at the old lady. "Don't worry," she said sounding much more confident than she felt. "He's harmless I think although I'm not certain what that remote control thing is for. His name he says is Kreshnik. Apparently, it means knight in shining armour and it can also mean the man from Krajina, wherever that is."

Turning to Kreshnik and wrinkling her nose as she took in a waft of the man's odour and that of the dope, Janine said as firmly as possible, "This is outrageous! I shall leave now to fetch the police and let me tell you there are a lot of them around!"

"Shut up. Fuck off. Sit down."

"Don't be so rude! I shall do no such thing. Let me pass. I've had enough nonsense for one day!"

Kreshnik waved his gun in her face. "Sit!"

"I think he means it Mrs Bishop. Sit next to me."

Janine sat down on the beaten up settee and Bethan put a protective arm around the old lady's slim shoulders.

"OK," snapped Kreshnik trying to sound decisive but actually having no clue as to what he should do next. He tittered, pointed his gun at Janine's head and said, "Bangs."

Constable Scott shot a smile at DCI Poole. "Preliminary interviews all done sir and the incident unit's just rocked up."

"Good," said Julian.

"Sir," Evie said sharply.

Instantly Julian was aware that a problem was about to be declared. "No Carmichael yet I suppose?" he asked.

Evie took a deep breath. "Yes, sir. We've found him. But…"

"But?"

"He can't be here sir."

Stanley guessed what was coming.

"Sir, he's dead."

Evie led her chief and Stanley to a stretch of grass towards where the portaloo toilets were standing like blue sentinels. She walked up to the third toilet next to which were two police officers. The door to the toilet was ajar.

Julian and Stanley stepped up to the lavatory while Evie, wearing gloves, opened the door wide. Inside was the body of a man kneeling on the floor, his head partially immersed in the toilet bowl's sanitation liquid. The liquid, once blue, was now a brownish purple. Jammed into the back of the man's neck were the wooden struts of a kite reminding Stanley of a bullfight's conclusion. Over the man's shoulders were the kite's wings.

To Stanley, the tableau of the kneeling man looked humiliating and dreadful. We should never ever look like this he thought. The man's legs and feet were at odd angles, a shoe was missing, the grey flannel trousers were stained and creased, the jacket was ripped and rivulets of blood were oozing down the man's back. The kite's struts were deep in the neck and sticking out from all angles. The smiling dragon's face on the kite's wings was at total odds with what they partially covered.

"Who found him?" asked Julian quietly.

"Webster, sir," replied Evie.

"How?"

"As you agreed sir, the portaloos had been emptied less than an hour ago and the contractor sent a truck to collect them. Arrived ten minutes ago. All the toilets' doors had been locked from the outside ready for transport. The lock to this one has been forced."

"In a minute tell the contractor that the portaloos will all have to stay for the time being. We have proof it's Carmichael?"

"Wallet with initials, credit and debit cards, driving licence, dry cleaning ticket with his name on it, photo of a lady with 'To Malcolm from Mummy' and a date on the back. Some cash. Bagged."

"Anyone else seen this?"

Stanley winced at the speed at which the body of Malcolm Carmichael had become 'this'.

"Not as far as we know sir," said Evie, "apart from the two guys from the portaloo company, Webster, Scotty and me. And now you and Mr Accrington."

"Get busy – I want the police surgeon or one of the FME team back here and, in the meantime, get hold of Bindman. Get the SOCO and forensics' teams back pronto."

Questions whirled more than floated in and out of Stanley's head. Were the two deaths connected? Three if you counted Tobias Bishop. Was that too far a stretch? The whirling in his head increased. If Carmichael's death was somehow connected to the vicar's, then how? Had Richard Threadgill been killed by mistake? Had Ray Berkley been the real target? David Horsham had changed his mind at the last minute over who should announce the fifty-fifty winning number, so could the vicar's murder have been Horsham's doing? Why though? And how? Or maybe the vicar hadn't been murdered at all. Natural causes of some sort. But what about the black specks in his friend's mouth and nose? Which were also on the fifty-fifty drum. What about those? Coincidence?

Stanley tried to calm his thinking. The murder of Carmichael might be easier to explain. A kind of Cluedo scenario – the brilliant man in a portaloo with a kite. Stanley shook his head. Not funny. Many people might have wanted Malcolm dead. A rival company perhaps? A jilted lover? A pissed off father of a jilted lover? What was definite though was that Malcolm's death had been premeditated. Was someone in cahoots with Carmichael? Had they planned Richard's death together and then fallen out?

"Hello – another one?" asked Dr Bindman cheerfully. The doctor nodded greetings at Stanley and Julian, snapped on plastic gloves, put on a face mask, knelt down, peered at the neck wound, checked the pulse and examined the face, or as much of the face as he could see. Then he got back to his feet.

"Yep, that's Carmichael all right. Killed by what looks like partial strangulation and drowning. There are marks on the front of the neck where his head was held down in that lavatory solution. And the whole thing topped up with the assailant slamming those sharp wooden struts into the poor fellow's neck. By the looks of scuff marks around the inside here and the disarray of the fellow's body and clothing, I'd say there was an almighty struggle. Death not long ago. Less than an hour, I reckon."

Julian nodded. "No sign of small black spots anywhere?"

"Can't see anything of that sort no, but it's a bit difficult until he's been… taken out of the… Your chaps will sort that out. But this was very different from the vicar."

"Thanks doctor."

"No problem." Ellis nodded at Evie who'd just returned. "I'll wait for your forensic people and then stick around for as long as I'm of use."

"Sir," said Evie looking at Carmichael's body, "the right hand. There." She pointed down. "Look at the index and second fingers."

Julian crouched down. The two fingers of the dead man's right hand were almost raw and bloody especially from the fingernail to the first knuckle.

"Scrabbling at something?" Julian suggested, wondering whether to call Ellis Bindman back again.

"Looks as if the fingers have rubbed hard against something rough for some time. It's as if he or someone's put the top part of those fingers into something like a pencil sharpener."

A police shelter was put up over the scene to stop prying eyes as the returning specialists got to work. Two constables were positioned to stop any curious members of the public.

Julian excused himself and went off to talk to his teams. Stanley walked away to think. How could Carmichael's killer have done what he or she had done without being seen at all? Maybe Carmichael had known the killer. Perhaps they'd had a chat near the toilets. Bundled into one and then killed? But the murderer would have had to break the toilet door lock and, anyway, bundling a tall man into a small space wouldn't have been easy. And without being seen by anyone? Someone would have heard noises or shouts. And the murderer coming out of the toilet would have had blood on him or her. The risks of discovery would have been a mile high. And why use a kite for God's sake? That was obscene on top of what was already obscene.

Mrs Monteith walked by and, seeing Stanley, stopped to say hello.

"A difficult day Barbara. Thank you by the way for your help with Mrs Bishop and ditto for your hard work in the tea tent. Oh and the amazing kites." He looked up. "Some still flying. Great job."

"Thank you Mr Accrington. Just heard about Dr Carmichael. Terrible news! Terrible. The poor vicar, what happened to Mrs Bishop and now this."

Stanley nodded. "Dreadful – all of it."

"Do you think the village is safe Mr Accrington?"

"I think so Barbara. Lots of police about now… Barbara, did you manage to sell many of your kites today?"

"Kites?"

"Yes. I just wondered if many were sold."

"Oh yes… thank you. Yes, we did quite well. And sales from your shop were encouraging last week. Thank you for that."

"Do people tend to buy a particular type or do all the designs sell equally well?"

"Oh the ones with the smiling dragon do best of all!"

"The ones that fell during the day. What happens to those?"

"Oh we just let people help themselves. I…"

"That's a kind thought. It's a marvellous idea to make them of course. Really good. How many of your ladies are in the business now over at Darkwater Hall?"

"Nine now. It's… a growing business." She smiled. "Well, I must go. My Jack went to get fish and chips for supper, but I expect that mine will be quite dry by now. And I'm to be interviewed by the police you know at some point this evening. So I'll need to come back when they ring. No peace for the wicked!"

"One more thing Barbara. Do you take on new recruits when you need to make more kites?"

"Oh yes, but we only employ ladies who have excellent detail skills and who can put together the kits quickly and accurately. We make everything ourselves you know. Mr Berkley converted a barn into a workshop. All mod cons! We do all the machining there, design everything, print all the designs and pack everything up. Everything!"

"So, if Pat or Bethan wanted to help, could they?"

"Oh well… that's very kind but they'd have to be in the WI

first and, anyway, it wouldn't be my decision alone you see. And… at the moment we don't need any more recruits. Now then, I must…"

"Amber Cooper – is she a new recruit?"

"Amber Cooper?" Barbara laughed briefly. "Oh no, not Amber. That wouldn't do at all. Now please do excuse me. Good evening, Mr Accrington."

"Scotty," said Julian. "I'd like Bindman next and please try and find Mr Accrington."

The constable was soon back to usher in both Stanley and the doctor.

"Dr Bindman, you OK with Mr Accrington sitting in? Might save time in the long run."

Smiling genuinely at Stanley, the doctor said, "No problem at all."

"Mind if I record this?"

"Please do and, before you ask I, Ellis Bindman, general practitioner in Little Peasen, give you, DCI Poole, permission to record this interview. And, yes, I'm happy that Mr S Accrington of Little Peasen general stores and postal office sits in on the same interview."

"Doctor, what do you know about the Threadgill couple?"

"Nothing that's going to help you I'm afraid chief inspector. Richard wasn't one of those stick-your-nose in, holier-than-thou type of vicars. As far as I'm aware, he didn't push religion where it wasn't wanted and neither did he get on anyone's nerves; he knew when to leave well alone. There've been some ne'er-do-wells in the village from time-to-time as I'm sure you know and he would offer help but only when it was wanted. Or needed."

"Anything else?"

The doctor shrugged. "I'm not sure what else I can tell you.

He wasn't a great man but he was a good one and they're scarce. He stepped up to the plate. The marriage seemed to be steady. Happyish as far as anyone can ever tell looking in from the outside. It's no secret that they'd wanted children. No hobbies as far as I know, apart from his theology, book collection and recently, bees."

"Bees?" asked Julian.

"Bees. The vicarage garden is large and he wanted to do something for sustainability. Meliponines…"

Evie interrupted. "Doctor, Tobias Bishop was stung…"

"I wasn't the doctor on the Bishop case and I don't know what the precise details were. If he was stung to death, unusual by the way, then either he had a propensity towards anaphylaxis or…"

Julian interrupted. "Let's get on with the vicar."

"Let me say for the record that meliponines don't sting," offered the doctor. "Well, the females don't or, if they do, the stings are mild and won't bother anyone. Even multiple stings shouldn't be harmful. The males can't sting. Anyway, it's academic because as far as I'm aware Richard never got round to getting any bees. It was just something he was considering."

"Anything more on the Threadgills?" asked Julian who'd had enough of bees.

"If there'd been anything much out of the ordinary in the Threadgills' lives, you can be sure the whole village, down to the last seagull, would have known about it. But in all lives, as we know only too well, some things are missed. Not much else to say really; being labelled a decent man is sufficient in my book. He knew how to make himself useful without yelling from the rooftops. Gave lifts to those who were carless – and dropped everything if dropping everything was necessary to help somebody. Spent time with parishioners – of the faith or not – when they were in hospital or ill at home. Or just in need of a shoulder. Went to court to help people too if he felt he could make a difference and sometimes went anyway even if he knew he couldn't. Richard was a rational voice in local affairs, as you might expect, but he wasn't the steamroller type." He paused. "Unlike Ray Berkley."

"You don't like Mr Berkley?" Julian asked.

The doctor laughed. "On the contrary, I do like him as it happens. But he has a way… of doing things and isn't everyone's cup of tea."

"And you liked the vicar?"

"Yes," admitted the doctor. "I did."

"No health history of anything that might have caused a problem?"

"No, he was fine. Bit overweight perhaps what with all the tea and cake that were part of his duties but, other than that, no. So, anyway, voila."

Julian asked, "Does that voila include the fact that you supported Ray Berkley's application to turn Darkwater Hall into a hotel?"

"My word, you have done some swift homework!"

"Well?"

"No secret. Mr Berkley wanted my advice on a medical matter and in the course of that conversation he told me of his plans. I have some family money that needs investing and he asked if I'd be interested in supporting his hotel venture. Nothing terrible about that is there?"

"What you do with your money is none of our business. I hope it stays that way. But, undoubtedly that would have upset Captain Horsham."

"As they say in the movies, it's just business."

Julian stared at the doctor for a moment but decided not to pursue what the doctor wasn't saying.

"Doctor Bindman, there's nobody you can think of who had any possible grudge against Richard Threadgill?" asked Evie.

"No. Can't think of anyone."

"Dr Carmichael, perhaps?"

The doctor pursed his lips. "I doubt that they'd have had much to do with one another. Carmichael lived close to the church as I'm sure you know, but I don't think he was particularly religious or of the faith. Would they have had anything in common? I don't believe so. Carmichael didn't socialise much as far as I'm aware, although I'd seen him out and about with a variety of girlfriends. Came to me for a couple of minor things but nothing else – and our social paths didn't cross."

Once the GP had left, Julian added some notes to his phone while Stanley went outside to breathe some non-air-conditioned air. He was puzzled. If Carmichael had somehow killed the vicar, why was Carmichael then killed and by whom? Retribution? A former comrade in arms? Could Jessica Threadgill be the guilty party maybe? Surely not. But perhaps she'd wanted her husband out of the way for some reason. Could Jessica have killed her husband following which she'd killed Carmichael? That made no sense either. A woman her size couldn't have killed Carmichael in the way that he'd been killed. With help though? But who? And that would have been even more obvious in plain sight. What about Ellis Bindman's business relationship with Ray Berkley? That was a new one. Strange bedfellows. Other questions hovered. What about the mysterious, oozing package that had been left outside the post office? What about the strange men dressed in black? What about…?

"Mr Accrington," Evie said in as sultry a voice as she could manage. "The DCI would like to see you again."

Inside the incident unit, Julian looked at Stanley. "Something's on your mind. What?"

"You know the day before yesterday I picked up a parcel left outside the post office? It had no labels, no markings, no name –

nothing at all. DS Harris here kindly came over and I'm sure you're up to date. She thought that it could have been a gun."

"It was a gun." Julian paused as if carefully deciding what to say next. "It's a 3D printed, automatic, light-weight, high-powered, rapid fire machine pistol. In the package was a completed plastic version, another made of some kind of metal and a third of a new substance that I'm not allowed to talk about. It's the last that's the hot potato. The gun is terrifying in any of its forms and anyone could make as many as they wanted with the right materials and a 3D printer. The metal version was wrapped in Cosmoline. That's what was leaking. There were some fingerprints on the box of which one set is yours and we're trying to match the others now." He paused. "If there are more of these things hanging around, then we're worried. And, if we don't find the source, then we're frightened."

"Nothing to do with today then you think?"

"Do you?"

"What about the surgical knife, the scalpel?"

"Being checked. Possibly something to do with whoever shouted the Nazi stuff. Or maybe some oik out to do mischief, but then why would a local thug have a new, highly specialised surgical knife? By the way, what do you know about Bindman?"

"Ellis? Why?"

"Anything?"

"He's been in the village for about eight years. Joined the Beech Hill practice and he's a partner there. Regarded highly. People like him. Good at what he does. No nonsense. Only medic in the family. Father and brothers all army through and through."

"You knew that Captain Horsham was responsible for getting Bindman's father cashiered?"

"No, I didn't know that."

"Did you know before today that Bindman had money to invest in Berkley's hotel development?"

"No. Didn't know that either. You're concerned about Ellis?"

There was no answer.

Stanley changed the subject. "I called on Will Benedict – he runs the bookshop opposite the post office – to see if the package had been his. But he wasn't in. And that's odd because when he's out, he tells Sheila Prewer. She works for us from time to time and is his neighbour. If he can't tell her for any reason, he'll normally tell someone in the shop. Or put a sign up on his front door. None of that happened. Sheila thinks there's something odd going on in the bookshop. She says she's spoken to William but only through shouting – her from outside, him inside. Says he sounded odd and wouldn't let her in which is unusual. William apparently said he had a visitor from overseas and was busy with his visitor. Sheila said she'd seen a big guy dressed in black go into William's house via the back door. She didn't see him come out."

"Go on."

"Today I caught Tony Helliwell and his sidekick Stevie Devonport trying to nick something during the fair. You'll possibly remember the Helliwells and the Devonports? Not quite the Montagues and Capulets, but the families had form. Anyway, the lads grabbed a bucket of money that Pat was carrying. We got it back. A kind of magic." He smiled slightly. "What matters though is that the boys now owe me and they came to say that they'd seen a man dressed in black at the top of green not fitting in with the fair at all. Occasionally we do get oddballs and a few weirdos at the fair, but they're usually obvious oddballs or weirdos. This one seemed different. I'd seen him myself. Apparently he and a few others like him had been seen lurking around the area for a couple of days. The boys took some photos. Obviously without the bloke knowing…"

"Stan!"

"Hold your horses," said Stanley quietly. "As I say, this guy roughly matches the description of the one who might be in the bookshop."

He handed Julian his phone. "Here. Look at these. There are seven shots."

Julian took the phone.

"Difficult to see…" he began. "Oh hello. The guy's holding something. I'd say a remote control… And I'd also say from this shot that he has a weapon stuffed down the back of his jeans."

Julian showed his DS the images. Stanley took back his offered phone and immediately sent Julian the photographs.

"This Sheila Prewer. We need to get her in?"

"Possibly."

Julian asked Evie to transfer the photos to the crime website. She gave orders to two officers to check local bed and breakfast outfits, hotels, car hire outlets, takeaways, cafés, beach huts and camping or caravan sites.

Julian rang his boss to update her on the current situation. He agreed with the superintendent that, yes, speed was paramount and gave strong assurances that, no, he didn't need another DCI on the double deaths.

"Over my dead body," he muttered under his breath after he'd closed the call.

Fifteen

Being fed up was something of a current common state for Stephanie Berkley, but right now her irritability level was stratospheric. She'd come all this bloody way, she fumed, to get one over on her soon to be ex-husband and the plan had been a spectacular failure. Sure, she'd watched the bastard grinning all over his stupid, fat face and it was true that her plan to grab a microphone that she'd seen unused on a table in the administration marquee had gone pear-shaped.

She stamped her foot. That idiot Horsham, she bristled, had said he'd help but hadn't. Then the bloody vicar had inconveniently died followed not long afterwards by Malcolm Carmichael's demise, something that had shocked her not only because of who it was but because that death seemed – according the rumour mill anyway – to have been murder.

Stephanie shrugged away images of death. She knew that Ray had been kept behind for questioning probably treating the police to his 'do you know who I am?' routine. It was unlikely that she'd have another chance to embarrass her husband into doing what she wanted. She swore. Time was running out. As she made her way towards the tea tent with no real plan of action, her musings were halted by a police officer.

"Sorry madam, but you can't go that way and anyway you need to get clear of the village green please. The whole area's cordoned off as you can see and nobody's supposed to be on here who shouldn't…"

"My 'usband's in that red an' white stripy tent there," interrupted Stephanie in an intentionally loud and belligerent tone.

"I probably didn't make myself clear, miss. What you need to do is leave. Now if…"

"Put one finger on me arm and I'll 'ave you in court. There are witnesses and I'm sure someone would be only too pleased to take some video. Where's your superior officer?"

Constable Scott sighed and tapped his lapel. "I'm taking some video, miss. You're on it. Come with me."

"Please."

"What?"

"You mean come with me please."

"Come with me please, madam."

"No. Fetch your superior officer 'ere."

Scotty's patience fled. "Sarge," he said to his collar radio. "I have this… lady here on the wrong side of the cordon who says she needs to see her husband who's apparently waiting to be interviewed… What's your name madam?"

No answer came from Stephanie who had just folded her arms and looked insolently at the young officer.

"She won't give it sarge." He listened for a moment. "OK. Will do."

"Madam," Scotty said to a smirking Stephanie, "if you don't leave now, you'll be put under arrest and charged with obstructing the police in the course of their duties, viz mine."

"Viz? What's a viz?"

"Will you leave or be arrested?" Breaking the rules, he added in a very much lower voice, "For the record, I don't much care which, but I do have a preference."

"What? What didjya just say?"

"Madam, your time for choice is running out. This is a crime scene and…"

"You're sayin' that if I walk over there, you'll arrest me?"

"Yes. In a heartbeat. And if you don't shift you'll be arrested here never mind there."

"In front of them reporters?" An idea was forming in

Stephanie's head.

"Yes."

Stephanie flung her bag over her shoulder and walked towards the five representatives of the local media who were on the right side of the cordon tape.

"My name's Stephanie Berkley," she greeted them pompously, "wife of Ray Berkley what owns Berkley Technologies 'ere in Little Pissing. My 'usband employed Dr Malcolm Carmichael, the bloke what was killed today. You interested in an exclusive?"

Deliberately mispronouncing the name of the village was not a smart move on Stephanie's part and the point was duly noted by the media representatives. But, while filing that away for future use, they each liked the idea of a story, even if they each instantly couldn't stand the woman.

"Sure," one said. "What you got?"

"Let's talk money first."

"Ha ha," said another.

"I'm not giving you a story for nothin' pal."

"Then don't. Pal."

Stephanie thought quickly. Her aim was not on this occasion to make money, but to cause mayhem for her husband. She shrugged.

"Can't blame a gel for trying," she said. "Let's go and sit under that tree – on that bench up there near the shed." Glancing over towards Alfie Scott, she yelled, "Away from the bleedin' law!"

Marching off as fast as her heels would allow, she was followed by two representatives from Norfolk Coast Radio and one from North Anglian News. A photographer and another reporter stayed put in case something happened in or near the tea tent.

"So," Stephanie said when the group reached the bench. "Do

we 'ave a deal or what? I give you some dirt on Berkley and you agree to a second piece the following week, just as damning, maybe more so. You in?"

"Why would you do this? He's your husband."

"He's a prat and you can quote me. So, you lot in or not?"

"Exclusive?" asked one.

"Exclusive," lied Stephanie.

The man from North Anglian News looked at his colleagues who nodded.

"Deal," he said to Stephanie.

Bethan was fed up with sitting in the dank, dark shed. She was also concerned about Janine Bishop who was looking pale and strained. Worse, nothing was happening. She made a decision, straightened her back and stood up.

"What you doin'?" asked Kreshnik who was having difficulty keeping awake.

"I'm leaving now with this lady. She's not well."

"No. Si'down."

"No. Enough. Come on Janine, we're leaving right now."

Janine Bishop got unsteadily to her feet and Bethan supported one of the old lady's elbows.

"I said si'down!"

"Drop dead! I said no!" Bethan shouted.

There was a sudden tapping at one of the windows and a number of surprised faces looked in at the surprised faces that looked out.

"Evie, I want those reports on the life and times of Dr Malcolm

Carmichael immediately they come in. I take it that someone's interviewing his family, friends and colleagues?"

"Seems that he didn't have any friends here to speak of and zero family. There's the girlfriend, Amber Cooper – the girl who was pushing for a scrap with him – and a couple of other women he dated. The team hasn't been to his house yet, but they will."

Julian sat down at the incident unit's central desk. "Someone's talking to the Cooper girl?"

"Yes – now."

"Check out some more background on her please and bring her in. What else?" Julian asked, waving for Stanley to sit down.

"Carmichael had a decent relationship with a few people where he worked," said Evie, "and in particular his own immediate team of four, but mostly it seems that he kept himself to himself."

"Speaking to the four?"

"Now."

"And?"

"They've gone all buttoned up and say they can't talk about their work."

"Get help from our friends at Five. I need to know what Carmichael did and everything about his work – and private life."

"Sir."

Julian glanced at the time. "Right. You OK Stan? Good. Evie, Horsham next."

"Captain," Julian said pleasantly as the old soldier was shown into one of the interview cubicles. "I'm sorry to have kept you waiting. We're a bit cramped in here but please make yourself comfortable. Glass of water?"

"Thank you."

Stanley pulled a bottle of mineral water from the small fridge, opened it and poured it out. David smiled gratefully and emptied half the glass in one go.

"Now, sir," began Julian, "firstly, do you object to Mr Accrington being present? He knows the village and villagers pretty well and that's proving to be helpful in our enquires. It's also saving us time."

The captain looked at Stanley and both smiled encouragingly at one another. "No, I don't mind at all."

"We're recording this," said Julian. "Alright with you sir?"

"Of course."

"Would you mind saying so?"

David complied. Julian thanked him. "If I could just have a few personal details."

"I believe that you have those already and I've given a full statement."

"You know, Captain Horsham," replied Julian patiently as he watched the man pick up the glass and drink some more water, "most police work is tedious beyond compare and I imagine that, as a decorated SAS captain, you also found that to be the case from time to time. Bear with me please. The rules you know?"

"Of course. Rules."

"Right," Julian continued briskly after the captain had been taken through his personal material. "Perhaps you can help me get the fair's setup straight in my mind. You're responsible for the awards, prizes and so on?"

"Yes, I've done it for years. I feel that the village…"

"Can you run me through the timetable of what you did when you got all of your people together in the administration marquee? I know you've been through it once, but it helps me. Detail please."

Julian listened for a good ten minutes as David Horsham

explained the various workings and order of proceedings for which he had responsibility and, unsurprisingly, the specifics were good.

"And, when you saw the vicar, he seemed untroubled? He wasn't unwell or anything?"

"I confess that I don't take that much notice of people once I know that they're all present and correct. But, yes, I think he was in fine fettle. He was genuinely looking forward to giving out the fifty-fifty prize. Maybe a little over-excited but, otherwise, he seemed his normal self."

"You say you knew him well."

"I like to think that he was a friend."

"Captain, did you notice anything odd at all in the administration marquee?" asked Evie.

"Odd? How d'you mean?"

"Anything on the periphery. Out of the usual. Something that anyone did or said? Anything that should have been there that wasn't and vice versa?"

The captain pondered but only for a moment. "No… I can't recall anything like that."

"You're certain? Please think back."

"No, truly, nothing."

"Sorry to be pedantic, sir," said Evie, "but you said that the vicar was on time."

"Yes, he was."

"But according to others, including Mr Accrington here, he wasn't."

The captain glanced at Stanley, his face darkening. "Wasn't?"

Stanley nodded. "He was late."

"Really? I don't recall that."

"But, sir," said Evie, "you live by detail and… rules. You must have known if the vicar was late."

There was silence. Evie broke it by asking, "Was it widely known that Mr Berkley was originally going to be giving out the fifty-fifty prize?"

"I'll say it bloody well was," the captain exploded, pleased that the focus had altered. "Maximum attention-seeking as per usual. Nasty piece of work, detestable man."

"Why did you change your mind about the fifty-fifty?" asked Evie.

"I felt that Threadgill does… did far more for the village. Berkley's offer of several thousand pounds for next year's fête was a bribe and one for which I fell."

Evie pursued the point. "When did you tell Mr Berkley that you'd rearranged that particular award?"

"About half an hour or so before everyone assembled."

"You cut it fine captain," said Julian. "No wonder Mr Berkley was put out. Look, it's warm, you're tired. We have a duty to perform. You understand duty. I feel that we're shoving water uphill here. Is there anything else we need to know?"

"No… nothing."

"Captain Horsham, I've been a police officer for some time and I'm also not daft. Neither is my DS. I'm patient but not that patient. Please don't push it."

David looked aghast, angry and resigned in that order.

"Waiting, sir."

"Alright. I threatened Berkley. I threatened to give a microphone to his tart of a wife so that she could say some unpleasant things about him and his business practices to approximately three thousand people. The first time she'd asked I'd said no, but then I thought it might be helpful leverage and it would be…"

"Sweet revenge for you?" asked Evie.

David looked abashed. "Yes. But eventually I refused."

"Stan," asked Julian. "Did you see Mrs Berkley and this exchange?"

"I did, yes."

"Hear it?"

"No. I saw David talking to Mrs Berkley but I didn't hear the conversation."

"It's common knowledge that they're getting divorced," Captain Horsham said. "Look, I couldn't in all conscience allow what she had in mind even if it would've been score-settling for me." He sipped some more water. "You'll know that Berkley bought Darkwater Hall and now threatens to turn it into a bijou hotel! Every bloody day, I stare out at what, for hundreds of years, used to be my family's home and estate! It's listed of course but he rides roughshod over everything and everyone. If he gets planning permission, I'll have to watch as he ruins it all… London luvvies and Chelsea tractors. And now he's trying to get hold of the small lodge where I live and my remaining bit of land. That's all I have left."

The captain paused and looked down at both sides of each hand as if undertaking a medical examination of his fingernails. The incident unit was quiet apart from the soft generator and some low conversations beyond the door.

"You know," David Horsham continued, "Syd Baxter was a corporal in my father's regiment. Rosie, his wife, was in the WRAF. They had nothing apart from each other and the forces. When they retired, my father offered them a very small grace and favour cottage. The cottage belongs to me now and it's on my remaining land. Syd does odd jobs as does Rosie but really this is their own time. They potter about and I'm very fond of them both. They were terrific when… my wife… Dorothy was ill." The captain took a sharp intake of breath. "Berkley has made it plain to me and to them that, once he gets his hands on the rest of

Darkwater, he'll throw them out. They'd have nowhere to go. He'd do it too." The captain mopped his face with a large handkerchief. "Chief inspector, it was unprofessional I grant you, what I did in offering a microphone to the ghastly woman. Forgive my language ma'am but she's a first class bitch. I did say no to her eventually and meant it. She was angry and, just before poor Richard… collapsed, I could see that she was about to grab the spare microphone anyway and simply take the stage and storm the barricades."

Stanley tried to picture Stephanie Berkley storming the barricades. He couldn't quite see her as a Marius Pontmercy and struggled unsuccessfully to imagine her having a role as a revolutionary in *Les Misérables.* How, he wondered, could anyone storm anything wearing high heels. He was suddenly aware of the captain and the two police officers looking at him. One of the officers was smiling but it wasn't DCI Poole.

"Well," the captain continued, "she said she wanted to embarrass Berkley and that maybe it would force him to put up a better divorce settlement. She said that she'd keep on telling people about his past deeds until he did. Dirty washing in public and all that. I believe…"

"Captain, where did Mrs Berkley go after you'd… denied her?" asked Evie.

"Don't know. I was busy with other things."

"Alright. Describe for us again exactly what you saw from the point when the vicar went from where you were in the admin marquee up onto the stage."

The captain was about to protest but did as he was asked.

"Let's say," suggested Evie, "that the vicar's death wasn't from natural causes. Do you think that whatever killed him might have been meant for Ray Berkley?"

"I thought you'd finished questioning me."

"What's the answer?"

"I thought we'd covered everything!"

Evie asked quietly, "Have we though?"

"What do you mean, meant for Ray Berkley? You believe that Richard was definitely murdered?"

"Don't be naive sir. We're considering the possibility, yes."

"I don't know anyone who would have wanted to harm Richard. Berkley on the other hand – well, I could name any number of people who detest him and would cheerfully ring his neck. And, before you ask, yes I'd be at the front of the queue!"

"David, may I ask you something?" Stanley looked at Julian for approbation. "Could anyone," Stanley asked, "have known that you were going to give the fifty-fifty to Richard? Apart from Ray Berkley obviously. Had you discussed your change of mind with other people?"

"No, I don't believe so. The only people who knew were Threadgill and Berkley."

"Certain?"

"Well, when I told Richard I'm sure nobody would have overheard. He might have told Jessica I suppose. Maybe others. Someone may have overheard me talking to Berkley. Anyway, he wasn't best pleased."

"Did he threaten you?" asked Stanley.

"He said something about making sure that he'd eventually get my lodge and remaining land. He also reaffirmed that he was close to getting planning permission to convert the Hall into a hotel and had local support. He wanted to gain prestige by giving out the fifty-fifty. To be seen as the village's face. He does nothing unless it's of benefit to him. And he's used to getting his own way."

"Who knew," asked Evie, "that Mr Berkley was supposed to be giving out the prize?"

"Everyone. The list was up in the pub, in Mr Accrington's

post office and it was on the village's website. I think it might have been on social media and in the local press too."

"Did you touch the yellow fifty-fifty drum?" asked Julian.

"Yes. I gave it a spin just before it was carried onstage. I always do. For luck you see."

"You said that only Graham Lambert and Juliet Corbell filled the drum with the tickets?"

"Yes. In the past we've had the odd occasion where some tickets were found not have been included in the drum. Hell of a hoo-hah. But Lambert and Corbell are trusted to do things by the book."

"Might anyone else have been involved in filling the drum?"

"I couldn't swear to it, but I'd like to think not."

Stanley looked hard at Hugh. Had the captain just gone pale because he realised that he'd just admitted to having the perfect opportunity of doing something to or with the drum? But why would David want Richard dead? And, surely, if he'd planned to kill Berkley somehow onstage, then he would have let the man give out the fifty-fifty prize.

"Sir," Julian was saying, "I understand that you discovered a medical scalpel on the ground near the admin marquee."

David gave Stanley a swift glance. "I... I just noticed something shiny on the floor, that's all. I... was going to pick it up but Mr Accrington stopped me."

"Odd thing to find, don't you think?"

"I suppose so, but there's always all kinds of rubbish found after the fair."

"Hardly an ordinary item of rubbish though," commented Evie. "Did you touch it?"

"No."

Julian leaned forward a little. "Back in the day, when you were a captain in charge of an SAS Mobility Troop, your main task was anti-terrorism. Sixteen men under your command, four corporals running four groups of four. You were based here in the UK for the most part but also in other parts of the world. On a rotation and advisory basis. You were attached to the Revolutionary Warfare Wing for a tour as well. How am I doing?"

David Horsham looked straight into Julian's eyes. "You're doing fine," he said quietly.

"Anything else we should know?"

"No."

"Tell us again," asked Evie, "the people who were in the admin marquee just before you gave everyone the green light to get on with the awards ceremony."

If David Horsham was rattled he didn't show it. He pursed his lips and went through the list again, counting each name on a finger. Then he sat upright, a light in his eyes.

"Syd Baxter. He was there! Shouldn't have been of course. We have strict rules because of the cash, but I thought him harmless. His son's gone missing you know, so I didn't have the heart to ask him to leave."

"And this is significant why?"

"Because he walked out just before we got going with the awards."

"And?"

"And he was holding his gardening knife. It's a big one too."

Julian tapped the table. "And?"

"The knife was open!"

There was a silence.

"Captain," said Julian, "you didn't think to mention this earlier?"

"Truly, I've only just remembered. Look, I've had a lot on my plate and with today's goings on… The blade was open and it had something very red on it. Blood red!"

Apart from some soft murmured voices, a few ringtones and the occasional laugh from beyond the interview cubicle walls, the command unit was peaceful.

"David," said Stanley gently. "Syd's knife was red I'm guessing because in his other hand he was also holding a very large piece of cherry pie which he was eating as he came out of the marquee with the stuff all over much of his face. I don't think the man committed some heinous crime other than to help himself to several large pieces of cake or flan and to fill his jacket with a few other goodies."

"Captain Horsham," said Julian, "you've been very helpful but something's worrying me. Your relationship with Ellis Bindman."

"What on earth are you talking about?"

"My patience, good as it is, might be now wearing thin."

"The doctor and I get on well."

"Sir…"

The captain slumped, resigned. "He was my doctor when he joined the practice here but we had a disagreement."

"You had his father kicked out of the army. Tell me about that."

David Horsham paused for a moment. "Bindman's father was a decent soldier but he was caught embezzling funds from a charity fund. That's a no-no in the army, no less so in the SAS. Without absolute trust between every soldier and the next, the unit's compromised. Money had been collected for orphans where they were stationed. The money went missing. It wasn't a vast sum I grant you, but enough – and anyway the amount wasn't the point. I was charged with finding out what had happened before calling in the MPs. It wasn't hard to discover that Bindman's father was the guilty party. And he admitted it. Said he had financial problems. Usual story. I had no choice but to report him and he knew it. Court martial and unconditional discharge. You can check the records if you don't believe me."

"We have. How did that affect future relations?"

"Ellis Bindman didn't put two and two together for some time. Then, one day I had an appointment with him and the receptionist said that Bindman would prefer it if I saw another doctor in the practice. It's been difficult ever since. Then… when Berkley bought the Hall, he and Bindman became friends or at least drinking pals. Anyone's who's a friend of Berkley isn't one of mine."

"You know Bindman is supporting Berkley's attempt to convert the Hall…"

"I know all about that and I suspect that Berkley has convinced one or two other good burghers from Little Peasen to invest as well."

"That makes you angry?"

"Of course it makes me bloody angry! It'd make you bloody angry as well! Now, unless you object, I should like to take my leave."

"We've seen Mrs Threadgill, Lambert, Monteith, Corbell, Bindman and Horsham. Cooper… not yet. Last on the list this evening is Berkley," Evie said.

"Let's have him in then," said Julian. "And Evie, get someone to check the captain's DNA from that glass."

Stanley, yawning, noticed a small fly that had given up the struggle in the captain's glass of water and he wondered for a moment if this case was dead in the water too.

Sixteen

His lethargy forgotten, a snarling Kreshnik leapt out of the shed, grabbed Stephanie, ripping part of her cardigan in the process, and pointed his gun at the three media people. Too shocked to do or say anything, the four allowed themselves to be bundled into the shed where Janine and Bethan were standing ready to leave.

Kreshnik waved his gun. "All of you," he shouted, totally unused to addressing people he didn't know in such close proximity. "Shut up, fuck off and sit down!"

There was a silence in the small hut as the newcomers absorbed the words and situation. Kreshnik muttered something to himself in a language that nobody understood apart from one of the Norfolk Coast Radio people.

Stephanie, coming out of her initial shock, suddenly shrieked and made everyone flinch including Kreshnik.

"What the bleedin' 'ell do you think you're doin', you scumbag?" Stephanie shouted. "Let me out!"

She lunged to get past Kreshnik, whose reaction was to hit her with his gun. Gasping in pain, blood spurted from her nose.

Kreshnik pushed the gun hard into her temple, his hand shaking. "Here there have a silent," he rasped, spittle flying.

"What did he say," asked a shocked Bethan. "A silent? A silent what?"

"I think he means a silencer," said the recording technician from the radio station.

Stephanie, tears in her eyes borne out of frustration more than pain, pressed an already sodden handkerchief against her nose and fell back onto an ancient leather armchair in a puff of dust while Bethan and Janine subsided again onto the settee. The others sat on bits of moth-eaten rolled-up carpet and rickety garden furniture.

The man from North Anglian News asked as firmly as he could, "What do you want from us?"

Kreshnik could think of nothing to say because he didn't know. He equally had no clue about what he should do next. In addition, he needed to clear his head after smoking dope all afternoon. He wanted more sweet things, but his M&Ms had all gone and he even thought for a moment of finding the green ones that he'd flicked away. To top it all, he also had to remember to hold on to the remote control and avoid pressing any buttons, particularly the red one which he thought fleetingly actually looked like an M&M.

"Stan," asked Julian, "how long's the Baxter son been missing?"

"Paul? Over six months."

"Anything we can do?"

"The Met and the HO were involved for a while, but nothing's turned up. Border Force came up with nothing either."

"When did he leave here?"

"When he went off to university. From there to London I think, but his parents never knew where. He used to visit Syd and Rosie pretty regularly."

"How old?"

"Not sure."

"What did or does he do for a living?"

"No idea. Seemed pretty well off whenever he visited the village."

Stanley excused himself so that he could stretch his legs. As he took in the smells of the grass, border flowers and the sea, he hadn't realised until now that the heat, the emotional stress of the day and the powerful sense of loss had weighed so heavily. He would have preferred at the moment to be sitting in his garden underneath the walnut tree, cooled by a welcome, evening breeze, looking out at the occasionally blue North Sea and sipping a glass of cold Chambolle Musigny. He could almost smell the closing roses and imagined the distant rim where the sea met sky marking the edge of his world. He salivated, remembering that Pat had made some anchovy tarts and damson cheese straws which would go down well with the wine. He wondered what it might be like to be sitting there with Evie, her hair lifting gently in the breeze and her… His thoughts were interrupted by an officer who was calling him back on behalf of DCI Poole.

"Just in," said Julian. "According to the latest interviews with Carmichael's team and Berkley's HR director, the company had no contract with Carmichael. No letters of appointment. Nothing. Doesn't make sense. Every other employee has documents galore including NDAs and all sorts of signed codicils. All sorts. For Carmichael nothing and nobody knows why."

Stanley turned to Evie. "May I ask when Malcolm Carmichael's house is being checked out?"

Julian knew that his friend changed tack often and annoyingly. The DS looked at her boss for approval to answer. Julian nodded.

"They're there now, under orders to report immediately if they find anything."

"Thank you," Stanley said frowning. "And I assume nothing's come up about the person who shouted at Mrs Bishop?"

"No, not yet. Slim leads though. I…"

They were interrupted by an irritated Alfie Scott. "I've got Mr Berkley here, sir. Waiting outside."

Julian noticed the constable's flushed demeanour. "Everything alright Scotty?"

Constable Scott felt that everything wasn't alright. He wanted to swear. "Something wicked this way comes," is what he said instead.

"What?"

"Mr Berkley, sir. *Macbeth*. Did it at school sir. One of the witches says it about Macbeth.

"Not in a good mood then is he, our Mr Berkley?" asked Julian.

"Not as such sir no."

"Where does the quote come from in the play?"

Scotty blushed. "I don't remember that sir."

"It's one line of a couplet spoken by the second of the three witches in Act 4, scene 1. Nasty bastards all three of them," said Stanley.

Ray's brown hair was short with any early grey carefully dyed out. He was good-looking in a clean-shaven, rugby club sort of way. There was a self-satisfaction about him with the behaviour of someone who could do as he liked and expected to be allowed to do as he liked. He was wearing designer jeans, a soft cotton white shirt with half rolled up sleeves, an Omega watch, a signet ring on his left hand's little finger, deck shoes and no socks. His chest filled out the shirt with muscle beginning to run to fat.

"Evening, Mr Berkley," Julian offered as Ray was shown into one of the interview cubicles. "We'll try to keep this short. I'm DCI Poole and this is DS Harris. Mr Accrington you'll know I think."

"I hope this won't take long," Ray Berkley said languidly as he sat down, fitting his bottom firmly on the seat of the chair, "I think I've used up enough of my valuable day waiting around with the hoi polloi of the village. I also don't appreciate being repeatedly told that I can't leave a stifling tea tent let alone my village green."

"What you might appreciate is that that two deaths on the same day in a small Norfolk village aren't that usual. So a small amount of discomfort is always de rigueur in these situations I'm afraid."

Ray merely looked insolently at the DCI and then leered at Evie.

"What's he doing here?" Ray chuckled unpleasantly, jerking his head towards Stanley without looking at him. "I don't believe that Mr Accrington has changed profession – if of course what he currently does can be called a profession."

"Well sir, I invited Mr Accrington to sit in. He knows many of the people in the village and that kind of background intelligence saves time and, sometimes, more than time. Important in my line of work. You want Mr Accrington to leave?"

There was something about Stanley Accrington that Ray found discomforting and he would very much have liked the man to leave, but felt that it would be wise not to say as much. He shrugged pretending disinterest.

"Do you mind being recorded by the way?" asked Julian.

Ray was about to say that he minded very much, but Julian's look caused him to shake his head.

"As a man involved in technology sir, you'll know that for a voice recorder to hear you, it actually needs a voice."

"No, that's fine," said Ray through what were fast becoming gritted teeth.

"What's fine?"

"It's fine for this conversation to be recorded."

A red mist was beginning to creep across Ray Berkley's eyes.

"And do you object to Mr Stanley Accrington sitting in on this meeting?"

"No."

"No what?"

Stanley hid a smile.

Ray looked at Stanley with loathing. "I, Raymond Berkley, do not object to Mr… Accrington sitting in on this meeting."

"Now, Mr Berkley," went on Julian in a relaxed way, "it's getting on and I'm sure you'd like to be elsewhere. Your relationship with Dr Malcolm Carmichael. Tell us about that please."

As the questioning went on, the answers became more abrupt or simply inadequate. After fifteen minutes and seeing Ray looking yet again at his watch, Julian's patience was wearing thin.

"Mr Berkley, for the third time of asking, how come you were meant to be giving out the fifty-fifty prize?"

"It was an honour bestowed upon me," was the languid reply.

"Then how come you didn't fulfil your destiny?"

"Because that fool Horsham chose to give the honour to a man of God. Are we done now?"

"Did you invite your wife to the fair?"

"Hardly!"

"But you knew she was here?"

"Eventually."

"Where were you when Richard Threadgill collapsed?"

Ray smiled. "Really, chief inspector," he said silkily, "nice try, but I think that I should have my solicitor present now, don't you?"

"You choose not to answer any further questions then Mr Berkley?" asked Evie.

"I should like my solicitor to be present or you will allow me to leave this instant. Chief inspector, you and your junior colleague here have insinuated that you are treating both deaths as suspicious and you have the nerve to point your grubby digits at me."

"I think," said Evie not remotely abashed, "you'll find that we haven't accused you of anything. What we have done is ask you questions the majority of which you've chosen not to answer.

Would you like to listen to what you said?"

The chair creaked slightly as Ray undid his body from it. "I'll call my lawyer."

"By all means Mr Berkley; you can use that phone if you wish," said Julian. "I've stopped recording now. Please tell whoever answers your call that we'll meet your lawyer or legal team down the nick in Great Yarmouth. Of course there are other stations we could choose, depending on your preference for the quality of hot drinks. There's Hoveton, King's Lynn, Sprowston, Thetford, Cromer of course… What's your pleasure? No, tell you what Mr Berkley, better yet, ask your undoubtedly expensive legal team to meet us in Norwich. I take it they'll be driving from London? At this time on a Sunday evening, that'll take… oh let's say three hours. While you wait, you can chat to one of the duty officers about… let's see, depending who's on this evening, Norwich City's form, Dante's *Inferno*, the roadworks on the A14 or your favourite episode of *Strictly Come Dancing*. If you're lucky, you can read yesterday's newspaper and take a look at your horoscope. I imagine your future's not looking dead rosy."

There was no response from Ray.

"Mr Berkley," Julian said, "I don't have time to sod about. Get on with it – invite your lawyer to Norwich. It might be a late-nighter of course. DS Harris, please ask someone to call…"

"OK, OK," Ray sat down with the pretence of bestowing a great favour on his audience. "Get on with it then."

Julian sat down too and switched his phone to record once more, explaining into the device the reason for the interruption, the current time and the revisited purpose.

To Ray, he said, "Did you have a problem with the vicar giving out the fifty-fifty?"

"What?"

"Very last warning sir. One more bit of nonsense and you're

on your way."

"I don't recall what I said."

Stanley leaned forward. "You were asked, 'Where were you when Richard Threadgill collapsed?' You smiled and replied, 'Really, chief inspector, nice try, but I think that I should have my solicitor present now, don't you?' The DS here, the one you keep leering at, asked, 'You choose not to answer any further questions then Mr Berkley?' You stopped leering and sneered instead saying, 'I should like my solicitor to be present or you will allow me to leave this instant. Chief inspector, you and your junior colleague here have insinuated that you are treating both deaths as suspicious and you have the nerve to point your grubby digits at me.' Then the DS said, 'I think you'll find that we haven't accused you of anything. What we have done is ask you questions the majority of which you've chosen not to answer. Would you like to listen to what you said?' You stood up and told the police officers that you wanted to call your lawyer. Then you curled your lip much as you're doing now."

If looks could have killed, Stanley would have been dead.

Stanley smiled slightly. "I can remember lines. I…" The smile and the sentence faded; instead a frown appeared. Julian and Evie noticed. Ray Berkley didn't, but just shrugged dismissively.

"Ask me your questions," yawned Ray.

"Let's try a different tack," said Julian. "Did you have a grudge against the vicar?"

"No, of course not. I hardly knew the man."

"Funny that, because you were seen today talking to him at some length. Twice. And we understand that you also spoke to him recently on several other occasions over the last few days."

Ray chuckled malevolently indicating Stanley with a thumb. "Is that what your pet poodle told you? I live here. I'm entitled to talk to my vicar aren't I?"

"You're a regular church-goer then are you? Keeping close to your vicar whom you say you hardly knew?" asked Evie.

Ray didn't answer.

"Do you know of any reason why anyone would have wanted to harm the vicar?"

"No. The man was totally usel… harmless."

"You thought the vicar useless?"

"He wasn't able to help me on a particular matter."

"What matter was that?"

There was no answer.

"The fifty-fifty?"

"That too, yes."

"You were annoyed at not giving out the fifty-fifty?"

"It irritated me."

"Why was the fifty-fifty so important to you?"

"No comment."

"Did you threaten him?"

"Don't be ridiculous!"

"What's the answer?"

"No comment."

"We have," said Julian placing both palms on the desk, "reason to believe that the vicar may have been killed unlawfully, undertaking a duty that you were meant to have performed. Perhaps you were the target. What d'you think?"

Ray flicked out a large, pink tongue and ran it over his lips. He rubbed a hand around his thick neck, eyes darting, his gaze ending up unwillingly on Stanley. He shrugged.

"Threats don't frighten me. I've had threats before now. I have to be a bastard sometimes."

Stanley hid a smile. Ray looked at him challengingly as if reading his mind.

"It's the way it is. Not everyone likes my decisions or methods. I couldn't care less."

For a very brief moment he lost his bravado. "You think that someone wanted to kill me today?"

"Is that what you believe?" asked Julian.

"You're the police officer. You think that however Threadgill died, that's what would have happened to me if we hadn't changed places?"

"You obviously think that's a possibility," said Stanley.

"What's this got to do with you, postman? Shut it!"

"You're not popular here in Little Peasen are you, Mr Berkley?" asked Julian.

"Says who?"

"Well, I'd say that Mr Accrington here may have a view and a fair few people to whom my team and I have spoken offered up frank opinions, often without being asked."

"Well surprise, surprise! They're jealous of my money and they don't like my plans for the Hall. They…" He hesitated.

"Sir?"

"Nothing."

"We understand that you're in the process of divorce proceedings," said Evie. "Why was your wife here today?"

"What's that got to do with you, you little…?" Ray stopped himself, nostrils flaring unpleasantly for a moment, his cheeks bright pink.

Ignoring the jibe, Evie took a different approach. "Tell us why you didn't like Dr Carmichael."

"Malcolm was brilliant. Helped the firm a great deal. I

respected his abilities. He understood propulsion technology like nobody else. He not only understood the automation elements of my… business, but he really got into the pants of… other factors too."

"Other factors?"

"No comment."

"You were telling us about his work."

"No I wasn't and no comment."

"You didn't like him much?"

"I didn't like the dumb hate in his eyes whenever I met him. I didn't…"

"What?"

"Nothing."

"Why is there no contract for him?"

"What do you mean? How…?"

"Under what circumstances did you employ him?" asked Evie.

"What do you mean?"

"Talk us through the process."

"I've told you!"

"You haven't actually."

"Is it relevant to your enquiries?"

"It's why I asked, sir."

"What was the question again?"

"The detective sergeant to whom you were rude just now asked under what circumstances Dr Malcolm Carmichael was employed. They're concerned that there's no paperwork for Dr Carmichael."

"You interfering little piece of…"

"Mr Berkley," interrupted Julian calmly. "I've had it with your intransigence. I'm more than tempted to arrest you for obstruction – then you can cool your jets in a cell. In fact that's what I think we'll do and then carry on tomorrow morning. Your best bud DS Harris here will do the honours. I'll see you in the morning. Maybe later tomorrow evening of course. Very busy you see. Cheers."

Julian made for the interview cubicle door. Ray Buckley began to get up from his chair. He glanced uneasily at Stanley.

"Alright…" Ray muttered. "Wait. I'll answer your questions."

"I'm not sure I want to ask you any more, so I think we'll just go for an arrest."

"I said I'll answer your questions!"

Julian sat down again as did Ray who now had a throbbing vein in his forehead.

"Last chance saloon then," said Julian.

"You alright, Ray?" asked Stanley wondering idly if the man was actually planning to make a run for it. Or have a seizure.

"It's Mister Berkley to you sunbeam and don't you forget it."

"What's the answer to my question, sir?" asked Evie looking at her notes.

"Which was?"

"In what circumstances was Dr Carmichael employed?"

"He… I… knew of his drone work and contacted him. I needed a brilliant technologist. He was a brilliant technologist. He was keen and we discussed terms. He agreed my terms."

"Why no contract? It seems, according to your head of HR, contracts in your business were detailed and watertight with attached DNAs. For Carmichael, nothing."

Julian, Stanley and Evie could see Ray trying to think up a good story.

"I… knew his work. And… he had a reputation. I needed someone in a hurry…"

"Bit lame sir, given that you run a tight ship?"

"Look, I just employed him quickly and we must have forgotten to sort out contracts! Who the hell cares? He didn't and, anyway, now he's dead, it really doesn't matter."

"You're not really as clever as you think are you Mr Berkley?"

"Meaning what?"

"Oh I don't know," said Julian. "You like to strut about, doing what you please, treating people like crap. You know the price of everything but the value of nothing. You have all the trimmings, but you still have a big chip on your shoulder. You don't give a stuff about Malcolm Carmichael. I reckon you never did. A means to an end that's all. You should have treated him like gold dust. But you didn't because you're a nasty piece of work. Your wife's in the exit room and I'm guessing she knows of a few little secrets that lie under your thick carpet. We'll ask her and we'll find them all I promise you. When the shit hits the fan, people like you suddenly discover they have few or no friends. The people who say they like you, don't. They like what you can give them. Period."

"You have no idea what you're talking about! The world will beat a path to my door, chief inspector. You'll see. Sure, Carmichael was key to all this. He was brilliant. But I didn't kill him."

"What did he do that was so brilliant? You make industrial drones. Big ones for delivery purposes. Most of your drones go to Africa or India. Good for you sir. But you didn't need him for that. Did he invent something better? I think he did and then he became a fly in your ointment and you needed to get rid of him. Right track d'you think?"

"I think we're done."

"You don't much care that Carmichael's dead?"

"You want me to say that I'll shed tears? Not my way. His legacy is what I wanted and I've got that. I'm leaving now," he said his voice high and angry, "so arrest me or don't but, if you do, you'd better have a good bloody reason!"

"Tell me," said Julian quietly. "About your relationship with Malcolm Carmichael's family. His father for instance. Let's start there and move on to his mother."

Ray, almost standing fully upright, froze for an instant, fear momentarily in his eyes. He scrabbled for the door handle.

Evie asked, "You been drinking sir?"

"Piss off."

Julian stood up slowly with a smile, but his eyes were flint as they locked onto Ray's.

"Mr Berkley, I've just turned off all recording hardware and my detective sergeant has stopped making notes. Mr Accrington will excuse himself on my say so. The video cameras that cover everything in this unit can be paused by me pressing this button here. All the other officers present in this incident unit will suddenly have become stone deaf. In sixty seconds I might arrest you on various counts and ask the ladies and gents of the press out there if they'd like to talk to you about the fact that you've been arrested and why. I will then have a problem remembering details. You on the other hand will be facing the front page, albeit the local front page, under media suspicion of what? Well, who can say? Oh yes and, quite possibly, you might enjoy an overnight stint in a cell. With all mod cons of course. One more thing. I very much trust that you'll not be driving home now because, if you do, I guarantee that you will be stopped, breathalysed and, as appropriate, booked. Sir."

Turning and almost losing his footing, Ray very nearly subsided on Evie's lap but instead, and luckily, stumbled out of the interview cubicle. Through the window, Stanley watched him as he struggled with the incident unit's steps, pushed past a duty officer and half-ran across the village green. Stanley smiled as he saw the man suddenly look nervously over his shoulder and veer away from where his silver car was parked.

The sun was on its downward slide, shadows lengthening and the village green strangely empty. There were now no onlookers behind the police cordon, just officers patrolling the perimeter. Everything was strangely quiet after the day's cacophony. Through the window Stanley saw that the evening had an odd, surreal, dreamlike quality to it as if the day was still waiting for something to happen before it slept. As he looked, Stanley thought of his friend the vicar, no – his friend Richard – and realised with a thump to his heart that his friend wouldn't see this.

"Evie," said Julian, "get someone to fetch Mrs Berkley."

"Now sir? I thought…"

"I'm struggling with the dead wood in this case. So, yes, now!"

Seventeen

Patricia Accrington tried for the fifth time to get hold of her niece but each call, including this one, had gone to voicemail. Normally she wouldn't have been particularly worried, but with two deaths, a fruitcake on the loose shouting foul abuse and a parcel containing firearms, she felt that she had every right to be more than a little concerned.

She'd cut herself a thin slice of strawberry flan made with fruit from the garden and, while the piece remained untouched, she was on her third cup of strong breakfast tea. As frequently happened when Sheila Prewer's instincts told her that tea and one of Patricia's vegan flans might be on offer, the old lady had popped in unannounced, but right now Patricia would have preferred to have been on her own. Or with her brother and niece.

"Look, Miz Accringter," said Sheila having just peered for the umpteenth time out of the dining room window which overlooked the bookshop across the road, "I just know that summat's wrong over there. Wills won't open 'is door and, when I went roun', 'e kep' shoutin' that 'e'd got a friend staying called Migraine or some such from Andalucía or Alabama or somewhere. Foreign anyway. I told your brother. Oh yeah an' I done a recce. Snuck up and 'ad a peep. The shutters was shut, but not totally shut. There were more than one man in there an' all. And none of 'em were Willy. When's your brother back?"

"I've told you Sheila. He's helping the police."

Sheila stuffed a large piece of flan in her mouth, swallowed, took a slurp of tea, swallowed that and spoke again. "I'm thinking that Wills is in trouble and I might need to get stuck in. You too."

"We can't just go and get stuck in as you put it Sheila. If you're really concerned, then we'll need to tell the police."

"Got their 'ands full, they 'as."

"Let's try ringing William again then."

"Won't do no good," Sheila said authoritatively through another large mouthful of flan.

Patricia didn't agree with the logic of this at all. Agitated, she walked over to the dining room window. There was no traffic outside and no people either. Everything was still.

"The light's going," she yawned, arms folded. "I'm a bit exhausted now, truth be told Sheila," she said talking to the window and in the vain hope that Sheila might take the hint. "It was hot today wasn't it? I think my neck's a bit burnt. That's odd."

"T'ain't odd Miz Accringter. It's what 'appens when you ain't got no 'at on. I got some 'omemade cream – good for sunburn it is. Made mostly o' turps and ol' butter. Ponks a bit but I allus teks it when we goes on manoeuvres…"

"No, not the sunburn. I mean the bookshop. The lights are off at the front, but you can see there's light coming from the back and, you're quite right, there are people moving about. Come and see."

As the women peered out, they could indeed see moving shapes in the bookshop.

"Maybe he's having a party," said Patricia.

"What, with two murders on the village green? Don't be daft Miz Accringter if you don't mind me sayin'. Anyways, 'e's bin closed today and Willy don't do parties. Well, 'is bloke, Vedansh, likes the odd knees up, but not Wills." She laughed. "Unless you count them affairs when 'e gets them people to talk about books in the shop and Vedansh and 'im gives out bits of fish on a biscuit and that fizzy wine. Once gave 'em summink called shizzel. Cut up into liddle pieces. Tasted 'orrible."

Patricia's curiosity was piqued. "What's shizzel?"

Sheila shrugged. "Dunno. Squashed chicken or summat in breadcrumbs and lemon juice. Cooden give that to troops I tells you that much!"

"Think you mean schnitzel, Sheila."

Stephanie Berkley was angry, frightened and in pain – probably, she thought, in that order although fear was beginning to take the lead. She could feel her bruised mouth swelling by the second, her nose was sore and her aching eye socket made her wonder miserably if she would end up with a face of purple, blue and yellow hues. Her overall fear however was founded now on the basis that a marbling face might be the least of her and her co-hostages' problems.

She took stock. Her new dress was torn, her cardigan was ripped almost in half and her hair was full of cobwebs. One of her shoes had a wobbly heel and her knickers were riding up her bottom. Her mission of the day had gone totally pear-shaped and now she yearned for a bath, a triple gin with a touch of tonic, a slice of lime and lots of ice accompanied by a large, thin crust pepperoni pizza and possibly that young trader from the American bank whose name she couldn't remember which was alright because he couldn't have cared less what hers was. The order might alter, but the ingredients were all there.

The sound technician from Norfolk Coast Radio had been secretly recording everything that had been said in the hut and he'd urged, through covert signs, that Ellie, his station presenter colleague, should engage Kreshnik in conversation. This wasn't easy given that the man's English was limited and, in any case, he said little when he said anything at all. Ellie didn't let on that she could speak some Albanian. Bernard, the reporter from North Anglian News had seemed hale and hearty to begin with but had now lapsed into a comatose gloom. Bethan was quiet but Stephanie thought she might be a good ally. Janine Bishop looked exhausted and a very tiny part of Stephanie's heart went out to her.

"Oi," she said to her current nemesis as she stood, hands on hips. "That fing in your left 'and, what's it for?"

Kreshnik, tough as he was and with a reputation for sustained violence, had in the last hour become drowsy. He'd been told again by Adidas to stay put and to keep the controller safe. He'd also been instructed to hold the hostages in the shed until advised differently. However, thought Kreshnik, what Adidas failed to realise was that he'd been in the hut now for several hours, was hungry, thirsty and badly wanted to relieve himself. He was also fed up to his back teeth with this whining woman and wanted any excuse to shoot her.

"I said, what does that actually do then?" insisted Stephanie pointing at the controller.

There was a look but no reply. Stephanie stepped forward, pulling down the front of her torn dress so that her cleavage was highly visible. Kreshnik didn't just look now; he goggled. In the immediate silence that followed, they both heard the definitive click of the recorder being switched off or on. Kreshnik immediately forgot about partly exposed breasts and stared in the direction of the click. Without hesitation, he shot the sound recordist. The report from the gun wasn't loud. What was noisy though was the scream of shock and agony from the injured man.

Everyone in the hut froze apart from the sound recordist who was writhing about in pain and bleeding from the wound in his upper left arm. At that moment, Bethan's phone vibrated again. While others were distracted, she eased it out of her jacket pocket, glanced down and saw that it was Patricia on her sixth call. Surreptitiously, she tapped out a message with a thumb, something she could do easily without looking at the phone's screen. She dropped the phone back in her jacket pocket, palming the nail scissors which had been so sharp and helpful when she'd trimmed her split fingernail.

Kreshnik was totally fed up now so he phoned his boss while the sound recordist sobbed, comforted by people who were at a loss as to know what to do. Bernard, the journalist from North Anglian News who'd had a little first aid training, staunched the wound after a fashion with handkerchiefs and Janine's silk scarf.

Even though she'd been born in Slovenia, Ellie's Albanian was actually pretty good. Listening carefully to what Kreshnik was saying on his call, she gathered that, whatever the remote control handset was for, it was going to be used soon. She couldn't glean any other information from only one side of the conversation but, like Stephanie, she realised with a cold shiver that the lives of all of the people in the shed might be at a dead end.

"Sir… it's Mrs Berkley," said Evie ending a call. "She's done a runner."

"Share her description and let's find her," sighed Julian, wondering if this was more than a missing person case. "Get her phone tracked. Border Force to have a description, high alert. The Met to check out the London flat soonest with a warrant. The place searched, overnight if necessary."

"Looking for?"

"No idea," Julian snapped. "Brief the search senior officer on the whole situation. I mean whole. And let's get any concierge, delivery people and neighbours questioned. Boyfriends, girlfriends, other friends. Taxis, local cabs, limo firms."

"Sir."

"Not done yet. I also want Darkwater Hall daylight searched with a warrant. Tomorrow morning. Top to bottom. See if Derek Johnstone can lead. He's thorough and then some. Computers, documents, the whole nine yards. And the grounds. Video the whole thing. Any problems, they answer to me, the chief constable and my grandmother whose birthday lunch I missed today. I'd be most fearful of the last if I were them."

"Sir," said Evie with a smile that wasn't reciprocated.

One of the uniformed constables asked to speak to Evie. She listened, nodded, pointed in Julian's direction and went off to make some calls.

"Sir. Excuse me sir," said the uniformed constable.

"Yes?"

"Apparently the head WI lady, a…" she consulted her notebook, "a Mrs Monteith, has offered some sandwiches. All freshly made she says. And a veggie option. Oh yes – and there's cake too she says. Lemon drizzle apparently. Sir."

Sensing Julian's tiredness and rising temper, the constable stepped back a little. "They mean well sir – and everyone could do with something."

"Including you…" added Stanley to Julian. "Not the same fare that your grandmother might have offered, but a sandwich and a slice of Mrs Monteith's lemon drizzle cake…" Suddenly Stanley stopped speaking and sat bolt upright. "Cake?" he asked, looking up at the anxious constable. "You just said cake. You said lemon drizzle cake."

The constable wondered if the man who'd spoken was a senior something in the force, a psychiatrist maybe. She knew that they could be an odd lot sometimes.

"Yes sir, cake," she nodded, puzzled by the exchange. "Lemon drizzle. Apparently, they made spare for the fête and they've got a few left over…" She stopped and wondered why the man was still staring at her with a wild glint in his eye.

"OK, constable," Julian muttered wondering at his friend's sanity. "Do it. Please thank Mrs Monteith."

Constable Patterson tried a smile, nodded at the DCI, glanced warily at Stanley and went off on her mission.

Julian turned abruptly to Stanley. "OK, what?"

Stanley stared at Julian. "It wasn't that cake! It was the wrong cake!" He stood up and shouted, "The wrong bloody cake!"

Those closest to Stanley were surprised and concerned that the normally quiet man from the village who was helping DCI Poole should have even raised his voice at the governor, let alone shouted. People didn't shout at DCI Poole. Not twice anyway.

Stanley took a deep breath. "The cake that Richard Threadgill ate wasn't seed cake. There was no seed cake, caraway or otherwise. The cake he ate was lemon drizzle."

Julian tried to say something but didn't get a chance.

"Those black spots in Richard's mouth, up his nose, in his mouth and on the fifty-fifty drum weren't seeds or pepper or whatever. Those specks were something else entirely. Ray Berkley's in the business of drone technologies. Big drones. Industrial drones. Martha – my sister Martha – did her PhD at Imperial College where Dr Carmichael did his. At exactly the same time. She's a micro-technologist. Not in Carmichael's league maybe but she always had time for him. Pat talked to her about all sorts of things this afternoon – mostly about Bethan wanting to go to drama school. They talked about today as well of course and the topic of Carmichael came up. She knew of him quite well and was aware of his speciality which was nano-technology. I'm so stupid! I didn't put two and two together. These things that looked like seeds weren't seeds at all. I think that they're microbots. I think Berkley's been making tiny, tiny drones. That's why he wanted Malcolm to work for him. According to Martha, Malcolm always wanted to produce micro-self-propelled robots. I think that's just what he did. He made miniscule flying robots. Not seeds."

Julian was about to tell his friend to calm down a little, but didn't get a chance. Stanley raced on.

"When Carmichael was trying to get away from Amber Cooper, he yelled, 'Leave us alone!' I thought at the time he was talking about himself. But he wasn't. He wasn't telling Amber to leave him alone; he was telling her to leave him and his invention alone! Everyone who saw him said independently in their statements that he kept waving at something or gently brushing something in front of him. Gently, brushing things away or encouraging them. These things were his babies. I bet you my Triumph Bonneville Bobber that he had his micro biomechanical invention with him during the fair. Why? I don't know. Testing it? Using it to kill Berkley? Both those things maybe. But I also bet my Bonneville Bobber that he wasn't fully adept at controlling the microbots. He didn't know how. Not properly. The things were brand new and not road tested. I think he had a small swarm. Hundreds not thousands of amazing, tiny machines emulating flying insects, the size of a pepper speck! No bigger than a seed or a tiny fly. That's what he was controlling and why his waving hand movements looked odd. He was trying to make his swarm work and at the same time he was trying to protect it. Protecting an instrument of death."

Julian called for Alfie Scott.

"Scotty, get the WI people to confirm one hundred percent what cake was available in the admin marquee during the fair."

"Cake, sir?" asked the puzzled constable.

"Cake! I want to know precisely what cake was available in the admin marquee at any time during the fair. Nowhere else. Just there. Go!"

Julian went into one of the interview cubicles and made three calls, one to the lead SOCO, another to Norfolk's chief pathologist and a slightly longer one to a specialist Home Office science director in London. As a result of the last call he phoned Porton Down and then Julian Poole smiled. He came back into the main area of the incident unit and shared the smile with Stanley as well as adding a nod before giving Evie a number of instructions. Scotty returned, out of breath and with his notebook open.

"Sir, Mrs Monteith says that the only baked goods in the administration marquee were…" He paused to read. "Four strawberry, three raspberry and two apple tarts, three cherry flans, four lemon drizzle cakes, a chocolate log and no end of shortbread. And there was an assortment of sandwiches. Plus jugs of mixed cordial and bottles of water." He grinned at the DCI, delighted with his concluded project.

"You've had a piece of apple something or other en route?" asked an unsmiling Julian.

The constable went bright red. "Sir… I did. Sorry sir. I'm…"

"Just remove the bit of apple from your shirt front."

Turning to Evie, Julian began to say something, but was interrupted by a small cheer from his teams. WI members and a number of Boy Scout helpers had arrived bearing huge trays of sandwiches and thick, yellow slices of lemon drizzle cake along with bowls of fresh fruit and three very large pots of tea.

Evie, on her way out to talk to some of the team, picked up a sandwich and asked for some of the fare to be held back for the officers outside. Julian grabbed a roll without checking its contents, bit half of it in one go, pulled a face and peered inside, confirming the fact that coronation chicken wasn't his favourite filling.

Evie rushed back into the incident unit and, without any preamble, pushed through to Julian who was about to finish the coronation chicken filled roll.

"Sir," she said, wide-eyed, "there's been a shooting at the top end of the green!"

Julian looked up sharply, food forgotten. "A shooting?"

"The village green shed, sir. Six hostages I believe and one man with a gun who's holding a device of some sort. One of the hostages has been shot!"

Julian rubbed his face with his hands.

"Sir," she said, now hesitatingly, "apparently Mr Accrington's niece is one of the hostages… She somehow managed to text Mr Accrington's sister. Who's just phoned in sir."

Stanley sat down unsteadily, not sure what to say or do. There was a hiatus when time and movement seemed to halt. Officers waited for the DCI to act. Julian looked at his friend and calmly asked him to wait in one of the interview cubicles which Stanley did without demur. He rang a tearful Patricia who told him that the text had been short but it seemed that so far Bethan was fine. Patricia forwarded her niece's text to Stanley who sent it on to

Evie. He asked his sister if she wanted him to come home or if she'd prefer to be with him on the green. Patricia told him to stay put and that she would do the same.

Finishing the call by promising to keep his sister in the loop and vice versa, Stanley felt useless. He lifted the window blind and looked out at the familiar village green. Everything appeared strangely ordinary even though he could hear snippets of conversations and people on phones. Nothing seemed panicked or rushed. That added irritation to fear. He wanted people to get on with it, to do something.

A sudden sense of dread swept over him as he thought of the possibility of hearing more gunfire which would mean a macabre guessing game as to the outcome. He opened the window and could immediately smell lavender and the sea neither of which comforted him in the way that both normally did. The day was coming to an end but, even though the sun had nearly lowered itself, the air was still warm. Adding to the normality of the tableau, he heard a child's distant, clear, golden laughter, unabashed and full of some simple joy. That frightened him the most.

Things seemed to happen at once. An unmarked, high-powered police car roared up to the side of the village green from which three armed police officers ran to the incident unit. Within what seemed to Stanley like no more than a minute, the same officers made their way slowly towards the hut, stopping frequently, speaking and listening over their helmet headsets to someone and then continuing. The sound of a huge army vehicle's air brakes punctured the air. Three army technicians immediately began erecting floodlight pylons on the roof of the army vehicle. Within minutes, the high powered LED lights were ready to go as were some additional, heavy-duty mobile spotlights. All lights and people on the green were pointing at or looking towards the hut next to the big oak tree.

Two bomb disposal experts donned protective outfits and awaited instructions. Several police officers exited the incident unit and spread out along the periphery of the village green creating a semi-circular net.

Listening to various external conversations, Stanley worked out that police blocks had been set up to stop any vehicle from entering or leaving the village. Everything was quiet as if Little Peasen was holding its expectant breath. Stanley suddenly remembered what Scotty had said – 'Something wicked this way comes.'

One of the armed officers was now positioned behind the stage area and the other adjacent to a tree not far from the big oak next to the shed. The third officer, the leader, obvious from helmet markings, was kneeling near the village green entrance gate. Julian came out of the incident unit wearing a helmet, dark blue long-sleeved T-shirt, short-sleeved bullet-proof jacket, action fatigues and Kevlar boots. Two similarly dressed officers were with him. Walking carefully around the edge of the village green, gradually getting closer to the hut, the three met up with the lead armed officer. The second armed officer moved silently to one of the shed's windowless sides and affixed what Stanley imagined was a listening device. He expected that the police would have a gadget for looking through the hut's window but, just as he thought that thought, he could see that someone inside the hut had stuffed a piece of cloth over the window stopping anyone seeing in. Or out.

After knocking, not banging, on the hut's door, Julian lifted his visor and spoke emphatically.

"I am a senior police officer. My name is Detective Chief Inspector Poole. I have no weapon, but this hut is surrounded by police officers, some of them armed. Can someone tell me please how many hostages are in there?"

There was no reply, so Julian repeated the question.

"Six. One man's been shot," a hesitant voice could be heard, "but there's an old lady who's unwell. Please help us…"

The voice was cut off by the sound of someone being hit

followed by the noise of crying.

"Can I talk to the man with the gun please?"

"Are you really a policeman?" asked another voice.

"Yes, I am. What's your name?"

"Ellie."

"Hello Ellie. I'm here to help you all. Ellie, can I confirm again that one person has been shot?"

"Yes, but…"

"And that person is an adult male?"

"Yes."

"How badly hurt is he Ellie?"

"He's been shot in the left upper arm. He's in pain and has lost a lot of blood."

"Thank you Ellie. Has the wound been bound?"

"Yes… but not very well…"

"OK, thank you. Ellie, what work do you do?"

"I'm a reporter for Norfolk Coast Radio and I present an afternoon slot on alternate days during the week."

"Thanks Ellie. Can you please ask the man with the gun if I can speak to him?"

There was a pause.

"He won't speak to you," Ellie called out with hysteria not far behind the anxiety. "He's from Albania and I speak some Albanian. He says he wants to leave now. He's demanding an automatic, fast car to be brought to the hut with the engine running. He's just been on the phone to someone and he's pressed a button on a device that he's been holding…"

Ellie spoke in sharp breaths and Julian could hear the rising tension in her voice.

"Mr Poole," said Ellie beginning to sob helplessly, "we don't know what the controller does and he won't say… and now he's dropped it on the floor and stamped on it. We don't know if there's a bomb or something in here…"

"Ellie you're being really brave and very helpful."

There were sounds of someone being hit several times followed by more sobbing.

"Ellie, hello?"

"She's a bit… upset sir."

"Who's speaking?"

"My name's Bernard Springer and I'm a reporter from…"

"Hello Bernard," said Julian crisply. "Please tell me if the man is wearing a jacket or something that might be covering anything on his body."

"No, he's not," came the nervous reply. "Just a black T-shirt, black jeans and black boots. Can you help us now please?"

"Bernard, are you all sitting together?"

Another voice shouted out, "Yes of course we bleedin' well are! We're in a fucking garden shed! Where the fuck do you think we're sitting? Get us out of 'ere, you moron. Now!"

"Who's speaking please?"

"Stephanie Berkley. Just hurry the f…"

"Stephanie, sorry to interrupt, but does the man have a bag?"

"Who cares? Just get us out!" screamed Stephanie. There was the sound of a slap and more weeping.

"Mr Poole, it's Ellie here. The man with the gun doesn't have a bag, but the man who was shot has just fainted and there's an old lady here who I think is really unwell."

"Ellie, where are you all in the shed?"

"There are two people on a settee centre back facing the door, two on mats rear my left as I face the door, one lying on the floor my right and Mrs Berkley's on a chair my right. I think the man…" Ellie's voice was on the verge of panic. "If you come in, he says he'll shoot all of us. I… think he means it. Don't let him shoot us… I have a little boy and…"

Julian turned. The lead armed officer behind him had been joined by her two colleagues. He looked into the eyes of the lead officer. She stared right back at him steely-eyed through her visor, but there was no emotion whatsoever on her face. She was just waiting for an order.

"Ellie," called Julian turning back to the hut. "Tell the man with the gun that nobody will harm him if he comes out now and immediately puts the gun down on the floor."

There was no reply.

"Tell him please," reinforced Julian, "that he must come out now and then we'll listen to what he has to say. We won't hurt him unless he tries to hurt anyone else. But he has to come out now."

"He says he won't come out. He's angry… He… he's just wet himself."

"Tell him that he has to speak to me."

Through the silence Julian could hear the clatter of approaching helicopter's blades. For the first time in the day he felt sweat on his forehead, a condition that increased as the hut's door opened slowly. Julian stepped back a couple of paces and to his left, leaving a clear sightline for the Heckler & Koch MP5K behind him. Kreshnik came out of the hut very slowly, his gun held firmly in his right hand and pointing outwards. Immediately three weapons trained on his head and heart, red dots remaining in the same places even as the man moved.

Keeping out of the guns' sightlines, Julian stepped forward, his arms outstretched and palms face up and flat. Slowly, he dropped his hands keeping his arms slightly away from his body. Kreshnik glanced around him and took in the armed officers and the helicopter in the near distance. His eyes locked on Julian's for a second. Making a decision, Kreshnik tensed, pointing his gun at Julian's head. What happened next was swift. Bethan, already right behind Kreshnik, stepped forward, leaned across and stabbed him very hard in the back of his trigger hand with her nail scissors. The scissors went into skin and possibly bone. Kreshnik roared, dropped the gun and, turning slightly, swiped Bethan hard. Despite her pain, Bethan stumbled, righted herself and froze, wide-eyed in shock. Kreshnik glanced at his hand, muttered something, yanked out the scissors and was about to bend down to retrieve the gun. Julian barked something. Immediately Kreshnik collapsed and spasmed, shot at close range with a Vipertek VTS-989 taser. As he fell, two of the armed police shouted with enormous voices that Kreshnik shouldn't even think about moving, an academic request really because, while he could hear and twitch, he certainly couldn't move.

The lead officer covered Kreshnik while two bomb squad officers pressed the man on the ground none too gently, body searched him and used double plastic ties on his wrists and ankles. The lead armed officer nodded at Julian and strode into the hut.

Kreshnik's gun was collected, tagged and bagged as the lead armed officer walked out of the hut still with zero expression. She had a word with her two officers, talked into her radio and then nodded again at Julian. Kreshnik was dragged away and, as he went, Julian walked past him without a glance. Removing his helmet, Julian stepped into the shed along with two officers, each recoiling slightly at the smell.

"I'm DCI Poole. Please don't move yet." Julian smiled at the hostages. "Which one of you is the interpreter?"

Ellie identified herself and smiled bleakly back at Julian through cut lips.

"Thank you Ellie; you did a fine job. You all did. Sir," he said turning to the wounded sound technician who had just opened his confused and pain-filled eyes, "we'll get you off to hospital in a jiffy."

The lead armed officer had returned. "Sir," she said, "we need to know the whereabouts of the device that the gunman was holding."

"Can't we just get out?" bawled Stephanie.

Julian turned to her and even he was surprised at the extent of the damage on her face and upper body. "Mrs Berkley?"

Stephanie nodded.

"Please just be a bit more patient. We'll go as fast as we can, but we just need to be sure where everything is."

Stephanie was about to shout again but one of the armed officers pre-empted that by holding up a hand. Stephanie Berkley looked at the face looking at her and for once said nothing.

"It's there, in that corner," Janine Bishop whispered, pointing.

"Thank you. Madam, are you Mrs Bishop?"

"I am, yes… why?"

"Glad you're safe ma'am." He gave her such a warm look that Janine felt both reassured and a little better.

"OK everyone, let's move, single file," called out an armed officer.

Four of the hostages were helped by paramedics into one ambulance, while two were stretchered into another. Bomb squad specialists checked the hut and after a few minutes came out thumbs up. Crime scene investigators retrieved the controller pieces and the phone, bagged them along with what they initially thought were curious green pills of some sort. They also scraped and bagged some firearm discharge residue from the floor, found the spent cartridge, bagged that too and left the hut.

Both Janine Bishop, whose breathing had become shallow, and the wounded sound recordist were immediately taken off to hospital. Bethan wanted to go with Janine, but the police wouldn't allow it. Stephanie, Ellie, Bernard and Bethan were taken the short distance to the incident unit. There they were offered water or a hot drink, Datrex ration bars and, even though it was far from cold, a thermal blanket. Paramedics examined each person carefully, administering antibiotics and applying ointment, plasters, bandages or a modicum of comfort as necessary.

Stanley, desperate to see his niece, was refused access. He felt relieved at the outcome of what had happened, but at the same time bleak. He would have liked to have looked into the eyes of the man who'd held these people hostage. He'd seen him being driven off under armed guard at the same time as the sound of the helicopter had diminished and then disappeared.

Each hostage was finger-printed, photographed, thoroughly searched, relieved of some DNA and their phones, debriefed at considerable length, then sent on their separate ways, apart from Stephanie Berkley. Bethan was reunited with a joyful Pat and Stanley began to breathe more easily for the first time in what had seemed a long time.

The sound recordist's material was given up to the police despite Ellie's protestations. After a swift call by an officer to her radio station's controller, the material was left with Evie.

"Will we get it back?" asked the irked station controller.

"Of course you will, sir," was the deadpan and untruthful reply.

Eighteen

After some serious washroom time, protests, foul language plus a change of clothing into police joggers, trainers and an oversize sweatshirt, Stephanie was declared fit to be further interviewed on separate matters. At Julian's request, Stanley was again asked if he wouldn't mind joining. In truth Stanley wanted to have time with Pat and Bethan, but Julian repeated the request and Stanley acquiesced.

The conversation with a very testy Mrs Berkley didn't begin well and the woman, it seemed to Evie, disliked most people and was indignant about the remainder. After a few minutes, any sympathy for the ordeal through which she'd been put was hard to sustain.

"This bloke ain't a copper," was her first snapped opinion when Stanley arrived in the interview room.

"Mr Accrington," said Julian patiently, "is helping us in connection with two cases of unexplained death. He…"

"Big fucking deal. Secret service goon or summink is 'e then?"

"No. he runs the post office and shop here in the village. He…"

Stephanie sniggered. "Yeah, yeah, whatever… like I really care… I don't believe I 'ave to answer any questions wivout my lawyer 'ere and I also don't reckon that even then I need to answer any questions at all."

"Well, that's plain enough Mrs Berkley," said Julian calmly. "Of course, Mr Accrington can leave and I can postpone any questioning until MI5 officers arrive to escort you to a building the location of which even I don't know."

"Look, I ain't the terrorist, smartarse! I'm the bleedin' victim!"

"If you won't answer our questions, I'll hand you over to my colleagues. I'm not in the mood to mess about."

He clicked two fingers as if an idea had just occurred to him. "In fact," he said, "y'know what? I don't want to listen any more to your insolence and rudeness, so I think the best course of action would be to hand you over to other folk who may not be as cuddly as we are. DS Harris could you make the calls please?"

"Oh, ha fuckin' ha. Pull the other one mate. It's got bleedin' bells on… I don't frighten easily."

Stephanie happened to glance at Stanley and what she saw in his eyes bothered her. She shivered.

"OK," she said, turning to Julian. "What d'you want? I've just told your buddies everyfink what 'appened in the stinkin' shed!"

Having confirmed on record that she was grudgingly happy to be recorded and have Stanley attend the meeting, Stephanie Berkley continued being obstructive and unpleasant. After twenty minutes, the attitude and number of contradictions had begun to grate on Julian's tired nerves much as they had when interviewing her husband.

With difficulty, Evie and he took Stephanie through her day – arrival, reasons for being in Little Peasen, people to whom she'd spoken, anything she'd done, seen, heard or said. Reminded by Julian for the final time that his patience was wearing wafer thin and that, if she wasn't prepared to behave with courtesy and truth, then they would arrest her for police perjury and obstruction or just hand her on to other authorities.

"Mrs Berkley," said Evie, "you'll be the first to admit that today's been a busy one. I'm tired and you must be exhausted. Let's get through this, shall we?"

Stephanie made no comment, but crossed her bruised legs and looked contemptuously at the detective sergeant.

"You claim that you were in the tea tent at two o'clock. Yet you now say that you didn't arrive in Little Peasen until quarter past two."

"Calling me a liar again, then?" she snapped.

Stepahnie desperately wanted a cigarette and she also wanted to get away so that she could think. She needed to consider the possibility of another plan to stop Ray Berkley in his tracks and extricate the divorce money that she felt was her due. Right now, her plans had fallen short.

"We know from your driver," continued Evie, "and, by the way, before you contradict us, this has been confirmed by the driver's agency, that you were dropped off here at four minutes to two."

"Yeah, yeah, maybe I was… but I didn't go straight onto the green."

"According to the driver and also to other witnesses, that's exactly what you did."

Stephanie didn't respond.

"Did you come here to kill Dr Malcolm Carmichael?"

Stephanie stared at the officers in turn for a moment and then laughed high and falsely. She stopped, realising that this wasn't the best tactic. "Why the merry 'ell would I do that?"

"You were having a relationship with him weren't you?"

Stephanie happened to catch Stanley's eye and once again she felt anxious. Not bowel wateringly so, but something.

She collected herself. "Utter bollocks. I was not."

"Yes, you were Mrs Berkley," said Julian. "You want to see the photographs?"

"You took photographs?" Stephanie screeched. "You fucking pervert!"

"We didn't as it happens, but DS Harris has them in that envelope there."

"You bastards… you… utter bastards. How did you get them?"

There was no reply.

"Answer me!"

Again, nothing came back.

Stephanie sagged. "Sleepin' wiv Malc was a way of getting back at Ray. I liked Malc. 'im an' me was only… three or four times… just fun… why not? I want them pictures! You've got no bleedin' right… I didn't kill Malc. And you ain't got no proof what says different."

"Your affair with Dr Carmichael was more than the three or four times you say it was."

Abjectly, Stephanie looked at the table top. "'ow did you get them photos?" she asked again more quietly now.

"No comment," said Julian.

"Has Ray got them then an' all?"

No answer was forthcoming.

"Tell me!"

"Mrs Berkley," said a tired Julian Poole, "this is a two way street. I've eaten one and a half sandwiches today neither of which I liked, I've overdosed on coffee, I'm trying to find out the reason for two deaths at a village fair and the cause of one, I've managed a hostage scenario which included you and I've missed my grandmother's seventy fifth birthday. So far you've been unhelpful, rude and not remotely grateful for any support you received in freeing you from a man who liked bashing you in the face with a gun. Now, I can do without the thanks – I'm used to getting none and I'm certain that our armed and other colleagues couldn't give a rat's arse. But, I'm not having you continue in the mean-spirited and nasty way that you have so far. Let's cut to the chase. Get your lawyer on the phone and, while you're doing that, my detective sergeant here will arrange for you to be collected by our national security people. Whilst you're in their custody my colleagues in the Met can interview you as well. They'll perhaps make a better job of it than me."

"I liked Malc," Stephanie said suddenly, everything about her subsiding, "and yeah we had a fling. But, Malc… well, 'e went a bit crazy over the weeks after. I reckon 'e 'ated Ray more'n I do and that's saying summat I can tell you. I reckon 'e wanted to get 'is own back for what Ray done to 'im and 'is mum and dad. You'll know about that I guess. Well, I…'elped 'im with… information…"

"Go on," prompted Evie.

"I suppose with them pictures you got, that'll put the mockers on everyfink." She paused. "You think I wanted Malc dead?" She shook her head and became watery-eyed. "I liked 'im as it goes. If I'd wanted anyone dead, it wasn't 'im. If I'd wanted anyone dead, it'd 'ave been Ray. And, believe me, I still do."

There was a knock on the interview room door. An officer thrust an iPad at Julian.

"Sir, sorry sir," the officer said glancing at Stephanie, "but you asked us to get these to you asap… the lab reports and the forensics just came through."

Julian thanked the officer and apologised to Stephanie while he and Evie read for a minute or two.

"So," said Evie, "that tells us something."

"Dead right it does," Julian said, looking at Stanley.

Stanley arrived home late, but Patricia was still up with Bethan slumped next to her on a settee fast asleep.

"Think she's had enough excitement for a while," Patricia whispered, nodding her head in the direction of her niece in pyjamas, fluffy dressing gown and fluffier slippers. "You OK?"

Stanley nodded wearily.

"Sure?"

"Yes."

"Want something to eat?"

"Not really, but thanks."

"So," said Patricia softly, "what news?"

Stanley sighed, wanting nothing more at that moment than to have a drink, a shower and a decent night's sleep. He didn't feel much like talking or, as a matter of fact, listening. He flopped into a chair.

"Martha was right," he said. "Richard Threadgill was killed by something called a botswarm."

"Sounds like a nappy rash. You mean the tiny robots?"

Stanley nodded and looked at his sleeping niece. He got up and poured himself a decent measure of bourbon. Before he stoppered the bottle, he turned to his sister to see if she wanted some. She didn't.

"A botswarm," he said collapsing again into a chair, "is a large cluster, could be hundreds, thousands, maybe millions, of tiny flying robots working together as a well-disciplined unit. A force to be reckoned with. An army. Pat, it beggars belief as to what these things could do. Martha was spot on and big thanks to whoever's up there that you spoke to her."

He smiled at his sister. Taking a sip of his drink he paused for a moment. Patricia had the sense to let him collect his thoughts. She could see how tired he was but there was also something else she couldn't quite fathom.

"Malcolm Carmichael invented the smallest winged drone ever. And I do mean small. And I do mean ever. Those are what were in Richard's mouth and nose… dozens of speck-sized flying robots… and apparently there are more in his lungs and stomach. And similarly on the top of the fifty-fifty drum."

"Poor, poor man!"

"According to the emergency autopsy report, the toxin that the tiny flying robots introduced to Richard's system – and what probably actually killed him so quickly – was botulinum. That's a powerful and pretty much instant poison – one nanogram per kilogram can kill a person." He paused to sip his drink again. "Did you know Evie Harris has an MSc in chemistry specialising in toxicology? No, neither did I… Anyway, a very small intravenous dose of botulinum is fatal… causes instant muscle paralysis by preventing the release of the signalling molecule. Apparently the same paralysing property is the basis of the botulinum toxin in cosmetic Botox."

"But how does anyone get hold of stuff like that?"

"Any pharma company would probably have it or a manufacturer of medical Botox. Most chemical users or manufacturers could get it."

"Berkley?"

Stanley knocked back the rest of his drink. "Maybe. According to MI5, it seems that when Malcolm was doing his PhD he had a strong link with Wageningen University and Georgia Tech Institute. Either place could have provided any raw materials that he might have needed over the radar or under it. Whatever the case, Dr Carmichael would have been able to source pretty much anything even, maybe, from the dark web."

"Was this botulinum poison necessary? Surely…"

"Maybe he'd flipped his lid or maybe he wanted to be sure that his enemy was well and truly dead. It could have been an experiment, a grotesque one. If Ray had been the target, killing him with a Berkley company invention and finishing the guy off with poison could've satisfied Dr Carmichael's need for retribution."

"But," said Patricia through a yawn, "if some of these… bots were on the drum, how come anyone else who touched the drum wasn't poisoned?"

"I asked the same thing. Inside each bot there's a microscopic syringe delivery device used for whatever purpose; in this case to inject the poison. But the poison could only be released or injected when the bots knew that the time was right. Or, when the original programme would have made them release it.

Whichever way you look at it, the bots would have only discharged their nasty payload when the target was reached. The swarm must have assumed that Richard was Ray. Once released, apparently any remaining poison would have evaporated or just become dormant."

"This is the stuff of movies… Stan, you said retribution was Carmichael's motive…"

"I think he was being blackmailed. Big time."

Stanley had played the blackmail story round and round his head and every time he thought about it he felt revulsion. More for his own sake – a kind of therapy perhaps – he wanted to say out loud what Ray Berkley had done. So, he talked to Patricia. About how an acquaintance of Ray's had wanted Malcolm's father to help the acquaintance's eighteen year old son avoid prison for appalling violence against a younger boy at the public school where Malcolm's father was a housemaster. He told her that the eighteen year old had been a seriously nasty piece of work with a history of violence. He told her that Malcolm's father had refused to falsify academic reports or provide a character reference for the eighteen year old. He told her that Ray had produced fake photographs of Malcolm's father having sex with two young pupils. And that the photos had been sent to each of the school governors. He told Patricia how the resultant firing, publicity and shame had ruined Malcolm's father's career despite the fact that he was an innocent man. Stanley said that the story had been front page news and that there had been a pending court case. He told her about Malcolm's father's suicide. He told her about how Malcolm had initially refused to work for Berkley and how Berkley had produced some disgusting photos featuring Malcolm that Ray had threatened to share with his current employer. And Malcolm's mother. Malcolm, Stanley said, had been given no choice but to join Berkley's company. He said that Dr Malcolm Carmichael must have been ever haunted by what had happened to his parents and that his own mental health must have been in serious doubt.

Whether Pat had known some or any of the blackmail case

information or not wasn't, for Stanley, the point. He had just wanted to tell the story and now felt a modicum of uplift at having told her in detail what had happened.

"It's impossible to understand the kind of hate that Malcolm must have felt towards Ray Berkley," he said.

Patricia said nothing for a moment or two. She looked at her brother and, had she not had her hands full with her niece, would have given him a hug.

"Tell me more about these bots."

"They're extraordinary. They can hover for hours, move in any direction, fast, slow, up, down – basically go anywhere and a decent distance too. They can be controlled as you would control a normal drone. However, and this is the very big deal, Carmichael's bots were controlled remotely only to a point and, after that point, they were able to work together as a pack – on their own… with their own intelligence, not just as individuals, but as a co-ordinated group."

"Intelligent as in sci-fi intelligent?"

"Intelligent as in AI intelligent. Intelligent as in properly communicating with each other, sharing and storing information, getting the best solutions to reach their target and then doing whatever they might have been programmed to do. After their initial programming, they wouldn't need any remote or third party control. At all. Not just intelligent but clever. In other words, they could think."

Patricia mouthed wow. There were no sounds in the apartment or from the outside world. Stanley stared at his empty glass.

"However," he said, "I think that Dr Carmichael was still working on the AI side of things. I don't think that the botswarm was perfect yet."

"Was he trying to kill Richard?"

"No. I don't think he was. Neither does Julian. I think at the fair Malcolm was in a confused state and he had a swarm with him. Perhaps not a full swarm. I don't know. Maybe he was finding it hard to control. He had it there for a reason. Practice? Maybe. As an instrument of death? Yes, probably. Malcolm was probably trying to kill Ray Berkley, but Ray wasn't onstage; Richard was. David Horsham found the courage to tell Berkley that Richard would give out the fifty-fifty award. That I think was Richard's death warrant. Once Malcolm thought that the swarm was good to go, he could have left it to get on with its job."

"Or," said Patricia, "he might have realised too late that it was Richard onstage and couldn't change the botswarm's instructions."

Her brother nodded. "Let's say Dr Carmichael discovered that his plan had gone south and met Ray for some kind of showdown. Perhaps Malcolm was going to tell his boss to stuff his job and do his worst. That would have been Ray's green light to get rid of Malcolm. But that doesn't explain the awful way Malcolm was killed. Ray couldn't have done that alone. I don't think."

For a minute or two Patricia just sat holding her niece's hand and pondered over what she'd been told and a bit of what she hadn't.

"He had a fling with Stephanie Berkley."

Patricia's eyes widened. "You're kidding! How on earth do you know that?"

"She told us."

"What? Just like that?"

"No, there were some photographs. Lucky really."

"Lucky?"

"There was something about their body language at the fair when she was with Malcolm. Hers particularly made me think that they'd been or were close. When we interviewed Ray Berkley, he was a bit drunk and definitely agitated. Just as he left the incident unit, he pulled his handkerchief out to mop his fevered brow. I saw a card drop as he walked past and I picked it up."

"Stan, you can't do that! Anyway what's that got to do with anything?"

Stanley got up to refill his glass. "The card was of a very expensive and exclusive London security firm that specialises in photographic evidence. I shared my thinking with Julian and, hey presto, the police got the pictures."

"Blimey… did you see them?"

"No and don't want to."

"But they were definitely of Mrs Berkley and Dr Carmichael?"

"Yes…" He paused and his sister saw the shadow over his eyes. "Photographs featured heavily in poor Dr Carmichael's life."

"Stan, you think that the terrorist in the shed was connected with either of the two deaths?"

"The police think not."

"And you?" asked Patricia.

"Not sure yet," said Stanley smiling wanly. "Worrying though," he said. "Close call. The guy who was shot was very lucky. They all were. Including," he said inclining his head towards his niece, "sleeping beauty there."

Bethan stirred.

"Bedtime you think?"

"Yep," replied Patricia. "You should get some kip too."

"I will. Julian's asked me to join them to see Berkley again in the morning. Can you manage here?"

"Sure. What's Julian's thinking in terms of what's going on over the road in the bookshop?"

"If he's addressing that, he's not mentioned it to me. Anything happening there then?"

Patricia brought him up to date with what little information she had. After helping her niece to bed, she went to her own room thinking carefully about what her brother had told her, realising quickly that such thinking wasn't good for the dead of night.

Nineteen

The following morning, it being a Monday, the post office and shop were busy as was always the case the day after the village fête. Sydney Baxter had come in to get a flat tin of small cheroots for which he had a fondness. He saw the purchase as a monthly treat, each little cigar a delight often smoked as he lay on his garden bench at night, staring at the stars.

Behind Sydney, an irritable Sir Jon Appleyard tapped a Scarosso-shod foot and looked alternately at the queue in front of him and his phone. Lady Appleyard was absorbed in a loud, lengthy phone call which featured shrieks of high decibel laughter from and to both parties of the conversation. The Appleyard pair stood in the post office queue which was moving at shuffle speed. Eventually, having purchased his cigars, Sydney stepped tentatively over to the post office counter. Other customers didn't mind this manoeuvre at all, but the famous director and his wife, who were directly behind Sydney now, did.

"A book o'stamps please, Sheil," Sydney requested, politely and quietly.

Sir Jon had been waiting for an opportunity to vent some spleen and saw now as the ideal moment to do so with enthusiasm.

"Excuse me!" he bellowed. "You've just pushed in, you cretin! There's a queue you know! We," Sir Jon declaimed loudly as if he'd just discovered religion, "are in a hurry."

His wife, neatly attired in white, skinny-leg, high-rise stretch-denim, Paige jeans and a white Veronica Beard shirt, finished her phone call with several anaemic air kisses after which the gash of a red mouth snapped shut. Seeing the forthcoming confrontation, her eyes gleamed.

Sheila Prewer scowled and leaned forward as far as the counter and her bosom would allow. "We're goin' as fast as we can, sir, madam," she said firmly to the Appleyard contingent.

"I'll serve Mr Baxter 'ere and then I'll be with you. 'e only wants a book of 'is usual stamps."

"Well, can this Mr… Maxer hurry it up? We," Lady Applewood said imperiously, "have things to do."

Sydney went very red in the face which was quite something given his already ruddy appearance. He turned to look around at the man behind him and also glanced at the sour-faced wife standing next to her husband.

"Yes?" enquired Sir Jon with a curled lip. "Help you at all can we or are you just staring for the hell of it? Perhaps you'd like an autograph?"

Sydney said nothing, but went redder still and turned back to pay for his book of stamps.

"Oi, numbskull!" shouted a spiteful Lady Appleyard. "My husband asked you a question!"

She tapped Sydney on the shoulder, a bit as a woodpecker might attack a tree and called out as if she were hailing someone on the far side of a wide river. "I'm talking to you," she declared. "Are you deaf as well as stupid? Sir Jon asked you a question."

All chatter on the premises ceased as if on cue. Sydney flinched but said nothing, waiting for his change, his held out hand shaking. Fed up with irritably tapping the small man on the shoulder, Lady Appleyard committed a heinous crime. Leaning forwards, she firmly flicked Sydney's ancient flat cap so that it fell to the floor.

If anyone had still been talking – even quietly – now there was absolute silence. Not a word or a footstep, not a clanking of one can of beans against another or the rustle of a bag. All who knew Sydney stood stock still with mouths agape. Sydney never ever took his cap off. As far as villagers were aware, he slept in it and rumour had it that he even had his bath wearing it.

"Pick up 'is 'at," said a young but steely voice.

Sir Jon turned to see Tony Helliwell, all five feet and not

much else of him, standing as close as anyone could possibly get to another person without touching. Next to Tony was a taller Stevie Devonport, similarly close to Lady Applewood.

"I said… pick 'is 'at up."

"Or what?" demanded the famous theatre director. "Get out of my way this minute you prick!"

"When you've picked 'is 'at up and given it back to 'im, you're to apologise."

"I shall do no such thing. Where's the postman Accrington?"

"I'll count to three," said Tony.

"Do you think you can manage that though?" asked Lady Applewood.

The two boys stepped back as did the queues. Isolated now, the famous theatre director and partner in crime sneered malevolently. "Thought not," said Sir Jon.

"Three," said Tony.

Recollections afterwards varied as of course they always do, but all agreed that to begin with neither Sir Jon nor his wife noticed the two extra large plastic bottles of ketchup. What they did see though were simultaneous jets of bright red purée arcing towards their heads. Lady Applewood shrieked and did a kind of agonised pirouette while flapping her arms up and down. Within seconds, her hair, face, neck and white clothes were covered in tomato so for a short while she looked like a Jackson Pollock painting. Sir Jon stepped back into Sydney who, laughing silently with small gasps for air, pushed the famous theatre director back for more ketchup. The bottles of sauce empty, the two boys placed them on the counter.

"Mrs," said Tony to Sheila in a voice that he had copied from an Amazon Prime series, "these people are leaving now, but first they'll be payin' for the two bottles of sauce and ten packs of kitchen towel. Oh yeah and eight of wet wipes."

"I shall do no bloody thing, you… you… little sod! I'll sue," spluttered the famous theatre director. "You'll go to jail for this. We've got witnesses!"

"I don't reckon you do 'ave any witnesses though," said Stevie gesturing at the laughing audience. "Although I do reckon there'll be some fun online later on. And if you don't pay up we can allus 'ave a go next with the brown sauce, mayo or mustard if you both want."

The new weapons were waved as menacingly as anyone can when flourishing large bottles of brown sauce, mayonnaise or mustard. Sir Jon was aware that something like twelve or even more pairs of eyes were looking at him and half that number had phones out taking video. He took out his wallet from his back pocket, withdrew two twenty pound notes and, despite the fact that they had small dollops of tomato ketchup on them, slapped the notes on one of the counters. He glanced at a frowning Tony Helliwell who wagged a finger at him and shook his head. The hapless director snarled, placing another two twenty pound notes on top of the first. He and the now hysterical Lady Appleyard turned, rushed, slipped and finally slid out into the sunshine. Instantly, everyone in the shop applauded.

"Well done Tone and you too Stevie," laughed Sheila Prewer. "Clean it all up now will you boys?"

"We will… What about the change from the cash Mrs?"

A voice came from the back of the shop. "It's yours Tony. Forty each. We'll pretend that didn't happen," said Stanley.

Stevie stood looking abashed. "Mr A, we… just… Mr Baxter there… he's a decent bloke like and… they…"

"I know Stevie and it's fine. You did a good, but messy thing. Remember though that ketchup in the face isn't always a good idea and I really don't want to be sued thank you."

But, as Stanley turned away, anyone watching would have seen that he was grinning. He walked over to pick up Sydney's cap which somehow seemed to have escaped any ketchup and gave it to the old man who took it gratefully and stuck it firmly on his head.

"Is it on straight, Mr Accringter?" asked Sydney anxiously as he looked up.

"Dead straight, Syd," smiled Stanley.

Ray Berkley seemed delighted to see his guests.

"Inspector. Constable… And Postman Pat too. Quelle surprise! Good morning, good morning! How good to see you all again and so soon!"

"The pleasure's all ours sir. As arranged, a word?"

"Of course, of course. Mi casa es tu casa."

"I'm glad of that sir because I have a team searching Darkwater Hall as we speak."

Ray Berkley's smile fell off his face. "What?"

"Your housekeeper has kindly let in my officers. With a warrant of course. Anything we might find there do you think?"

"Come through to the boardroom," Ray said. To his PA he snapped, "Ted, organise tea or coffee for these people."

"Nothing for us Mr Berkley," said Julian.

"As you wish. Then, coffee for me, Ted."

When Berkley's PA had left the room and they were seated, Julian began politely.

"I should like to record this meeting if you're comfortable with that, sir?"

"This again? Sure. Fine."

"Sure, fine what, sir?"

"I, Raymond Berkley, am delighted to be recorded during this meeting and yes I am beside myself with joy that Mr Accrington is in attendance."

"Thank you," replied Julian adding date and time.

Ray looked pointedly at the soundless, nuclear clock on the wall. "Might we press on?"

"We now know, Mr Berkley," Julian began conversationally, "that immediately after Richard Threadgill announced the winner of the fifty-fifty prize, there was a massive nanorobotic invasion of his airways, lungs and stomach. The invasion stemmed from the rotating ticket drum aperture and thereon directly into his mouth, ears and nose. Many of the nanorobots were able to administer a poison – botulinum. We're advised that the invasion would have caused severe internal damage and most definitely death without the poison."

Ray stared at Julian and was about to say something but seemed to be finding speech difficult.

"You want to add something Mr Berkley?"

"No."

"There was," continued Julian, "evidence of the bots not only on the vicar's mouth, on the inside of his cheeks, his inner ears and in his nasal cavities. On the lip of the drum's aperture there were more bots stuck to whatever residue was there – perhaps sweat, spilled liquid, anything moist. It wouldn't take much to cause a tiny robot the size and weight of a seed to stick. Imagine such a way of dying Mr Berkley… You seem to want to comment again."

"No. I don't."

"Dr Carmichael was an extraordinary man. He was working on minute robotic swarms. It's why you blackmailed him to make him work for you. The botswarm he invented was branded as Pixie. You had a number of forward sales of Pixies even though testing was incomplete and hence that's partly why you wanted Dr Carmichael to stay. But he wasn't going anywhere because you had him over a barrel, didn't you? A very big, nasty barrel.

Anything to add yet?"

Ray's big tongue licked his lips. "No. I hope the police have good lawyers these days. Slander carries a hefty penalty."

"As does murder of course. And blackmail. Now, we know that someone managed to get a Pixie botswarm from this secure building to the fair and into the fifty-fifty drum, there to lie in wait. A lethal mugging if you will. We know that the perpetrator of this particular ambush could only have been Dr Carmichael." He paused. "Or you."

Ray, trying to look unconcerned, folded his arms and tucked his hands under his armpits. He glanced at Stanley. "I see that you've brought your pet poodle again."

"I'm obviously not making myself clear for which I apologise," said Julian ignoring the comment. "The definitive origin of the bots is from this facility. You may shake your head sir but it can be proven. Unequivocal proof as some of your staff will testify. What else? Oh yes. I'm advised – and therefore I must advise you – that your enterprise can be shut down with no notice whatsoever if it's even suspected that you or your company are endangering the public. Several agencies are now involved in investigating you and your business as are the security services. You've become a bit of a risk."

"I see," said Ray, unsettled but trying hard not to show it. "Well," he said standing, "thank you for bringing me up to date with your findings and I congratulate you and of course your colleagues, even," he pointed at Stanley, "that one. Now, if that's all, may I wish you good morning? I shall of course immediately be in touch with my lawyers and you can be sure that any damage done to my home will be met with the full force of the courts."

Julian didn't move. "By the way, we've had some interesting conversations with a Mrs Barbara Monteith. She's a JP you know. But of course you know. But what you didn't know is that now she's in custody. As is your rotten gang of WI ladies. Your little earner on the side was very clever. Quite a big earner actually as it turns out. Bringing in and sending out class A drugs by industrial drones to and from all over the UK. Clever. Cocaine and cash by drone. Surprised that Amazon hasn't got in on the act. But of course they can't can they sir because what you've done is illegal? All under the cover of a kite business. Fancy the WI being involved in flying drugs around. Who'd have thought it? Not going to look good when the WI ladies and you get tucked up for a few years. Or, in your case, many. Anything yet you'd like to say?"

"No."

"Perhaps understandable in the circs. You'll need your brief. Clever stuff Mr Berkley – I will say that. Of course none of the drugs or the drones could go to or from this building here, but they could go from Darkwater Hall, couldn't they? The pretext of making kites under the aegis of your charity in favour of helping local children with learning difficulties was clever too. What I find particularly disgusting is the fact that none of the money from kite sales went anywhere except into Mrs Monteith's pockets and those of her team of workers. Plus the fat fees that you gave the ladies for their drug work and silence. And of course you and she made sure that each so-called kite lady was under literal pain of a nasty death to keep quiet. Well, we have a big file of statements admitting guilt each with a very interesting set of stats and facts. Smart ladies. You OK Mr Berkley?"

"Yes, I'm fine."

"By the way, said Julian. "The four members of Dr Carmichael's team and indeed a number of your other senior staff are, as you may know, not at work today. They're having in-depth conversations with specialists. Way over my pay grade of course."

Ray remained standing. "I should think that most people are. If you're threatening me chief inspector, it won't wash I'm afraid. I know nothing about drugs via drones and the kite-making is simply my way of helping poor unfortunates. Also, this company has very good connections with government departments and believe you me I shall be speaking to my contacts there."

"We'll get to that," Evie said. "Please do sit down sir," but

Ray remained standing.

"We now know about Dr Carmichael's work in some detail," said Julian. "Not all I grant you, but most. Oh, and one of his team is of the firm belief that your top scientist was working on something else without your knowledge. Something at home. Something even better than…"

"Total crap! Now, I really have had enough… I'll be speaking with all my senior employees and reminding them about their non-disclosure agreements. I shall also discuss matters concerning your collective behaviour with the local council, the chief constable and the media."

Stanley tried to hide a smile.

"You think that's funny do you, you interfering shit?" barked Ray. "Why don't you bugger off and run your sweet shop?"

"Mr Berkley, we believe," said Evie pleasantly, "that now might be a good time to remind you that the Official Secrets Act is very clear. The security of the country comes a bit higher than your employees' NDA small print. It's the government's big print that you'll want to consider. And, by the way, according to the text I've just received, we have all of your employees' NDAs as of two minutes ago although the text declares that there's still no sign of Dr Carmichael's NDA or indeed his contract. In fact, no file at all. Funny that."

There was silence.

"So, we're done?' asked Ray lazily.

"Lying comes easy to you doesn't it?" Julian commented casually. "You truly don't know what we know. For instance, full access, stress full access, to the three Pixie swarms you have, or had, was limited to two people. One's dead. We also have reason to believe that you had a motive to get rid of Dr Malcolm Carmichael. Several in fact."

Ray's cheeks and neck were rash red. A film of loathing crossed his face. "You have no proof of anything!"

"Do you know, Mr Berkley," asked Julian, "how our colleagues will react if they believe for a second that you're involved in making and possibly using something rogue that could threaten the safety of this country and its citizens? And that's apart from the problems you're facing regarding your cocaine dealing. Or your various adventures into blackmail. Mr Carmichael, Malcolm's father, killed himself because of you. And his mother's death was hastened because of you. Maybe Dr Carmichael died because of you. Then there's the crooked kite business. Added to which are attempted bribes to local councillors and others. The charge sheet has spaces left."

"No comment. Now get out."

"Have you," asked Evie as if she was asking about the weather, "been having a recent relationship with someone from the village?"

Ray looked as if he'd been thumped. "No, of course not!"

"The police believe that you're being blackmailed, Ray," said Stanley gently.

"Shut your stupid, fucking face!"

"Mr Berkley," said Evie. "Someone knows what you're up to in your personal life, manages somehow to get some photos taken and threatens you. It's called blackmail. As of course you'll be more than aware from your own experience at initiating that particular crime."

Ray licked his lips and pressed a section of the table. Immediately there was a telephonic connection. "Where's my coffee? If it's not here in one minute, you're fired!"

"We know sir," continued Evie, "that you arranged to have photographs taken of your wife and Dr Malcolm Carmichael in compromising situations. You wanted them as leverage against your wife. But you didn't use them. Maybe you were saving that up for a final showdown? Anyway, Mrs Berkley knows about the snaps. And she's seen them."

"How…?"

"What you may not have known," continued Evie, "is that the very same specialist company that you used had been commissioned by someone else to take pictures of you and… another party. A local other party. Amazing coincidence! But life's like that sometimes. Want to see them?"

"I don't believe you!"

Evie opened her briefcase and took out a large, hard-backed, buff-coloured envelope which she pushed across the table. Ray sat down heavily, picked up the envelope, opened it and drew out the ten large, colour photographs. After a quick glance at each picture, he put them back in the envelope and looked up. Stanley noticed a tic in Ray's right eyelid.

Shakily, Ray said, "Right." He exhaled a big breath. "Caught in sharp focus. I can guess who's responsible for this."

"Tell them who's blackmailing you," said Stanley. "They know the answer."

There was no response.

"Ray, the police could bring both parties here now," said Stanley.

Ray stared at Stanley and for the first time there was no hate, no disrespect, no arrogance, just fear and, thought Stanley, somewhere there was a plea for help. Ray floundered a little like a schoolboy who had run out of excuses.

"No… please…" he begged of Julian. "Don't do that. There's no need."

"What's David Horsham demanding of you?" asked Stanley.

It was clear that a myriad of possible answers were running through Ray Berkley's head. The arrogance returned.

"If I go ahead with the hotel plans, he'll release the pictures. If I don't pay him a very large sum of money, he'll release the pictures. Hoist by my own petard." He laughed mirthlessly.

"*Richard III.*"

"No," said Stanley. "*Hamlet.* Act 3, scene 4. And I'd say you're just as hoist as Hamlet was having just killed Polonius. That didn't end well for the Prince of Denmark either… David Horsham also wants money for another reason, doesn't he?"

"I don't know what you're talking about."

"Mr Berkley," offered Julian, "would this have anything to do with the fact that the captain knows about your cocaine business? You know he knows and that's another noose round your neck. A bit more leverage for him. You see, old Mr Baxter lives near the fence dividing what is your property now and the captain's. Mr Baxter has time on his hands and he sees things. He knows the estate like the back of his hands and your ladies were a bit sloppy. He hears things and they talk to him. They think he's a harmless old duffer but he isn't. The captain used to be in the SAS and has good contacts still. Didn't take much for Baxter to talk to Horsham and for Horsham to cook your goose. He wanted a lot of money for that as well. But, you see, something else came out of the captain's discoveries. It wasn't only cocaine that you were pushing around the country, was it?"

"What do you mean?"

"You forced Dr Carmichael against his will to design weapons that could be easily copied with basic materials. He did that and you arranged for a sample set to be made. They couldn't be made here of course, but they could be made secretly in Holland. The package was sent over from Rotterdam with a much larger consignment of arms and ammunition. All sorts of cock-ups, but you'll like this one sir. Unfortunately for you, the package was left outside Mr Accrington's premises and handed to us. It should have been given to a contact in London and then to a Mr Big. But it wasn't delivered to London. It was here. Pig of a thing to track down but we did with some help from insider info and our Interpol friends."

"I don't believe you!"

"I don't much care whether you do or don't. You see, Captain Horsham was good mates with your Dr Carmichael. They met for walks, mostly at dawn because neither slept well. Both shared a common hatred against somebody. Who was that d'you suppose? The captain made some discrete enquiries and it didn't take that long to discover that you had a link with the Hellbanianz. They were helping you with your nice little earner weren't they? As I say, someone on the inside was given a tickle and is now leaking information like there's no tomorrow. Under police protection of course. Turns out that he was the brother of one of the blokes recently found in the Thames wrapped up in black, rubber matting. Both shot twice. Double tap. You alright? You seem a little warm."

The room was quiet.

"What does my wife know?"

"Most of everything. She's declared under oath and in no uncertain terms considerable detail about the work you've done although the technicals are sketchy. Be that as it may, it's enough and she talks specifically about the people you've met on a regular basis and some of those to whom she believes you sell your work. Much of this is of course hearsay, but names and roles are very clearly mentioned. The names are prominent. And each will be followed up, Mr Berkley. The nationals, the main TV stations and social media… will gobble this up. Juicy and tasty stuff. If it's allowed to reach the gobblers."

"The bitch. I'll…"

"Kill her?" asked Stanley.

Ray, looking at Stanley with revulsion, stood up and began to move forward, fists clenched.

"I wouldn't if I were you Mr Berkley," cautioned Julian. "I'd say that Mr Accrington here would be within his rights to protect himself and I'd also say that would worry me if I were in your shoes. He's… he's not as soft as you think he is, not by a long chalk. Anyway the video cameras that you undoubtedly have in this room will show a court what occurred here this morning. I'd say you had enough on your plate without bodily harm added to the charge sheet… Talking of which, do you think that it would be fair to say that you killed Malcolm Carmichael because he tried to kill you?"

Ray stared.

"Let's say," Julian went on in a business-like way, "that the botswarm at the fair was meant for you, but the vicar became the unwitting victim instead. You discovered or probably guessed what Dr Carmichael had done and that made you very angry. So you met him near the toilets. Odd place to meet, but needs must in trying circumstances. He probably thought he was in for a bollocking or maybe he assumed it was to be a conciliatory chat. You know, an opportunity to be pals again. Or maybe he'd had it with you and was going to clear off and take whatever consequences a nasty person like you would throw his way. I reckon you managed to shuffle him into one of the toilets and, hey presto, you heaved his head into a toilet bowl and held it there. You're a strong chap. Add a bit of strangulation and then a kite shoved hard into the back of his neck. Job done. One of your problems solved."

Ray stared at Julian. "Is that how he died?"

There was no reply.

"I didn't kill Malcolm Carmichael. Is that how he died?"

"In agony Ray," said Stanley.

"You're in a pickle sir," offered Evie. "Now might be a good time to get your lawyer."

"I think you're bluffing."

Julian walked to the door, Evie and Stanley following.

"Of course you do," said Julian smiling. "We'll be off now. Oh, yes, by the by, you should know that in your reception you'll find a team waiting to search these premises."

Ray Berkley was now on the verge of panic.

"If you or your goons want to look over this facility, you'll need a search warrant."

"A warrant like this, sir?" asked Evie taking out and waving a document. Ray stepped forward tucking the envelope containing the photographs under an arm. He snatched the search warrant from Evie and scanned the contents. He made to tear the sheet in half, but Evie put up a hand.

"Wouldn't if I were you sir. You could end up in even bigger trouble for destroying an official police document handed to you in good faith. Remember the cameras. We're going to ask our government agency and specialist colleagues outside to effect the search immediately and accompanying them will be members from our force. Any obstruction will…"

"No! I demand to hear this from a higher authority than yours!"

"Not an issue, sir. Bear with me please."

Evie handed her briefcase to Stanley, stepped up to Ray relieving him of both the envelope and the warrant and tapped a number on her mobile. She had a very brief conversation with the person at the other end and waited for a moment.

"Thank you ma'am," she said to whoever was now on the phone. "I have Mr Berkley for you now." She handed her phone to Ray who, ashen, took it with a slightly shaking hand and listened.

At that moment the smiling Ted came in with Ray's coffee, a large pristine banana, a crystal dish of pale blue, sugared almonds and a white, linen napkin all set out neatly on a silver tray. Ray dropped the phone on the table, rushed towards the door, pushing an astonished Ted out of the way causing the banana to fall, the coffee to spill and the almonds to fly all over the place like candied bullets. In his panic, Ray slipped on the banana and Stanley put an arm out to stop the man from falling.

"Steady now," said Stanley.

Ray shook himself free. "You're all dead meat," he roared as he reached the door. "Dead meat!"

Twenty

Sydney Baxter was sitting on a sunny wall near the post office smoking a small cigar and chuckling happily to himself as he relived the sight of tomato-drenched Sir Jon and Lady Appleyard. That had made his day he thought. He looked forward to telling Rosie all about it. He just knew that it would make her day too and maybe her week as well.

On her way back from visiting the pastry chef at The King's Head where she'd placed an order for the shop, she stopped. "Hello Syd. Enjoying the sunshine?"

"I am that missus," grinned Sydney. He proceeded to tell Patricia all about the delicious tomato incident and left no detail out, such was his delight. Patricia wasn't sure of the truth of the tale, but smiled at the exuberance of the storyteller.

"My boy," said Sydney eventually, smile slipping, "woulda smiled an' all."

"No news about Paul then?"

Sydney's smile and good humour disappeared like music being turned off. "No missus," he said, looking down, "Nothin'."

"Syd, I'm so sorry. I was stupid to ask, but I'm sure that he'll be fine and, before you know it, he'll be back. You'll see. He's probably working abroad on a project and has to keep moving about."

As she spoke, she realised how utterly pathetic the words must have sounded and could only guess at how it would have been had she been the recipient of similar, empty words. Sydney said nothing but moved to go on his way with a dismissive shrug, then turned back as if something had just occurred to him.

"This murder…"

"What Syd?"

"The murder. I saw…" He stopped, struggling with

something. "I saw that tall feller, the one who worked at Berkleys, the one what died. Saw 'im standin' near the toilets."

"Well that's not so strange."

"The toilets 'ad just been emptied an' I thought it were odd that someone would stand there knowin' that they couldn't be used. They was all locked up you see, ready for collection."

"Perhaps he was just waiting for someone."

Syd shook his head. "The tall man was talkin' to someone but I couldn't see the other person. Then somebody asked me summat and when I looked back I saw 'em both goin' into one of the toilets. Don't know 'ow cos I thought they be all locked."

Patricia wasn't sure what to say. Other people's peccadilloes were their own but in this case the result had been death.

"Seemed to be talking to the someone as 'e went in. Then 'e waved over his shoulder an' I thought 'e was wavin' at me an' so I waves back, but I don't think it were me 'e was wavin' at."

"Did you see anything else?"

"No missus. When the police talked to me I should 'ave said summat about seeing 'im there. But I thought I'd get into trouble and I got enough on me plate."

All this came out in something of a rush. Patricia touched the old man's sleeve. "Would you like a cup of tea Syd?"

A sea breeze flew up the Little Peasen street and clouds scudded at a pace as if on a mission out over the water. The old man looked down at his shoes and didn't answer, big tears dropping at his feet. He collected himself with deep breaths and an anguished effort.

"Syd…"

"I'm… sorry missus… but I miss me boy and 'e's all us 'as got… I done a stupid thing an' all…" He could say no more and Patricia knew, as is often the case when guilt competes with anguish, that the telling of a truth that's been waiting to get out is very painful even if a relief.

"A stupid thing? What do you mean?"

Sydney shook his lowered head and said nothing, but Patricia could see his shoulders heaving.

"I miss my Paul. I miss 'im… I jus'…"

"Let's go and have that cup of tea Syd."

There was no reply, just agonised sobs from someone who rarely showed any emotion. A couple with two children passed by on their way to the shop and each stared curiously at the weeping man. Patricia ignored them and guided Sydney up to the flat where she sat him at the kitchen table and said nothing for a while. Sydney took out an enormous blue and white bandana and blew his nose more than thoroughly.

"I bain't been up 'ere afore," he said, sniffing, wiping his eyes with the back of his hand and looking a little more cheerful. He examined the contents of his handkerchief and then the kitchen with interest.

"Big ol' place you an' your brother got 'ere… Your niece, she's a nice gel ain't she? Allus sez 'ello when she sees me and Rosie."

Patricia brought over a tray on which there were two mugs, a pot of strong tea, a small jug of milk, a sugar bowl and a plate of homemade, currant buns. Sydney eyed the buns appreciatively and took two when they were offered along with three heaped spoonfuls of sugar for his tea.

"No news at all about Paul then, Syd? Nothing?"

"No. The police cooden find out anythin'. Them Foreign Office blokes don't say much. The MP what your brother asked ain't done nothin' yet far as we knows. Mr Berkley 'e offered to pay for a private 'vestigator o' some sort, but 'e said if 'e did that, we'd 'ave to sign summat to say that we 'ad no claim on our cottage when 'e bought the captain's lodge. Miss Accringter miss, the captain's father gave us that place and our bit of garden. The captain says it's our'n until we both dies. It ain't our'n to give away. Besides, the captain ain't sold the lodge and 'e don't want to. And, any'ow, where would we go?"

"Mr Berkley had no right to say any of that to you!"

Sydney's eyes became watery again. Patricia put an arm around his shoulders for a moment as the old man finished his tea with a wobbly hand and hoped for more which he duly received. As he added sugar, he seemed to recover his spirits a bit.

"Next time I come over this way," he said, "I'll bring you a big bunch of them freesias you likes," he said. "Your ma liked 'em an' all."

"That's kind Syd, but no need."

"Dretful this murder… and the vicar… 'e was a decent bloke," Sydney said after a pause.

"The police talked to you nicely?"

"They did… an' that chief inspector one, 'e was kind. Sort of knew I wus telling the truth – an' I was too missus! But…" Sydney paused and again his eyes became watery. "I didn't tell 'im everything and I did a bad thing and 'aven't said nowt."

"About the two men in the toilet? Well, we must tell him about that Syd."

"I did a bad thing."

"What bad thing was that?"

Sydney said nothing and just stared at his tea as he stirred it. He seemed to come to a decision.

"It was me what shouted at that cow Bishop, 'er being a Nazi an' all."

For a moment Patricia froze. She might have cried out, but later couldn't recall. She wondered if she'd heard right, but she also knew simultaneously that she had.

"But Syd…" she said hesitantly. "Syd, why? Why would you

do a terrible thing like that? You're a good man."

Sydney stared into his mug as if seeking a suitable response from the depths of his tea. Eventually he lifted his head and there was venom on his face.

"My uncle was tortured by them Nazis. Much older'n me 'e were. Stan were 'is name. Stan. I loved that uncle o' mine. 'e was my 'ero. I was only a tiny nipper when 'is call-up came in 1944 an' 'e joined up faster than you could say knife. Parachuted into Poland 'e was. Well, 'e didn't come back. There was a telegram and then after the war it came out that Stan'd been tortured as a spy and shot. I didn't know that then o'course and my ma kept saying that Stan would be 'ome soon. Years later I found out the truth. Stan was dead and I couldn't get that straight in me 'ead. All Germans are scum and that one… that Bishop woman, she lives 'ere as if butter wouldn't melt in 'er mouth. I was right glad when 'er 'usband died, the bastard. Bee stings weren't it? Good job. I 'ated them two and allus wished 'em dead."

"Wished then both dead? Mr and Mrs Bishop?"

"S'right," Sydney said as if to justify his cause. He began to stand up and had to hold on to the back of the kitchen chair as he stood.

"Syd," said Patricia finding speech hard. "Sit down. Please. Let me tell you something about Mr and Mrs Bishop."

"I don't need to know no more 'bout them and their sort! They can burn in 'ell!"

"Please, Syd."

The old man sat down heavily, staring at the plate on which had sat the buns. With a stubby finger, he played with three recalcitrant currants.

"Bishop isn't the name Janine was born with. Janine wasn't her name either. Syd, she's Jewish. You know what happened to millions of Jewish people in the war?" There was no reaction from the old man. "Syd, she was German yes, but Jewish too. She became British many years ago and changed her name when she was very young. She changed her name because not many people here liked Germans then. Or Jews." Patricia swallowed. "She's not a Nazi Syd and neither was her husband. They were German Jews, that's all."

Sydney looked up and stared at Patricia uncomprehendingly. "What yer mean?"

"Syd, her name was Wilma Katten and she was born in Heidelberg. It's a city in Germany. She lost her grandparents, parents, her brothers, sister, aunts, uncles, cousins – her whole family – every single one – all sent to Dachau concentration camp where the whole family was killed. Gassed. Like… many others. She had nobody left. Nobody. And she was two years old."

Sydney continued to stare at Patricia who held one of his hands. Abruptly, as if it didn't deserve to be held, he snatched it away.

"She was one of the lucky ones Syd. She'd been visiting some Catholic friends of her parents with her nanny when the rest of her family were taken. The family friends hid her, looked after her and sent her to England on something called Kindertransport. It's a German word and means transport for children."

Patricia took back one of Sydney's ice cold hands. He didn't object.

"Syd," she said, "Janine was adopted by a family in London. Not a Jewish family, but they respected her religion and so she kept up with her German and Jewish roots at a synagogue in Belsize Park; that's an area in North London. You know what a synagogue is – like a church. When she was fourteen, she met a Kindertransport boy of the same age at the synagogue and they kept in touch. He was called Tobias or Toby if you like. When they were both nineteen, they married, but they never had children. They moved to Little Peasen when Toby retired."

Patricia paused and wasn't sure how to proceed. "Syd," she said eventually, "you did a terrible thing. Janine's a good woman.

She was desperately hurt by what you said. And terrified. Imagine how you or Rosie would have felt! She didn't deserve that… and in front of all those people!"

Sydney just continued to stare at Patricia.

"Let me show you something," said Patricia, leaving the kitchen and returning a few moments later with a large book.

For the next ten minutes, Sydney gazed in silence at photographs of Kristallnacht, Dachau, Gurs and Auschwitz. When he looked up he was shaking his head and his eyes were wet again. He could hardly speak and, when he did, his voice was clotted.

"That's what 'appened to the Bishop woman's family? All of 'em?"

Patricia nodded.

"I never knew. I never, ever knew," he sobbed.

"That's what many people said then, Syd. And still do now."

"I… I bin dead stupid, ain't I?" asked Syd but received no answer.

"You've arrested Berkley?"

"Not yet. He's not going anywhere."

"Helicopter? Plane from Norwich? Boat?"

"Stan, he's not going anywhere. He wants to cut a deal. Unless he gets face surgery in the next day or so he won't get as far as Cromer. He's holed up in his office and there are officers and MI5 people on the premises. We don't know who the munitions main man is yet but Berkley knows. The ex-inside guy who's been talking doesn't know, so we need to get Berkley to talk. He will. I want the main man."

"He'll walk free?"

"Not a chance but he might get a lesser sentence."

"OK. What about Barbara Monteith and ladies?"

"Still in custody for the moment. All singing loud and clear. They'll get some prison, particularly Monteith."

"And the gun shipment you think is here?"

"Can't say. Sorry."

Stanley nodded and changed the subject. "You noticed Ray Berkley's right hand?"

"His right hand? Why?"

"You didn't notice the index finger on his right hand?"

"Stan!"

"It was red raw. The finger. All the way round. As if it'd been scraped. Exactly like Malcolm Carmichael's fingers."

"And?"

"And this," said Stanley as he put something wrapped in a handkerchief on the table. What he saw in the handkerchief looked to Julian like an elongated open-ended thimble.

"It's based on something originally designed by Nokia years ago," said Stanley. "A flexible rubber and silicone cell phone concept that goes on a user's index finger. The device fits the finger like a ring. When you get a text or phone call, the ring vibrates and you can simply hold your finger up to your ear to talk and listen. Daft these days and old technology that wasn't that great then. However, this protype isn't for a phone and it's not made by Nokia. It's to control something. I think your people will find that it operates like a conductor's baton. But this thing was a work in progress – not smoothed out properly on the inside. Look."

"And you believe this controlled the swarm?"

"Yes but only as a training mechanism. I think the swarm had to be taught. The bots had to learn, like children if you like."

"You got this thing how?"

"When Berkley did his pieces in the boardroom and knocked banana, coffee, sugared almonds and his PA all over the place, I steadied him because he lost his footing. I can pick an occasional pocket."

Evie hid a smile. Julian groaned.

Stanley shrugged.

"Will he know you've got it?" asked Julian.

"Possibly, but he'll be more worried that it's gone. He would have insisted that only a few controllers were made. Both Malcolm and Ray wouldn't have wanted too many of these things around. And I reckon he'll have other things on his mind right now."

Stanley thought of something. "How's Janine Bishop doing?"

Evie smiled. "Sitting up and taking notice apparently. She was suffering from exhaustion and shock more than anything else and her blood pressure was low. Bethan did a good job by the way looking after her and what she did with the scissors was very quick thinking."

"Can Janine have visitors? I think Beth'd like to visit."

"Don't see why not. They'll keep her in I think for a couple of days. The floor sister said that she's had a visitor already. Sydney Baxter. Stayed a long time apparently."

"I should think," said Stanley, "that Syd will have taken her some freesias. And," he added, "I'd guess a beaten up, wooden sugar beet race plate and a silver bracelet with two people's initials inscribed and entwined on the inside."

"What do you mean?"

Stanley shook his head. "Nothing. Sorry."

"Stan," said Julian hesitantly, "Maybe you've done enough now? Paid at the door and all that. Let us take up the slack and do the rest."

Stanley nodded, stood and smiled. "I'll see you in a bit."

As he came out of the incident unit, he started walking towards a trellis on which a fragrant rosa rugosa Rosierie de l'Hay was stretching out in the sun. Captain Horsham stood alone. Stanley leaned over the roses to breathe in the bouquet, angrily dead-heading a couple of finished flowers with his fingers.

"Accrington."

"David."

Stanley eyed the old soldier carefully, wondering what might be the best way to tackle him or even if he should.

"How're the investigations going?" asked David airily.

"Not my place to say. There seem to be a lot of machinations, dark corners, nooks and crannies."

"The police nearing any conclusions?"

"You'd have to ask them."

"You're assisting though. I imagine…"

"David, I can't comment on detail. I do know that they're more than grateful for your help so far on several fronts and the SAS connection's been crucial."

"Glad I could help. Makes my view of Berkley easier to sell."

"I agree. Good that Berkley's drug business as well as the gun-making are closed down – both very big and bad ops."

"What's on your mind? There's something else isn't there?"

"David, you'd be amazed at the facts that the police dig up in the process of putting the jigsaw pieces of a case together. Old secrets, things that one might have thought buried and long forgotten. Perhaps seemingly irrelevant but embarrassing misdemeanours which become relevant. You name it, they'll find out about it."

"Accrington, the police trust you. Surely…"

"I'm not party to everything. There are lots of avenues down which I can't or don't go."

"You implying something?"

"Not at all. You know what they're like though, David. Questions and more questions – until they get what they want."

"What they want?"

"In cases involving deaths, people of interest are questioned, backgrounds checked, facts revealed, untruths exposed, enigmas explained. It's extraordinary the things they're capable of finding out about these days, things that seemingly have nothing to do with the… business in hand."

"The business in hand?"

"Take the situation between Richard and you for instance," Stanley carried on conversationally. "Whenever I've acted as the fête's MC, I see things. Can't be avoided. I don't aim to be nosy, but I do notice what goes on. For example, when you were talking to Richard, just before you hurried over to the admin marquee, you seemed distressed. As did he. Awkward and uncomfortable. An argument of some sort."

"Now look here, Accrington…"

"Oh, I know it was and is absolutely none of my business and it's probably nothing," Stanley said cutting off the bluster.

"That's right. It's none of your business. And it was nothing."

"You both had a lot to do. And it was hot. But it's interesting you'd agree that perhaps we all have things that we'd each of us like to keep below the radar. I do."

"You do?" asked the captain hopefully.

"Everyone does David. Look, the stage at the fair is like a lookout post. You understand that. You must have defended hills in your time."

"Hills?"

"If I noticed something at the fête, then you can bet your bottom dollar that someone else did too. And human nature being what it is – and Chief Inspector Poole being a good officer

– well, he's bound to hear about it in the end as well. Sooner or later, he'll discover that you and Richard might have been at odds with one another about something. David, I know how these things can escalate. People start looking at those at whom fingers are pointed with suspicion, anger… or fear. It's the way of the world. 'Suspicion always haunts the guilty mind.' You follow?"

"Shakespeare?"

"Yes."

"You're fond of the bard aren't you Accrington?"

Stanley looked away and was angry with himself for doing so. "Sure," he said.

"Where does that quote come from?"

"*Henry VI*." He paused. "Part three, Act five, scene 6."

"Shakespeare has a bon mot for most occasions doesn't he?"

"Possibly. That quote is followed by 'the thief doth fear each bush an officer.'"

"You see me as a thief?"

"I see you with some guilt. And fear."

"He says a fair amount about the quality of mercy too, doesn't he? Guilt and fear run hand in hand of course. Like the persecution of those whom people thought were witches. Actually in this very village once upon a time. Mathew Hopkins had a field day here in Norfolk as Witchfinder General. Self-appointed you know. In a couple of years he was responsible for the executions of over a hundred so-called witches. The topic may have changed, but not human nature."

"You're right."

David Horsham paused. "Are you trying to make a point, Accrington?"

"No, not really. I know that Richard and you were good friends. You also had some kind of a history together. No, let me finish. You knew him for many years. You were close. I think that DCI Poole and his team will eventually find out more about that history. So, not only would it be for you to explain whatever needs explaining, it gives you the opportunity to do so discreetly and sooner rather than later. David, if you've done something that you shouldn't have done, perhaps now's the time to say so. Don't you think?"

"What I actually think Accrington, is that this conversation is at an end and you should mind your own bloody business!"

Angrily, David turned and began to walk away.

"David, the police will want to talk to you. I'm talking to you first."

The captain stopped, frowned and thrust his hands deep into his trouser pockets, jingling coins or keys and shuffling one of his feet.

"It's a private matter," he said gruffly, "one best left buried."

"Yes?"

"Yes."

The captain had begun to turn away again but stopped once more, turned back and looked hard at Stanley. "As I say, Accrington, best left alone. Some people's business is not yours…"

"I'm not interested in your business. I'm not your enemy and I don't want anything to become difficult, but it will."

David's shoulders suddenly slumped. He glanced at Stanley. "You know don't you?"

Stanley said nothing. David walked back towards him.

"Accrington… I'm going to tell you something in confidence. I suspect that it will confirm your thinking. Do what you like with what I'm about to say."

"Not my job. You'll have to do any telling yourself. It's what you'd expect of a good soldier. And I imagine that you were a very good soldier."

The captain nodded ruefully. He took a deep breath. The air on the village green was still. In the distance the two men could hear children playing some kind of game in someone's garden. Light, joyous laughter redolent, thought Stanley, of childhood's long, summer afternoons.

David cleared his throat. "Walk with me."

The pair walked away from the green towards the sea, the sea that in different ways and for different reasons both men loved.

"When I was newly married, I'd just finished my last tour of duty in the SAS. We settled here of course at Darkwater where my parents and grandparents were still in situ. One day I was contacted by my regiment to join a task force on a very hush-hush job that involved some work in the UK and some overseas. I can't say more. Anyway, the job was difficult – very difficult – and a number of my chaps were wounded and one was killed. These things happen of course and it's part of what all soldiers know they've signed up for."

The captain paused and just walked, looking down at his brogues. Stanley had the sense to say nothing.

"We came under attack. I can tell you that this wasn't in some jungle somewhere, but in the heart of one of our major cities here. The task was, as I say, hard but that's what the SAS is good at. Everything was completed successfully but I made a mistake the result of which was that one of our own was killed. My fault. The man was Richard Threadgill's brother."

"If it was a mistake…"

"It could have been avoided and the fault was mine… Mine alone. Just mine."

David coughed and studied his brogues again carefully as he walked.

"Every action has consequences," he said, struggling with expressing a painful memory, "and there are always consequences, aren't there? Anyway, I told Dotty, my wife, about what had happened. Shouldn't have of course. Not supposed to talk to anyone about anything. Dorothy was angry that I'd never told Richard and urged me to tell him but I didn't. Fear I suppose. Small, close community. Him a vicar and so on."

"People do die in warfare and sometimes accidents happen I suppose."

"They do but I deliberately put this man in harm's way. To save my own skin. No other reason. To save my own life I ended his."

Stanley felt as if the colour of the day had suddenly been washed away like rain on a freshly painted watercolour. He didn't want to continue. Prying into someone else's misery or sadness wasn't his business. Irritably, he kicked a stone.

As the pair walked through the back streets of Little Peasen, David looked up and out towards the grey sea, tinged with speckles of bluish white.

"Well," he breathed. "after Dotty's death four years ago, I sought solace from Richard. I'm not at all religious, but he offered friendship. He, and Jessica too, helped me to move on a little. They didn't have to do that but they just did. I have few close friends and my only sister is, as you know, in America so Richard's friendship was very dear to me. I was invited for meals and they made sure that I looked after myself, that sort of thing. Stopped me drinking or thinking too much."

"David, this is none of my business. I just want to do the right thing for Richard. He was a good friend… to us both. True?"

David nodded. "Without question."

Suddenly David put out a hand and tugged at Stanley's left arm, something that Stanley didn't mind.

"The thing is Accrington," he said clearing his throat, "the thought of what happened to Richard's brother preyed on my mind for years. Every day. Richard had always believed that his brother had died a hero's death in protecting citizens of this country. Richard talked about it. And I knew that to be incorrect because I'd killed him!"

"It was an accident."

"I can't comment, but no. The man's death was down to me alone. As time went on I felt that I had deceived Richard and of course I had. At some point I knew I needed to face up to my wrongdoing. We all need to do that at some point Accrington, don't we?"

David paused again thinking of something.

"Your Hamlet feller says something on this if I recall. 'Confess yourself to heaven…' or something?"

"Yes. 'Repent what's past; avoid what's to come.' Hamlet tells his mother to admit her sin in marrying her husband's brother and avoid damnation."

David shrugged. "Well, I suddenly decided to put things right at the fête. Totally inappropriate timing. Just felt that it was more than high time that he should know that I'd been responsible for his brother's death. But…" and here the captain found it hard to speak for a moment.

"It's OK David."

"I discovered that Richard had known all the time, but had never raised it with me. That's the conversation you saw us having. He was angry only because he didn't want me to feel any guilt. But I did of course. And do. Now more than ever."

David stopped walking for a moment and gazed out at four container ships, more like black smudges crawling across the horizon.

"It turns out that it was my Dotty who'd told Richard. Not out of malice but I suppose in the hope that telling him would bring some peace. Or closure. But, it should have been me who confessed to Richard not… her. And I hadn't the guts to do that. Until now."

Stanley watched David struggle and fail with the process of controlling emotions while trying to speak. Nothing was said for a moment. A piece of the previous day's newspaper floated along in the breeze. Stanley caught it and screwed it up.

"Why did you discuss it? Opening old wounds surely?"

"I wanted to say how very sorry I was. Apologies are often thin or hollow, but I wanted him to understand that I'd been living with guilt for a very long time."

"You wanted forgiveness?"

"Possibly, yes. We all do. Age puts some things into clear perspective and also, because of my other… problems, I needed to… wanted to rid myself of guilt, even though Richard insisted that I should feel none."

Stanley shoved the screwed up newspaper page into a bin. He looked across the expanse of sea. There'd been a time when he had longed one day to play Prospero staring out at the island's seas, throwing away his magic and offering forgiveness. There must be a point to all this he thought, but at the moment he couldn't put his finger on what it was and felt grubby at prying into someone's heartache. It was, as David intimated, absolutely none of his business. How would he feel if someone poked about in the embers of his own history?

"That's not all."

"What do you mean?"

"You know about Bindman's father and why he was cashiered."

"Yes."

"That's only half the story. Bindman's father had stolen much more money from army charities and, more particularly, refugee funds over which he had some serious control. He'd done it all very cleverly too. Hundreds of thousands of pounds. People suspected what was going on but there was never sufficient proof – not until I got him cashiered. But, alas, I could only nab him for the one case, not the rest. The vast sums of money were never repaid of course. They went with Bindman's father's estate and ended up in Ellis Bindman's pocket. Of course I tackled Bindman about it and said that he should do the right thing and give the money back to the army authorities so it could be used properly. He laughed in my face and told me that if I said a word or cast any aspersions, then he would tell Richard Threadgill about Richard's brother. I'd made the silly mistake of confiding in Ellis before I'd properly joined the dots about who his father was. Naive and basic stupidity on my part of course. But it was when Dotty was very ill and I wasn't thinking straight."

"That's why Ellis had money enough to invest in Berkley's scheme to develop Darkwater as a hotel?"

"Exactly."

"The police will want to talk to you again – and Jessica too – about what you've told me and in much more detail. You need to tell them everything David. Everything. Including what you've just told me about Ellis."

"I suppose all this would have come out, but I don't want Jessica to suffer any more than she has."

"Truth is a tough boss," Stanley said suddenly. "I don't mean that pompously at all, but we sometimes avoid it because we're frightened of the consequences… There's something I need to talk about David."

"Something more?"

Stanley stopped walking. "It's about Ray Berkley."

David stopped walking too. "Oh yes?" he asked far too quickly.

"You've been blackmailing him with photographs that you commissioned of Jessica Threadgill and him in bed together and… elsewhere. Did you know they were having an affair? Did Richard?"

Stunned, David stood stock still, his complexion grey.

"Blackmail is a criminal offence no matter what Ray Berkley's ever done to you."

"Poor Jessica! I never meant that..."

"What? You mean that she did that for you? You engineered it?"

Stanley hadn't meant to be or sound judgemental, but he was horrified.

David was defiant, "I... did. Yes, I did. What I did is unforgiveable. Indefensible. I know that! She... was aware that I was a busted flush. Most of the money from the sale of the estate had gone to my sister in repayment for what I owed her. It was her money that had funded the estate for so many years. And I couldn't let Berkley get the lodge and what little remained of my family's land! I couldn't allow him to convert Darkwater Hall into a bloody hotel. And throw the Baxters out. I just couldn't."

"So you enticed..."

"She offered. Yes I know it's horrible, but I had no other choice..." He trailed off. "She said that for a sum of money she'd do it."

Stanley was stunned. "But you had all that other leverage on Berkley didn't you?"

"Not then I didn't. There was no choice."

"There's always a bloody choice David! She agreed to do that so that you could blackmail Ray and you'd both share the spoils?"

David nodded. "Yes. She never loved Richard. She was fed up to the back teeth with being stuck here in Little Peasen doing vicarage and church things. She'd done it for years she said and felt that she'd done enough. She wanted out and a different life."

Thoughts twirled around Stanley's head again. So, had Jessica – mild, vanilla Jessica – had she been the murderer aided and abetted by David and possibly Malcolm too?

"If Ray had paid you and you'd given Jessica her cut, what

then?"

"Jessica wanted to go to France with her money. She'll still do that I suppose. And there'll be insurance money that she'll get on Richard's life. My home is here."

Stanley didn't know what to say.

"Of course," said David, "Berkley would have had to die."

"Is that why you had this?"

Stanley took out of a jacket pocket a reinforced, clear plastic, police specimen bag. "You attempted to pick this up outside the ambulance when you pretended to tread on it as if you'd just discovered it. I saw you drop the thing by mistake, as you transferred it from one pocket to another – a daft move given I was standing there and the knife is literally razor sharp. You pretended to find it because you knew I'd see it. Knives like this don't get carried around naked. They're kept in a sheath. They also don't appear on a Norfolk village green."

Stanley was suddenly tired. He wasn't a police officer. It wasn't his job to point fingers. And yet, he'd encouraged Julian to let him talk to the captain before the police pulled him in. For the purposes of what? His own self-importance? Because he really was minding other people's business? Or because he cared?

"David," said Stanley wearily, "Ellis Bindman hates you because of what happened to his father. And you knew the full extent of what his father had done. You hate him because he was blackmailing you over the death of Richard's brother. This knife would have been more than suitable for your purposes... of killing Ray Berkley. So why would Ellis give the knife to you? He likes Ray."

"I didn't get the scalpel from Ellis. I got it from Carmichael. He could lay his hands on most things. I befriended Carmichael and discovered that he and I shared the same hatred for Berkley."

"David, you know you could be in seriously big trouble on various counts, don't you?"

"Sold me down the river Accrington, have you?"

"Unworthy of you to say so and I haven't. I told you, I want the truth. For Richard. And Malcolm Carmichael."

"From my military days I knew that a scalpel like that would go through soft tissue and, because it was so sharp, it'd cause little blood. Initially anyway. I…"

"David go and see the police before they pull you in."

"Even though I hated the man and still do," David said in a low voice, "Berkley was much more use to me alive than dead. He was about to pay me too – an enormous sum of money. To make the photographs disappear. And to shut me up about what I knew about the drug business and the gun manufacture. The money would have solved all my problems. The financial ones anyway. But I feared what would happen to me after that. He would haunt me. Hunt me. Punish me. Make my life impossible. And probably have me killed. I knew too much. He told me as much when I gave Richard the chance to give out the fifty-fifty. But I didn't care any more. I did know that, if I got him to pay, I knew immediately after that he would have to die."

As they made their way back to the green, the two men didn't speak. The silence was thick and uncomfortable.

What, wondered Stanley, if Jessica had really wanted Richard out of the way? Maybe that had been her plan for years. Collect some life insurance money and bugger off somewhere as a grieving widow. But then she'd found out about David's plans and that financial opportunity would mean that she would want for nothing even if it meant sleeping with the enemy. In practice it would be hard to see how she could have garnered the help of Malcolm Carmichael and the botswarm. But with David's friendship with Carmichael, then it all would have fitted together pretty well for them. There was another thought that fluttered about. Even if David and Jessica hadn't been involved in Richard's death, had his death actually done Jessica a favour perhaps? Certainly it had. But then Berkley's death would have done David and Jessica a favour too. After the blackmail money had been paid. Either way, Jessica might have got away.

"David, go to the police."

Stanley turned to leave. The captain grabbed one of his arms.

"Will all be well, Accrington?" he asked urgently.

Surprised, Stanley thought the question odd and somewhat archaic. He didn't know what to say. Would all be well? Who the hell ever knew? You had to just move forwards, sometimes a day at a time and then do your best and hope that all would indeed be well. But sometimes all just wasn't well. Not well at all. The key was hope. But then hope could be dashed against life's walls. Would all be well now? Such a difficult question and one that demanded reassurance and comfort, both of which weren't always available.

He saw a small, loose branch on the lower reaches of one of the nearby oak trees. Grabbing and waving the dead branch in farewell to the captain, he wished that he believed it when he called out, "I don't know."

Twenty One

William Benedict had been untied and allowed to put on some underpants, but nothing else.

"In case you try an' run," said Adidas by way of a rationale. "And them're pretty knickers," he added pointing at William's watermelon print underpants.

William now thought of the three men as terrorists hell-bent on some venture to harm as many innocent people as possible. The crates of weapons and ammunition crowding his large kitchen, dining room, lounge and shop were a constant reminder of violence and death. The gang had opened a few more of the crates to examine the contents and there'd been a number of low whistles when they'd seen the standard of fare. William had listened carefully for any clues, but nothing gave him comfort.

Each of the three men had made it plain that they didn't want any witnesses and had become even more irritated by William's presence than they had been at the start. He'd been close to tears on several occasions and was almost resigned to the fact that he was probably going to be shot or blown to bits. He tried to imagine whether either option would hurt before the oblivion that would follow. He also tried and failed to imagine what the people in his life whom he loved would think, say or do after his demise.

"Make us something t'eat," ordered Adidas.

"What… what do you want? I only have mostly tinned things and some bread and eggs… I could get something from the shop," he added hopefully.

Wilf flicked a tea towel against William's exposed thighs. "You think we're stupid or what?"

"No, no…" said William hurriedly, desperate only to be helpful. "OK, so how about some fried eggs, tomatoes, mushrooms, baked beans and chips? Actually, I don't have beans, but I do have spaghetti hoops. Would that do?"

"Yeah, fine and no tricks, otherwise you're dead," snarled Wilf who wished fervently that he could fry William's head.

"And no musher rooms on my plate," barked Terence.

"Bread an' butter on mine," added Wilf. "Five slices. Fick butter."

Adidas was agitated on two counts. They had no truck to load and, for a long time, he hadn't heard from Kreshnik. Adidas could see from the controller's app that the button had been pressed and therefore the device had been armed despite the fact that no order had been given. That was a very big worry indeed, he thought, because he still had no clue where the device was.

Terence had views. "You sure you didden order 'im to press the button, boss?"

"Course I didden. I got no instructions and so Kresh got none neither. You callin' me stupid?"

Terence thought that Adidas was very stupid. "No boss… Reckon e's scarpered."

"Yeah," said Wilf, "maybe 'e pressed the button by mistake and did a runner. Or, 'e was zonked and thought 'e'd bin told to press the thing. Or pressed it by accident? Or, the filfth 'ave 'im. And so 'e pressed it anyway. Cooden 'elp it. Summat like that."

Adidas walked round the kitchen thinking. Each time he passed William busy at the Aga, he snapped the tea towel at the bookshop owner's thighs which didn't help in the cooking process.

"Kresh said 'e had one 'ostage," he muttered almost to himself. "Then more 'ostages. So what 'appened? Did they overpower Kresh? Or maybe 'e put 'em down?"

Adidas boggled as he envisaged a possible blood bath in the village green hut. Whatever the situation, Adidas thought yet again that he and his men needed to move. Things, he thought, were getting out of hand.

As William nervously went about heating up spaghetti hoops, cracking eggs, frying mushrooms and putting chips in the oven, he thought about Sheila Prewer and the fact that she hadn't returned. He knew that she'd be worried about him, but hoped that she wouldn't do anything silly. He also hoped – no, prayed – that she'd gone to the police. Worrying about the current possibilities within his world caused tears to fall into the saucepan of spaghetti hoops. Heaving a huge sigh, he wished that at least he might be allowed to die with some clothes on.

By the main Little Peasen sea wall, Stanley enjoyed the crashes of occasional waves as they hit the boulders and submerged concrete. A few hundred yards further down, groynes split the big waves which made for a mesmerising pattern as each wavelet rippled towards the beach.

Amber Cooper thrust her face out towards him. "Yeah," she said, "I nearly decked him. So?"

At The Basin of Porridge pub where she worked, Amber had been flirting with a used car salesman when Stanley asked if he might have a word. Various customers, her bar staff colleagues, friend Jules Tinkley and the pub proprietor all looked on with group curiosity. There were very few people who had any animosity towards Stanley, but they all regarded Amber as one of their own.

"Nearly," Amber went on defiantly as she perched on the sea wall, "don't mean I did smack 'im. Anyway, 'e was muckin' me about. I was pissed off. You would be an' all."

"In what way was he mucking you about?"

"Screwin' someone else, weren't 'e?" Amber exclaimed.

"How d'you know he was having a fling with someone else?"

"He was seen with some skirt over Cromer way. I reckon it was Sharon Benford. Tart. Me mate Jules at the pub reckons she saw 'em bookin' into some 'otel. The Poseidon I fink she said."

"And at the fair you just decided to shout at him and call him names – causing a rumpus?"

"A what?"

"A scene, a show-down, a row."

"Yeah, well. So?"

"You were about to hit him."

"Yeah. I was. I would've if 'e 'adn't scarpered."

"You were angry."

"I'd drunk a bit that's all. Voddie as it goes. 'e tried shovin' me away. Then suddenly 'e cupped 'is 'ands like what you do if you capture a moff, but there weren't nuffink there."

"What was in his hands do you think?"

"I don't bleedin' know do I? The bloke was always a bit off wiv the fairies. Maybe 'e was protectin' an animal or summink." She shrugged and lit a cigarette.

"What do you think that was?"

"Fink?"

"You said he might have been protecting something. What do you think he was protecting?"

"You're not the fuzz. Why all this? The bloke's dead."

"He was murdered. Don't you care?"

Amber shrugged and blew a chewing gum bubble. She looked expectantly at Stanley. "So we done now?"

Ignoring the question, Stanley asked, "A few years ago, you were mixing with a bunch who smuggled alcohol from Holland."

"It weren't much. Mates that's all. They brought in a foo cases of Scotch and voddie from the 'ook is all. I wasn't involved. So?"

"But it wasn't just alcohol though, was it? There were lots of trips from the Hook and several from elsewhere. Not all of it booze."

"I didn't get nicked or nothing."

"What I'm interested in is where they took the drugs. Uncut cocaine, wasn't it? On three occasions the boats were tracked from pick-up to Holkham beach. The cocaine and heroin were never found. Destined for the Mafia Shqiptare?"

"I'm going now," Amber said as she slipped down from the sea wall.

"OK, no problem. See you."

"What do you want?"

"The drugs needed to be processed," went on Stanley, "and that could only happen somewhere very safe and clean. So clean that you could eat your dinner off the floor. So clean that the cocaine could be cut without contamination. The drug cutting place was smart. Did well for a few years. Made a lot of money. Remind me, where was it?"

"If you know, you know," said Amber. She smiled. "You stood up for me mum when she were done for shopliftin' an' that. She reckons you," said Amber. "Dad thinks she fancies you."

For the first time Amber grinned and Stanley saw that, despite her raw edges, Amber wasn't only beautiful but had some soul. He smiled back.

"So where was the cutting place?"

"What're you playin' at?"

"Where was it?"

"It was the 'ouse next but one to the vic'rage."

"You know who lived there?"

"Yeah," said Amber quietly. "Malc did."

"That'd be the man you didn't like very much. The one who is, as you say, now dead. Did you ever go to that house?"

"No… I did when it was a cuttin' place. A few of us did."

"Do you know who killed Malcolm?"

There was a heartbeat of hesitation. Stanley noticed.

"No," said Amber.

"Anything strange about the house next but one to the vicarage?"

"I wooden know."

"Yes you do. It had a cellar where they cut the coke."

"You know that 'ow? You a nark then? You should watch yourself mate. They find out an' you'll be toast."

"Is the passageway still there and the cutting room?"

"I'm guessin' you know the answer."

"I was involved in the bust at that house four years ago. I'm not a police officer but I helped stop the trade."

Amber was shocked. "What? It was you what broke up the cuttin' room operation an' that? You 'elped put them guys away?"

"Yes."

Amber looked worried. "Fuck a duck mate, but you could be in very big shit."

"Tell me about the cutting room."

"But you know."

"Tell me."

"Four years back, there was a passageway under the 'ouse between the church, the cottage and the pub. Most of the passages was all blocked off from the old days but… they built a cuttin' room under the 'ouse. Must've cost a fortune. Mind you, they 'ad fortunes, didden they? Clean as a whistle it were. Air tight… no dust or what 'ave you could get in. They was cutting pure for big time dealers. The real players would only accept pure. If they got a bad score, there would be murder…"

"And you never went to the house with Malcolm?"

"Nah. He wooden let me. Secretive sod. I wanted to go in case 'e didden know about the cellars and maybe there could've been some stuff left over or summink."

"Blow doesn't last that long Amber. I might look like a wally but I'm not. So why did you want to go there with Malcolm?"

There was a pause. Amber looked out to sea. Stanley wondered what she was thinking when she took in the choppy waves and, further out, the blue-green swell with flashes of white.

"The guy was me feller so stands to reason you go to where your feller lives. An' I thought there might be cash lyin' around. Malc 'ad loads of cash and, if I asked, 'e just gave me some. Thought I could 'elp meself."

"Crap. That wasn't the reason… Back in the day when the bust happened," said Stanley, "there was access to the secret passageway somewhere in the garden, but that access probably doesn't exist any more. Maybe your old mates concreted it in and put some begonias on top? So how do you get in down there?"

"I dunno do I?"

"OK, let's do this your way. I know you've been to Dr Carmichael's house when he wasn't there."

"Bollocks."

"OK, let's leave it there then."

Stanley turned to go. He walked about three steps before Amber called out.

"I wanted to 'ave a look round. Nick a bit maybe."

Stanley walked back. "So how d'you get down to the cellars now? Same as before?"

Amber stared at Stanley for at least a minute.

"By the big kitchen cupboard, there's a terracotta floor tile slightly darker than the others. You press it free times with your foot and Bob's your…"

"And a section of wall opens up?"

"Yeah."

"Airlock inside? Access to some stairs. Kitchen wall arrangement closes behind you with hydraulics. All the air in that area cleaned before the main door opens at the bottom of the steps. Another airlock where you put on a Hazchem suit. Each suit fresh each visit. Yes?"

"Yes. 'ow do you know all this?"

"Nearly done. How did you get that sore cheek and neck? Somebody thump you?"

"Walked into a door is all."

"Also crap. I saw you talking to Mrs Monteith at the fair but I couldn't hear the conversation. Not all of it. I did hear her say something about you being a recruit. A recruit for what?"

There was no answer.

"Mrs Monteith and all the ladies who were working at the Hall on kites are in custody. They're in deep trouble for the cocaine work. Were you involved?"

Amber smiled. "No."

"Who was it you talked to after Barbara Monteith?"

"I couldn't see 'is face but 'e gave me a right smack."

"Why?"

"For bein' lippy."

"Any idea who it was?"

"Nah."

"Also crap. OK. Thanks for helping Amber. Did you like Malcolm Carmichael at all? Even a bit?"

"Mr Accrington," said Amber softly. "A bit of advice."

Stanley stared. Amber's demeanour and accent had totally changed. Her accent was perfectly neutral and she could have auditioned for a part as a newsreader. She smiled and put a hand on one of Stanley's sleeves.

"Be careful. Please. You're a nice guy and people like you. You do good things, but in future leave it others. It's a dodgy world."

Stanley didn't know what to say. Amber leaned forward and kissed him on the cheek.

"Be lucky," she said in her posh accent and was gone.

Julian waved Stanley over to the main table where there was an array of filled rolls, fruit and fresh coffee.

Julian pointed to the spread. "That's cost me four evenings of Mothers' Union presentations… Now that Mrs Monteith and her cohorts are tucked up, a very nice Mrs Margaret McFlintock has stepped into the breech as have one or two from The King's Head."

Stanley sat down and Julian insisted that he should help himself.

"The intel on Carmichael's house was perfect, Stan," said Julian munching a roll, again without examining the contents. This time, cheese and tomato filled him with no dismay.

"Particularly since the case was years ago," said a smiling Evie. "They say that the case wouldn't have been sorted if it hadn't been for you…"

"Not all my doing by any means," said an immediately embarrassed Stanley.

"Amazing that the house was the one that Carmichael bought. He knew about the cellars beforehand you think?" asked Julian.

"I don't think so. Happenstance. You've talked to David Horsham?"

Julian nodded. "We have," he said indistinctly, mouth full of bread, cheese and lettuce. "Messy business, but not so unusual. Our feeling is that he would have definitely used the scalpel, so it was a close call. The point of no-return wasn't far away. But a dead Berkley wouldn't have paid him anything, although the thought of a dead Berkley was overpowering his need for cash. He dropped the scalpel to avoid what was becoming genuine temptation and had to get rid of it as soon as he could. He was relieved that you saw it. Better you than some kid. He was genuinely in bits about the vicar's brother and we've checked on the history with the MoD as far as we're allowed. Oh and he definitely knew a great deal about Carmichael and his plans. That gave him even more leverage over Berkley. The blackmail issues are clear-cut and undisputed. The photograph business is commonplace of course. Desperation breeds nasty solutions. Mrs Threadgill clearly had no great love for her husband, although I think she respected him. Maybe. You were absolutely right that she was in it for whatever big bucks the captain could leverage out of Berkley. Sleeping with the blackmail target isn't so unusual in cases like this. My guys are talking to her again now."

"You've taken David into custody?"

Evie shook her head. "No point at this stage. He's at home and knows that much of what he's done is certainly criminal. We'll talk to the CPS and he's being watched. He'll be charged in a day or two once we get some paperwork we're waiting for. But the positive stuff was good. The drone drug bust was down to him as was the intel on the gun manufacture and package delivery. That'll go in his favour big time. You speaking to him was key, Mr Accrington. His guilt was the driver to a confession."

Stanley felt grubby for all kinds of reasons. "Bit of a mess really," he said. "What about Ellis Bindman?"

"I suspect he might get struck off and the MoD are having chats with him about the stolen money. Bindman thought his father's loot was his by right. They want it back."

"Any news about the hut gunman?"

"Not a lot," said Evie glancing first at her boss who nodded. "He's not talking. They reckon they have a name for him now though. Likely he's been part of a Mafia Shqiptare cell from the moment he arrived in the UK five years ago. There may be a link between what happened here in the village then and now. But, apart from Berkley's drug drone business, which we're pretty clear was a totally separate operation, this whole thing doesn't smell like a drugs op. The specialists still don't know what device the controller controlled, even though the charge button was definitely pressed. But they're working on it."

Stanley looked closely at both police officers.

"The specialists don't know? Really?"

There was no answer.

"Doesn't that present a danger for the whole village?"

Again there was no answer and the sudden quiet was obvious. Almost as obvious as the almost imperceptible look between the two officers which caused Stanley's blood to run cold.

"So," asked Stanley. "We're in harm's way here?"

Again, there was no answer.

Stanley seriously thought about walking out there and then and knew that the officers wouldn't stop him. He looked at an apple and wanted to smash it with a fist.

"I think we're nearly done here Stan, one way or another."

Quietening his breathing and consciously steadying his voice, Stanley disagreed. "I don't think we're done in Little Peasen. I think you know more than you're telling me but that's of course your privilege. I'm a postman and shopkeeper as I keep being reminded. No! Don't interrupt! I'm concerned about the fact that Pat thinks Sheila Prewer's missing now. She's not answering her phone. Neither is William Benedict who runs the bookshop. Pat thinks something's very wrong in the bookshop. So, as a heads up to you, I'm going to take a look."

"What if there are some nutters in there all tooled up?" asked Julian. "This isn't a TV series Stan." He hesitated. "Apologies. That was uncalled for."

There was silence for a moment. Julian considered his resources and came to a conclusion.

"Look, Stan, seriously, we can take it from here. You look knackered."

"I'm fine," said Stanley untruthfully.

Both officers had noticed the same shadow they'd seen before falling across Stanley's face.

"Stan," said Julian, "sparing your blushes and forgive me saying this in front of DS Harris, but perhaps now's the time for you to step back."

Stanley stood up. "I'm going to see if William and Sheila are OK. Then you can do what you want. I imagine that I'm a bit surplus to requirements anyway. And, yes, I am tired. Very."

"Look, I don't have masses of spare troops, but take Scotty with you. Then you've got some law next to you, albeit young law. But he's a good lad and knows the village… and people know him. Just knock though, ask to speak to Benedict and see if everything's cool. Scotty'll make an assessment, not you. If there's a doubt, you step away."

When told of the plan, Alfie Scott beamed.

To both men, Julian was sharp. "Scotty leads, Stan. If he tells you to back off at any time, then you back off. I mean it. No heroics. None. Either of you. OK?"

"Sure," said Stanley.

"Yessir," reinforced Scott happily. To Stanley he asked, "Ready, Mr Accrington?"

"Hold on," said Julian. "Wear vests and first wait for one hour in your flat Stan. Keep watch. After an hour, call Evie or me here and we'll discuss. No risks! I mean it. Scotty, video on. Low profile. No Jason Statham stuff thank you. Keep me in the loop. I repeat, do nothing for an hour. Just watch and report."

No more than five minutes had passed since Scotty and Stanley had headed off for the post office.

"Sorry to interrupt sir," said a uniformed sergeant addressing Julian. "Apparently there's a problem with the phones. Landlines, mobiles, internet. All dead."

Evie immediately checked her own phone. Julian did the same with his and picked up the incident unit's. Dead.

"No phones at all?" Evie asked the sergeant.

"Seems none of the phones work anywhere in the village. And all our vehicle radios have packed up."

"Video cams?"

The officer shook his head. Evie looked round the incident unit. Everyone was shaking his or her head too.

"Geoff," Julian called out to an officer. "Satellite?"

The officer called Geoff swivelled round in his chair. "Just tried sir. It works, but we only have the one."

"I'll need that here. Sergeant," he said to the officer by the door, "I want someone to drive out of the village and see what happens then. Evie, get over to the post office. Check if they have phone access. Low profile. When you've had a good look and, if there are definitely still no comms, come back here. Do nothing else. Vest, phone, radio and bodycam just in case they work over there. You'd better check out what's going on in the bookshop whilst you're there. If you smell trouble, empty the post office. Slowly and low key. Take Chambers with you. But do it all quietly and don't panic anyone. Let people out in ones or twos. Get people to actually go. Properly go. No standing around. No shouting, no rush. Everything calm."

As Evie and Gus Chambers walked towards the post office, Graham Lambert ran up.

"Mr Lambert, I'm in a hurry and…"

"I'm coming with you. I was in the shop half an hour ago and saw that Sheila Prewer's big army truck's been moved from the back of the bookshop to the front."

"And?"

"Sheila's mad keen on anything military. Goes on war game manoeuvres. Stuff like that. She keeps the unit's truck behind her house. Rarely used so I was a bit surprised. Beaten up old thing…"

"She was beaten up?"

"The truck."

"You actually saw this truck being moved from there to the front of the bookshop?"

"Yep."

"Who was driving?"

"Well that's what's odd. Nobody."

"Mr Lambert I'm not in the mood to…"

"Nobody was driving."

"It was being pushed?"

"Nope."

"Mr Lambert," Evie said irritably.

"Nobody was driving or pushing the truck. I swear. Sheila's not anywhere and something odd's going on I reckon, so thought you lot could use some help."

"You saw Mr Accrington and my constable?"

"Scotty yes, but not Mr Accrington."

"OK thanks for your input, but this is a police matter."

"It's a village matter an' all. And d'you know that nobody's phone's working?"

Evie swore, checking her own phone and radio as did officer Chambers. Nothing. She studied Graham Lambert for a few seconds.

"OK. But you only do what I say. Or what this constable says. Nothing else. Clear?"

The three arrived at the back of the post office. It was quickly established that all the phones and computer links were dead. Constable Chambers stayed at the rear of the shop but with instructions to keep an eye as far as possible on the front and back. Evie made a swift decision.

People listened to her calm voice carefully albeit nervously, accepted what had to be done and began to leave at irregular intervals in ones or twos. Bethan was on discrete duty to politely stop new erstwhile shoppers from coming in.

"Where's your brother?" Evie asked Patricia.

"I don't know. Alfie Scott's upstairs, but he says that Stan just scooted off somewhere en route."

Evie moved forwards carefully so that she could look through the shop window at what was going on across the road. The old army truck was indeed at the front of the bookshop. She tried her lapel radio again, her video camera and then her phone. Nothing.

It was agreed that Patricia should stay in the shop with Bethan and Gus Chambers. Tony Helliwell and Stevie Devonport, both now regular assistants in the shop, were told to go upstairs to the flat and to be ready to help out wherever help was needed. Evie and Graham Lambert followed the boys.

Alfie Scott was using binoculars to look out of the dining room window across the street.

An irritated Evie snapped at him. "You and Mr Accrington were supposed to be here together!"

"Sarge," said the officer without taking his eyes off the target area, "he said he needed to sort out something first – wouldn't say what – and that he'd be over here as soon as he could. Then he legged it."

Scotty suddenly fiddled around with the binoculars. "Sarge! There's movement over at the bookshop. Something's being loaded on the other side of the truck. I've counted three sets of legs so far." He handed the binoculars to Evie.

Stevie and Tony munched on large chocolate bars directly behind the constable, eager to see what was going on.

"Tony," complained Scotty, "stop eating the sodding chocolate in my ear."

"Sorry Alf."

"Constable Scott to you."

"Yeah, whatever. I'll go down an' lock up the shop door shall I?"

"No," said Evie sharply. "Bad idea. If one of them comes over to get something, they'll smell a rat. Scotty, go downstairs. Keep a low profile. Stay out of sight of the front windows. Lend a hand only if necessary. Lads you go too."

Scott went downstairs with the two teenagers. Graham Lambert joined Evie at the window. Evie stiffened as she saw Alfie Scott walking over the road bold as brass and knocking on the bookshop door.

Evie yelled uselessly at the window. "Oh, come on! You're kidding me! You bloody idiot!"

Evie and Graham watched helplessly as the bookshop door opened. Their horror grew as they saw Scotty step back, only to be grabbed by two pairs of hands and pulled in. The door was slammed shut. Almost at the same time a metal grey, unmarked BMW X7 slid up to the right of the bookshop further down the same side of the road. Out of it came four armed, anti-terrorism officers each dressed in Nomex outfits, Kevlar helmets and

Valsetz RTS boots. Once the officers disappeared from Evie's sightline, she was suddenly aware of the dead silence.

Twenty Two

The King's Head, that Michelin-starred establishment about which gourmands and critics have written in various forms of rhetorical ecstasy, was quiet this lunchtime. Anyone who'd cared to observe would have seen a man in a lightweight blue suit, pale blue open-necked shirt and highly polished, tan Church's brogues sitting in the comfortable lounge. In front of him on a low table was a colourless drink, maybe a gin and tonic; a little had been spilt, creating a small puddle.

Something made the man jump which, if any observer knew him, would have been a surprise because, as a rule, the man didn't jump at much. As if trying hard not to disturb something, gently he put out a hand waving it up and down slightly as if trying to emulate a fish swimming.

Stanley smiled at the restaurant's receptionist whom he knew moderately well and asked to see the duty manager. Before the duty manager arrived, he had a brief chat with the receptionist to establish that the phones here as elsewhere weren't working. Questions put to the duty manager were dutifully answered. It was confirmed, when Stanley asked, that a particular guest was indeed in the lounge and he was kindly pointed in the direction of where that guest was sitting. Stanley thanked her.

"Hello, Mr Berkley," Stanley said smiling down at Ray who, startled, looked up. He didn't acknowledge Stanley but began examining the carpet again.

"I don't think your lunch date has shown up has he?"

Ray Berkley looked up again but didn't reciprocate Stanley's smile. He appeared glazed, said nothing and fiddled with his right hand.

"Ray, you alright? You've spilt some of your drink there I think."

"I… need to concentrate. No time…" Ray pressed his right

hand with his left.

"Ray, I know what you're doing. So do the police… and two of your MI5 minders are here. The man and woman sitting over there. What did you think was going to happen? Ray, I know what you're doing."

"No, no… you don't."

"You're trying to operate a botswarm with a finger ring device and I can see that your finger is very sore. I don't think the ring is working properly is it? Or maybe you don't know how to use it. Mind if I sit down, Ray?"

Stanley sat down and watched as Ray kept searching the carpet.

"Dr Malcolm Carmichael," said Stanley quietly, "had his own private version of the device you're trying to operate. Remarkable man you know. You should have been much kinder to him. What you did to his parents was disgusting and nobody should forgive you for that. Did you know Ray that Malcolm developed his own device at home and he wanted to sell it to a high bidder. He knew it was better than the one he'd developed for you – and it was. The bots in his version think for themselves. I mean totally think for themselves. No need for a finger ring with his version. His are literally point and go. Ray? You OK?"

There was no response.

"You never saw Malcolm's own version of course, but you suspected him of something and you kept on terrorising him didn't you with your lies? That fear made Dr Carmichael angry. Very angry."

There was no response.

"Anyway, the swarm that Dr Carmichael developed at home was a small one. Only about twenty bots. A baby swarm. All any operator had to do was programme the swarm once and let it go. His bots though were very powerful. They could work together and get any programmed job done come what may. His device wouldn't have made the mistake of killing the vicar. It would have sought you out and it would have killed you. It would have known that you hadn't been there onstage. It would have found you though. No hiding place. Extraordinary technology and terrifying really. Dangerous stuff. That's what Malcolm was going to sell. With some help from your lunch date who isn't going to be here for lunch. And that's the person the police want now. They've got you and now they want the person who's going to miss his lunch."

Ray was becoming more and more agitated and shaking his right hand as if trying to get something off it.

"Very late last night, Ray," went on Stanley, trying but failing to make eye-contact, "the police and other smart people went through Malcolm's secret laboratory at his home with a fine tooth comb. Quite a set up. A few years ago a drug gang used the house and the underground lab. The place was perfect for what Malcolm had in mind. Pure chance that he bought a house that more or less had what he needed. He must have spent a small fortune getting the lab just right though. Ray?"

There was no response.

"Ray, it's a great house. Not like Darkwater Hall of course, but I wouldn't say no to a place like Dr Carmichael's house. By the way, the police have the CCTV footage from a secret camera network at the cottage which has now gone to all sorts of important people. You weren't always careful enough, which is odd for someone so security conscious. The intruders, some even masked up, will eventually lead back to you. Several other curious people visited the cottage too you know. A regular Piccadilly Circus. Oh and you visited once as well didn't you? Couldn't resist? Bit silly that."

Stanley glanced around at the people in the lounge who were beginning to stare at Ray's erratic behaviour. He signed to the two MI5 officers that he was going outside.

"Ray, let's walk shall we? Get some air. Your date's not going to turn up. I can guarantee it."

Ray offered no resistance as Stanley gently helped him to his feet and the two made their awkward way to the reception area. Ray kept looking around and behind him.

"Let's go out to the garden," said Stanley kindly. "Lean on me." As they walked, Ray waved an arm as if trying to attract someone's attention. He stumbled a little.

"Ray," said Stanley conversationally as they walked, "You're trying to control a Pixie swarm now aren't you? Y'know I think that there were three finger controllers and three Pixie swarms. You have one of the controllers… and I took one from your pocket. I think that whoever killed Malcolm took his controller. Literally ripped it off his finger."

Ray now stared at Stanley. "You took my controller ring?"

Stanley nodded. "Yes. The one you're using now belonged to Malcolm's team. The other one's not been found yet. Same as the swarms. One swarm's here with you. Sort of. One was used by Dr Carmichael at the fair, not very well as it happens. And the third is being used now by the person to whom you sold it. Or who took it."

Stanley steered Ray outside to a wide teak bench facing a marble fountain that tinkled water into a lily-covered koi pond. Ray sat seemingly in a trance. Something suddenly caught his attention and he began to look around him in the air. He kept pressing his bloody hand.

"I don't think," said Stanley, "you killed the vicar. Your no-show did that with a swarm that he was controlling. It was a mistake wasn't it? Should have been you. But the vicar was onstage, not you. Think how lucky you were. Poor Dr Carmichael was trying to control one of the swarms but not doing so well. He was going to use it to kill you but, like you, he couldn't get the hang of it. His invention too."

Stanley paused, taking his own clean handkerchief out, removing the finger ring and pressing the handkerchief onto Ray's bleeding hand. Ray began breathing heavily. Crouching down so that he was level with Ray Berkley's pale face it was clear that something was very wrong. The man's face was shining with a veneer of sweat and his breathing had now become shallow.

"Ray, look at me. Focus."

"Mr Accrington?" gasped an out-of-breath, tousle-haired teenager in fashionably ripped jeans and a faded T-shirt featuring Usain Bolt and the runner's famous arrow stance.

Stanley looked up. "Stevie?"

Stevie was looking interestedly at Ray Berkley.

"I was sent to find you, Mr A," he said nervously. "DS summink sent me. I'm a kind of runner today. Bit of a gofer. You know, go fer this, go fer…"

"Why did she send you Stevie?"

"None of the phones work Mr A. She wanted to know if you was alright. Someone called Ted and a copper from Berkley Tech went over the incident unit cos they was concerned about 'im sat there… and I… Is 'e OK, Mr A?"

"Stevie, listen carefully. Go into the lounge. There are two officers. A man and a woman. The man's in a grey suit and the lady's wearing red. Secret service agents. Ask for the lady. Her name is Amber Cooper. Tell her we need an ambulance here urgently. And armed support for the post office. She's got a satellite phone and will know what to do. Got that?"

Stevie's eyes were wide. "Support? What, wiv guns an' stuff?"

"Stevie, get going! It's really important."

"What if she tells me to eff off?"

"Just run. Go!"

Stanley turned back to Ray Berkley who's facial skin was like putty.

"Ray, talk to me."

Stanley sat back putting a supporting arm round Ray's

shoulders. Ray leaned into the crook of Stanley's arm. There were some tiny flies around both of the men, some settling on Ray's face. Stanley brushed them away.

"Your botswarm's out there now isn't it Ray? It was with you and now it's gone. That's right isn't it? Forget it now. It doesn't matter any more."

Ray nodded feebly. "I can't do it," he said faintly his head now sinking onto Stanley's shoulder. "I can't make it work. I've messed up big time. The swarm won't do what I want…"

Stanley looked down and could see that Ray's unfocussed eyes were watery and his breathing barely perceptible.

"I've tried," murmured Ray hoarsely, "but someone else is controlling another swarm. Someone stronger than me. And I think I've swallowed some bots… Someone else's swarm."

Stanley nodded. "I know Ray."

"He made sure the swarm was ready in the drum. He killed the vicar. It was meant for me. I knew that. I wouldn't have killed Malcolm. But he did. Got pissed off with Malcolm's toing and froing. And anyway probably knew where Malcolm's personal swarm was and where the plans were. Didn't need Malcolm. Didn't need Malcolm talking too much."

Ray began to drift off and his eyes were fading.

"Ray, come on, stay with me."

Stanley slapped the man's face, much to the astonishment of an elderly couple who'd come out to admire the koi.

Ray tried to smile. "A bit late, postman… You were right. You're always bloody right aren't you? I should have employed you… you'd have been good for me… I was involved in a deal," he whispered, "to… Stupid mistake. Backfired. Got dumped. Me. Dumped."

"Lot of flies about today Aggie," said the old man who was pointing at one of the goldfish or koi.

Stanley waved away a fly and sat bolt upright as he watched in horror as a huge formation of black specks flew from the other side of the pond and more or less flowed directly into Ray's nose, ears and mouth. The man jerked backwards trying to claw the things away, but that was the last thing he did apart from falling into Stanley's lap, choking horribly. Stanley tried desperately to get as much of the black mass out of Ray's mouth and nose, but it was all too late.

As Ray Berkley's eyes stared open, sightless and out of focus, Stanley was startled to note how very blue they were. He could hear the ambulance siren now and his phone began to ring as did a dozen other phones from in and around the restaurant.

"The ambulance," someone called out. "It's here."

"Just in time too," said a diner who'd just finished a large lunch and who was peering down at Ray.

"They said five minutes and they're dead on time," another diner said although, of course, she was dead wrong.

Patricia was quietly scared stiff at what might have happened to her brother. Everyone was upstairs in the flat now apart from Gus Chambers who was instructed to keep an eye on things at street level.

Stevie, hot and breathless, had just returned to tell DS Harris what Stanley had told him to do. Halfway through the telling, a single gunshot echoed between buildings. Everyone in the room ducked down below the window sill. Peering over the edge, they all assumed that the shot had come from the bookshop. In the silence that followed the echo, through the open windows, children could be heard playing obliviously on the bales of hay that still marked out the sugar beet race course.

Another shot sounded out and simultaneously the bookshop's front double doors burst open, crashing back against the wall, causing the substantial doorframe to splinter. Two men wearing black balaclavas appeared, each holding machine pistols. Pushed out in front of them was a stumbling and terrified William Benedict still only in his underpants. Next to him was a badly beaten, cut and bruised Alfie Scott in his torn and bloody shirt but no Kevlar vest, uniform jacket, trousers or shoes. Evie automatically made a mental note to have a stern word with him later. If, she thought with a cold shiver, there was a later.

Another single shot rang out. Julian, watching from across the road behind a vehicle, could see the asphalt kick up just behind William and Alfie – presumably to indicate that these people meant business. The two hostages were forced at gunpoint to climb into the old army truck's four seater cabin. Nobody got in behind the wheel.

Armed officers moved swiftly to the rear of the truck as the engine came to life with a roar, accompanied by a huge belch of blue-grey exhaust. From deep within the bookshop there was a dull crump and almost immediately mustard-coloured, acrid smoke billowed out of the building. As the old army truck began to move off still with no driver, two officers fired shots into the four rear tyres; another marksman did the same to the two tyres at the front. The truck lurched, shuddered and stopped.

The two gunmen in the truck's cabin ripped off their balaclavas and began firing simultaneously out of the windows. On the street in front of the post office, everyone fell flat, one police officer grunting in pain as a flying chip of broken pavement caught an ankle. The street was quickly peppered with holes as powdered concrete and bits of road flew upwards and sideways causing a shower of sharp shards. The truck began moving again even though the wheels were on their rims, sparks flying from metal on tarmac. A spatter of gunfire aimed at the truck's cab resulted in grunts and shouts as both Wilf and Terence were hit. Smoke drifted out from under the truck's bonnet as again the vehicle stopped, but this time permanently. The only sound for a while was the tick-ticking of the cooling, ruined engine.

Evie was leaping downstairs two at a time when she simultaneously heard three things – the sound of increased gunfire, the dining room window panes shattering and a collective scream. Outside, she could hear sudden shouting, a lot of it. Calling up to see if everyone was alright, her relief that they were almost caused her to join Bethan in a flood of tears.

Without warning, there was a long burst of automatic fire from inside the bookshop and, backing out, wearing ill-fitting, army fatigues and, for some reason, a blue UN helmet, was the diminutive figure of Sheila Prewer. She was absolutely focussed on pointing her Uzi submachine gun at someone inside the house. Her outfit and slightly oversized helmet in any other scenario would have been funny. There was blood, her own or someone else's nobody could tell, on her legs and she looked ready to collapse.

"Everyone," Julian shouted in the street as if he was trying to overcome the sound of a hurricane, "now say absolutely nothing. Mine is the only voice."

Nobody had heard this tone before and nobody, police officer or civilian, was going to argue or disobey. There was a strange, anticipatory silence, the kind that can occur when it's very clear that something shocking is about to happen.

"Mrs Prewer," called out Julian. "Mrs Prewer," he repeated more urgently, "put your weapon down slowly and walk backwards towards me. I'm behind you to your right. Just walk backwards and I will guide you. You'll be safe. But do it now."

Sheila appeared not to have heard or had chosen to take no notice. She didn't look anywhere but straight ahead and her weakened legs stiffened with resolve. The gun she held was gripped tight and did not waver. Through the front door stepped the remaining gunman. He was limping, dripping blood from a wound to his thigh and pointing a pistol directly at Sheila Prewer. With Sheila in their line of fire, the armed police couldn't get an accurate aim on Adidas.

"Mrs Prewer…" called out Julian calmly, more calmly by far than he felt. "Sheila… I repeat, please move backwards to me. Now. You'll be safe."

"You let us go now and this old cow can live," Adidas shouted, snarling with hate, pain and frustration. He raised his gun.

Sheila Prewer shouted back in a thin, old voice but one that everyone heard clearly.

"You put that there gun down right now you scumbag or I'll shoot you!"

As Adidas smiled, that's exactly what she did. Only fractionally after Adidas died, an enormous explosion could be heard from north of the village. Instinctively everyone ducked down. The noise of the detonation was immediately joined by a pall of thick, black smoke and spouts of orange flame each attacking the high Norfolk sky.

Two officers grabbed Sheila Prewer who yelled all sorts of obscenities, gave up her gun only after a struggle and had to be lifted away. Other officers moved swiftly to the truck's cabin where Wilf and Terence were sprawled, badly wounded but still alive. An officer and paramedics were seeing to Alfie Scott and William Benedict each of whom was suffering from multiple, deep cuts, numerous bruises and severe shock.

Another single shot was heard from within the bookshop and the whole street seemed to freeze for an instant as all heads turned to look. Armed officers trained their weapons on the bookshop doorway from which smoke was still creeping out. Nobody moved as they saw a stumbling figure emerge. The man was wearing a crumpled grey suit and white shirt which now had bloodstains on it as if someone had painted red carnations on the material. His hands were raised as far as he could manage which wasn't very far given his wounds.

Patricia gasped. Despite his state, she recognised Syd and Rosie's son, Paul. His hands were covered in grime and he had dried blood caked on his face. Rocking slightly on his heels, he winced in pain. Behind Paul Baxter and holding some kind of gun was Stanley, very badly cut and bruised too, covered in dust and also not particularly steady on his feet. Patricia could feel panic rising in her chest and that was the moment when she fainted dead away.

Twenty Three

Bethan was fed up with the fact that she couldn't go back to the flat above the post office and get fresh clothes. She and her aunt had been put up in one of The Basin of Porridge's four bedrooms, but sleep had been in short supply given the subsequent celebratory, all night lock-in that Graham Lambert had organised.

Stanley had been taken off to London for a lengthy debrief along with others including Alfie Scott, Evie Harris, Julian Poole, a traumatised William Benedict and most of the on-the-ground senior police officers. Sheila Prewer had been taken to an MoD hospital north of Norwich for some immediate surgery to one of her legs. Overnight, fresh police and MI5 teams had gone through the village green shed, the post office, the flat, the bookshop, Sheila Prewer's house and the pond area at The King's Head – in each case examining and removing items. More people had been interviewed, some several times. The army truck, the Lexus, the crates of weapons and ammunition, the old armaments from Sheila's house – all these had been loaded onto an unmarked, pale grey, forty five foot Mega Cube truck that had long gone with armed outriders.

The whole village seemed to be a hive of activity with many people trying hard to mind everyone else's business. The conversations du jour of course were about the double murders, the village green hostage situation, the wounding of one hostage, the fear amongst and bravery of the others, Ray Berkley's death, the wounding of two terrorists and the killing of another, gunfire in the street, the now destroyed Berkley Technologies and the arrest of international arms dealer and murderer, Paul Baxter.

After each telling, the stories became unnecessarily, but expectedly, deeper and wider until any visitor would have thought that a small war had enveloped the small, north Norfolk seaside village which in a way of course it had. It was interesting to Mrs Margaret McFlintock that half the village claimed to have been nearly part of the hostage group in the hut on the village green. Top flight media were out in force, hounding people and, having cornered some, thrust microphones or cameras into faces demanding answers to questions about which the interviewees had little clue.

Stanley Accrington, William Benedict and Sheila Prewer were exhausted from their debriefings and, after hers, Sheila, in her hospital bed, was promptly charged with manslaughter. Stanley was given a reprimand by the Post Office higher echelons, the police and several government authorities for putting himself and others at risk after which he was formally and genuinely thanked profusely by the same organisations. Mention had been made by someone of an auspicious bravery award to which Stanley had paid no attention. A short, hand-written note from an MI5 officer was what he treasured most but showed nobody.

Bethan and Patricia had of course made enormous fusses of Stanley once he'd arrived back in the village. Many villagers, including the chef from the Michelin-starred King's Head and Mrs Margaret McFlintock had produced all sorts of homemade dishes mostly because they genuinely cared about the Accringtons and partly out of curiosity at being allowed close to the scene of battle.

Mrs Margaret McFlintock was deeply saddened at the loss of her vicar and felt that mourning him would not be something that could be managed easily. She was disgusted as were many villagers at the behaviour of Mrs Threadgill, although facts on that front were sparse.

Mrs Margaret McFlintock felt that, in the absence of Charlton Heston, Mr Accrington could be her warrior in chief now. Not marriage material she knew of course, but someone up to whom she could look for inspiration. She reminded herself to explain her views to him one day about the Battle of the Vale of Siddim in which she thought he would have an interest. She wondered if, despite the battle being two thousand years' old, Mr Accrington might identify with Abraham who, it seemed to her, had played an important role then in exactly the same way as Mr Accrington had now. She wondered, privately for the time being, if he might be interested in becoming Little Peasen's non-stipendiary vicar. Pro tem of course, she thought.

Sheila Prewer was recovering in the MoD hospital under unnecessary armed police guard. Sheila's two RAF nephews had driven immediately from Brize Norton once they'd learned about what had happened to their aunt. Right at that moment, at her bedside, they were both expressing mirth and shaking their heads in genuine amazement at the tales of their aunt's valiant efforts in protecting those whom she adored and the village she loved. They were also keen to ensure that Sheila should not remain under arrest for any accusation. A top barrister was on her way along with two solicitors. One of these was from the RAF and the other happened to be Mr David Grise's son, Henry, already a partner at Grise, Doughty and Pantile, a firm well known to Mrs Stephanie Berkley who now of course had very different needs of their services.

A warm, summer's evening some days later saw Julian, Evie, Bethan, Stanley and Patricia sitting in the Accrington garden that sloped towards the brown, blue and grey, white-flecked North Sea. Conversation was limited, not out of any awkwardness, but because relief and a gentle weariness pervaded each of the number now sipping chilled Sancerre, cold Peroni lager or iced, fresh fruit juice.

"Paul Baxter was clever," said Julian in answer to someone's question as he watched a flight of pink-footed geese. "He was behind an extensive gun-running project that had already fuelled untold violence and was destined to do much more. The amounts of money involved were eye-watering. And he'd been at it for years."

He followed the geese as they flew majestically into the distance. Helping Patricia to another glass of wine he smiled into her eyes. Bethan coughed pointedly.

"The idea," he went on not remotely embarrassed, "was to

use different teams to smuggle huge quantities of arms all over the world. The business was mainly based in parts of Eastern Europe and Russia, but also the States, Iran and Syria. And now the UK. Baxter used and worked with a number of well-structured criminal groups including the Mafia Shqiptare and Hellbanianz although the crew on this job weren't the finest. That was partly Baxter's own fault. He trusted nobody. Any smell of mistrust and they were gone."

Everyone watched a family of swallows offering up a short show of aeronautical acrobatics.

"As it happens," went on Julian, "the mix-up in book and arms' deliveries suited Baxter very well. He knew the village inside out of course and, in any case, he'd been trying for some time to do a deal with Berkley for the botswarm invention. He had wealthy consortia in the wings keen to spend enormous sums on anything that could wreak havoc on a single enemy, an army or even a country. While he was negotiating with Berkley, Baxter met Carmichael and, over time, fed Carmichael's hate as of course had Captain Horsham. It was easy for Baxter to promise Carmichael everything that Berkley hadn't and, once he discovered the secret, home-developed botswarm, well… he knew that Carmichael was the golden goose."

"How was Amber Cooper involved?" asked Patricia.

Julian glanced at Stanley. "Can't comment I'm afraid. And that's telling you too much." He looked again at Stanley who didn't reciprocate.

Bethan and Patricia waited expectantly for more information but there was none forthcoming.

People stood to yawn, ponder, stretch and smell the roses. The evening was muggy, the sea like molten glass, everything sluggish and heavy. Even the hedgehogs, which normally liked to wander in the gloaming along the sea wall, weren't in evidence. The only one remaining seated, Stanley could hear a few voices far along the beach – children calling other children. It was a series of merry calls full, he thought, of fun. He recalled his parents' voices when the family had played games on the beach at Lytham St Annes. He remembered the summer holiday performances of little plays that he and his sisters had written and performed there to assembled and assorted grown-ups, many of whom just happened to be sunbathing or passing by and who greeted the short shows with genuine applause. His father had…

"Uncle Stanley?"

He looked up and saw his niece standing in front of him holding a plate of small water biscuits each one scraped with some kind of soft cheese or a smudge of vegetable pâté topped off with a quarter of an olive or a bit of gherkin. Stanley smiled weakly, used his good hand to brush his eyes and winced as he felt a stab of pain in his damaged arm.

"You OK?" asked his niece with concern.

Stanley smiled at her, more strongly this time. He hoped that she hadn't noticed as he'd tried to blink back memories. She had and in his heart he knew it.

"The wind… makes my eyes water sometimes," he said unnecessarily.

Bethan leaned forward and kissed his cheek. "There isn't any wind… Go on, have a thing."

She held the plate out. He took a biscuit and held it, looking around as his niece moved away. Garden tables were covered with platters of sandwiches, two large quiches, all kinds of cheeses on a huge board and an array of salads kindly supplied by the village. Bethan had made some large, savoury cheese straws which, surprising her aunt, were very good. Batons of crusty, freshly baked bread had been ripped and chunks were being enjoyed with deep yellow butter the colour of which, thought Stanley, matched his sister's much loved roses.

As everyone sat down again, Evie made very sure that she was now sitting next to Stanley who, confused, smiled shyly at her and ate the biscuit with cream cheese and gherkin on it. Julian munched a sandwich that had some sort of green something in it along with a crunchy something else. He didn't examine the contents and regretted it. He watched swifts darting about in the powder blue sky that was beginning to gently darken.

"Will Paul Baxter be in jail for a long time?" asked Bethan.

"The Americans and two other countries want him extradited. Mind you, the Albanian lot will have him marked wherever he ends up and they don't mess around. There'll be scores to settle. Baxter was ruthless and the number of deaths by his hand or instruction over the years will take a long time to unravel. He'll be looking over his shoulder forever, wherever he ends up. And for as long as his forever is."

"Richard Threadgill's death…" began Bethan but was given such a stern look by her aunt that she clammed up. Julian glanced over at Stanley. Evie desperately wanted to hold Stanley's good hand such was the sadness showing on his face. Nobody knew quite what to say.

"By the way Pat, your two teenage sleuths did really well," said Julian. "According to them and our gun-toting friend in the shed, it was Baxter who handed over the bomb remote control."

"Didn't the police know where the bomb was?" asked Patricia.

No answer was forthcoming and there was another awkward, tumbleweed moment.

Bethan broke the silence and asked, "Did Berkley know that Paul Baxter was Syd and Rosie's son?"

"No he didn't," said Evie. "Berkley was a show off and told Baxter about his plan to kick Mr and Mrs Baxter out of their home if the rest of the Darkwater estate became his. Baxter would have loathed Berkley for that threat. Whatever he was or is, Baxter loved his parents."

"What about the Berkley Technologies' explosion then?" asked Bethan.

"Well," said Julian feeling that the conversation should move on to more everyday issues or, preferably, to the subject of asking Patricia if she'd like to go for a walk along the beach, "we know that Dr Carmichael placed the explosives. Clever. He knew exactly what to use, how to get it past security, how to fool the cameras and where to put the device. But the company had tertiary cameras and they were fire and bomb proof within the equivalent of black boxes. The explosion was Baxter's idea of course but by then Carmichael was his pawn so he was only too glad to help destroy Berkley's pride and joy. Sweet revenge if you like. Hate was the driver. Long, burning hate. Oh yes and Baxter had an overall control override on the bomb app; in the bookshop, knowing the game was up, he pressed the button. Luckily nobody was hurt."

"How come nobody was hurt then?" asked Bethan but again there was no answer and another silence pervaded the group.

Julian gazed out over the now grey North Sea. As a breeze rose, he noticed a distant, white cruise ship, crisply bright and sitting high in the mid-distance. He wondered where it was going and where it had been. And when he might get a holiday. And where he should take his grandmother for a late birthday treat. Maybe the Michelin-starred King's Head he thought. Perhaps with Patricia? Evie coughed slightly and Julian turned back to the eyes that were still upon him.

"Excuse me. Apologies. What?"

"I was asking about the truck being driven without a driver," said Patricia.

"Ingenious. The botswarm, the one invented at Berkley Technologies, could be made to do almost anything, but I can tell you no more than that. But if the future is tiny drone robots with full AI, then the possibilities for good are wonderful and for bad they beggar belief."

"How come the phones were all dead?" Bethan asked.

"Easy," replied Evie. "On a number of occasions… terrorist actions or similar… the government can ensure that there's a signal blackout across the whole of an area or city. It's often done so that nobody can collude. Nowadays, it's not difficult with the right kit."

Patricia had wanted William Benedict to join the gathering but, while grateful for the invitation, he'd politely refused. Instead, he was being cossetted by his partner who was supplying refreshing drinks along with piles of hot buttered toast covered in Marmite, a particular favourite of William's. He had vowed not to visit Sweden again for some time, although interestingly he was considering Albania but not immediately. He was wondering how he could use his experiences to attract more customers to the bookshop which he was determined to make a success. Already an offer had been received from a London talent agency for him to go on the after-dinner circuit and talk to paying audiences about books and bombs.

"Mr Benedict was resourceful," Julian was saying. "And, by the by, we got his books back – all present and correct as far as we know."

"How did he manage to avoid being… you know…?" asked Bethan.

"Despite the danger he was in," said Evie thinking now that she'd like to be alone with Stanley and tell him how she felt, "and he was in the gravest, he'd managed to put a large amount of antacid medication into the food that he made for the men. He knew that the stuff could cause pretty much immediate and intense… upsets if taken in too large a dose, but had no idea how much would cause a problem. He managed to crush heavy duty amounts of omeprazole, esomeprazole, lansoprazole and rabeprazole into the food. The result was more or less instantaneous. Unpleasant but that was what probably saved his life."

Patricia chuckled, "Surely the men could have just got going. As it were."

"In principle yes, but they needed facilities close by and, given that everything was unravelling, in every sense, they wanted instructions from Baxter. By the time Baxter arrived, the net had closed."

Bethan, who was looking at her phone, said, "Amazing. I've been asked to do an interview tomorrow for Sky."

"Whatever you do, don't say anything you'll regret," warned Evie.

"Don't worry," said Patricia, 'I'll be going with her. No way is she doing that on her own."

"Is Alfie Scott OK?" asked Bethan changing the subject.

"He's fine," said Evie. "Suffering from a few nasty wounds and shock, all of which will take time to heal. But he'll be OK. Going to the bookshop's front door was daft and he's in trouble for that. But he's a good officer. It was a very close call for him and Mr Benedict because I think that, sooner rather than later, the gang would have just done away with the pair of them for the hell of it. But when Baxter got there, his solution was that hostages could be used as bargaining chips. Scotty managed to get his hands free. God knows how though. He saw Mrs Prewer at the window in her full regalia signing to him what she planned to do. She went in by the back door, literally gun blazing. Gutsy lady even after she'd been shot. Mr Accrington followed seconds later having done a King's Head sprint."

Evie wondered when it might be appropriate to call Mr Accrington Stanley while Julian glanced at his friend hoping very much that he was still his friend.

"Will Jessica Threadgill go to prison?" asked Bethan.

"Sub judice," was all that Evie said.

"Who's was that last shot just before Baxter came out of the bookshop?" asked Bethan. This question wasn't answered although they all knew, including Bethan, what the answer was. They glanced surreptitiously or in their own way at Stanley and then, following his gaze, they all looked out to sea once again, that calming balm of a vista that can sometimes, but not always, soothe hurt and troubled minds.

"Paul Baxter murdered Tobias Bishop," said Stanley suddenly and quietly. "With a botswarm. The bots injected what was a mixture of melittin, apamin, MCD peptide, histamine, hyaluronidase and something else…"

"Phospholipase-A2. Replicates bee sting venom," added Evie softly.

"God!" exclaimed Patricia. "Stan you never said you knew… God. Why?"

"On behalf of his father's misplaced hatred of the Bishops," said Stanley.

Julian was about to add something but decided against it. Enough had been said and there was no need to say much more. Not now anyway. There was another silence, a lingering one this time and a general air of melancholy that all who sat in the garden felt, each in different ways.

"You were lucky," said Bethan eventually as she gently took her uncle's bandaged left hand. Evie wanted to take his other hand but didn't.

"Dead lucky," said Patricia and began to cry quietly making a bit of a mess of the makeup that she'd put on for Julian's sake.

The following day, as Stanley began to manage once again the business of running a shop and post office, his deeper wounds freshly bandaged and his lesser ones under ointment and plasters, he suddenly felt it necessary to get out. There were builders working in the flat and a glazier was expected shortly so there was no peace or quiet upstairs. Stevie and Tony, who'd been exemplary during the previous few days, were employed in helping to get everything shipshape. He and Patricia had in fact mulled over the idea of offering the two full-time jobs.

"Pat," Stanley said, "I'm just going out for a short while, OK? Just for a walk."

"Fine," she said and then grabbed a part of arm that wasn't either in a sling or bandage. "But please Stan… just a walk."

He winced and smiled. "Promise."

Getting out of the post office and shop was easier said than done since all the customers bar none wanted to either shake his damaged hand or thump him appreciatively on his bruised back. People were in a celebratory mood and Stanley sensed their relief. Eventually he was out and nodded at the police officer still on duty. Looking across the road at the mess that was the front of the bookshop and at the building work that had already begun, he wondered if William really would continue to sell books.

Turning away, he breathed deeply, looked up and saw that low, grey clouds tinged with light purple had covered much of the summer sky. Raindrops fell on a rosebush full of open, golden blooms, stems bending as if in homage to the weather. Thunder murmured and grumbled far out at sea. Stanley stopped walking, although his version of walking had been little more than a shuffle and, at best, a limp. He breathed deeply again as the short shower finished. The sails of three fishing boats seemed like copper in the sunshine that out at sea was still bright.

Everywhere he looked there was sharp focus and sudden appearances of bright colour as the sun split clouds. Phloxes, fuchsias and petunias glistened. A plum tree glittered with damp, dark red fruit. Someone had left pots of homemade tomato chutney on a wall with a sign indicating that anyone should take a jar and contribute something to a small biscuit tin which, Stanley was pleased to see, was almost full. He put the lid on the tin.

Continuing on his slow journey to see Syd and Rosie Baxter, he wondered what he could actually say to the old couple and realised that probably it had all been said or, if it hadn't, then it might be better said by others and at another time. Maybe, he thought, some things just shouldn't be said at all. Or didn't need saying.

He thought about his motive for going to see Syd and Rosie and concluded that he was going for his own benefit, not theirs.

There would be a time he knew when he could and would sit with the old couple and drink tea, look up at the stars and even smoke a small cigar. That time wasn't now. He wanted to believe that whatever happened to David Horsham wouldn't culminate in the Baxters being turfed out of their home. For many reasons, the couple would be hurting and Stanley had nothing with which to ease their pain, apart from friendship. That, he thought, had some definite value, but perhaps at the moment not enough.

Stanley imagined or, rather hoped, that Syd would, if he could, try to make things right with Janine Bishop. Emotional debts, along with guilt, were terrible burdens and, he thought, not easily lost or paid. When the old man had visited Janine in hospital, it had been reported by the ward sister that the old lady, sobbing, had accepted the embrace that the little old man had offered her, and it was the ward sister who had to eventually remove the still weeping visitor from her still weeping patient.

For some reason, he recalled David Horsham asking him if all would be well. He still didn't know. People, he thought, needed reassurance even if they knew that sometimes there was just none to be had. He felt the rising sea breeze on his bruised face and juicy drops of rain spattered once again on and around him. A miniscule fly landed on his white, bandaged arm and a swarm of summer, storm midges flew about his face which, in irritation, he waved away with his good hand.

About the Author

Simon has been a writer for many years. He started his career lecturing in Shakespeare and, following that, he directed corporate events around the world during which time he was often asked to write speeches, produce film scripts and step up as a keynote speaker on storytelling.

He looks at writing stories from two points of view – what everyone can easily see and what is often hidden.

Simon's books include:

The 100 - Insights from the Greatest Speeches Ever Delivered; Speak Like a President; Inspire; The Diary; In Any Event; The Evil Executive; The Other Side of History; Great Mindset Changing Ideas and *Silver Green: Volume I*. Each has achieved international success.

Silver Green: Volume II (Red Metal) will be the second book in the trilogy and the next novel in the Stanley Accrington series is being written now.

Available worldwide from Amazon

www.mtp.agency

www.facebook.com/mtp.agency

@mtp_agency

Printed in Great Britain
by Amazon

86611498R00155